Forgive Us Our Trespasses

by

Richard Davidson

The Lord's Prayer Mystery Series

Volume III

This book is a work of fiction. Any resemblance to actual events or persons, living or dead, is entirely coincidental.

"Forgive Us Our Trespasses," by Richard Davidson. ISBN 978–0-9976381-1-0

Cover photograph by Jim Davidson..

Second Edition June, 2016
Published 2016 by RADMAR Publishing Group, P.O. Box 425, Northbrook, IL 60065, USA. ©2016, Richard Davidson. All rights reserved. No part of this publication may be reproduced, stored in a retrieval system, or transmitted in any form or by any means, electronic, mechanical, recording or otherwise, without the prior written permission of Richard Davidson.

Manufactured in the United States of America.

This novel is dedicated to my mother who always forgave me whenever I got into trouble. She forgave me right after she punished me.

CHAPTER 1 – UNEXPECTED VISITOR

Pastor Arthur Blake, following his benediction at the close of the Parkville United Methodist Church Sunday morning service, waited in the doorway of the sanctuary to greet the exiting worshippers. As he chatted with each departing person, his eyes kept returning to a nervous and distressed-looking man who waited in the line halfway down the center aisle. This traditional greeting of departing congregants was usually a perfunctory matter consisting of a few words or murmurs exchanged as they shook hands. Today, when he wanted the process to be brief, everyone seemed to have a detailed personal story to tell him. He tried to concentrate on Sue Willoughby's chronicle of her recent vacation, Ed Jensen's plans for the next Church Council Meeting, and Florence Slovitch's animated description of her honeymoon with Rob, but his furtive glances at the lean man with the thinning gray hair and the vacant stare distracted him so much that his responses became terse and automatic.

At last, there was only one person to greet before encountering the target of his interest. Marge Irwin was a close friend of Shirley Hadley, the Church Secretary. She had also been an Army nurse during the First Gulf War. Today was her first time back in church after an operation to repair a left forearm bone that had healed misaligned after a wartime injury.

"Marge, you're looking well. Did the operation eliminate your stiffness and pain?"

"Absolutely, Arthur, I'm as good as new." Marge moved her left arm through a variety of positions to demonstrate that she had complete freedom of motion. Then she meandered off toward the coffee line to mingle with several of her friends.

The lean man approached. He was several inches shorter than Arthur, and what was left of his graying hair was similar in hue to his ashen facial skin. He forced a thin smile onto his otherwise somber face. "Hello, Son; that really was a pretty good sermon this morning. Quite a bit better than the first one I heard you deliver."

"Hi, Dad, it's great to see you, but is anything wrong? You've never before come all the way from home without giving me advance notice and without bringing Mother along. Is she ill?"

"She's fine. I wanted to see you to discuss some things that I'd rather she didn't know about. It's pretty scary stuff. I told her that I needed a father and son outing with you, and she went along with it. I'll grab some coffee and wait for you in the other room until you're free."

Arthur returned to his pastoral greetings. Peter Blake headed for the coffee line and then to a quiet corner of Fellowship Hall. His hand trembled slightly as he raised the Styrofoam cup to his lips. Despite his anxiety, he found himself wondering why the church didn't use recyclable cups. He'd ask Arthur sometime.

Peter had driven to Arthur's church in the northwest Illinois village of Parkville from his home in Richmond near the border between northeast Illinois and southeast Wisconsin, a trip of almost one hundred miles. Richmond, Illinois was a historic village specializing in antique shops. Peter owned one of the oldest of them. Arthur had grown up discussing history and antiques at the dinner table, and those conversations served him well as background for both his ministerial career and his engineering career that had preceded it.

After greeting the last departing worshipper, Arthur strode directly to Peter Blake's chair in the corner of

Fellowship Hall. "Sorry for the delay, Dad; do you want to talk here, or would you rather head for my office?"

"I think your office would be better. Is Irma around? I'd like to include her in our discussion."

Arthur spotted Irma talking with a visitor near the pastry table and beckoned for her to join them as they walked toward his office. She nodded slightly, but not so much as to distract the woman who was explaining the fine points of her son's latest hobby, butterfly collecting. Irma Custis, the former County Medical Examiner, was Arthur's closest friend, although they had not yet sorted out the other dimensions of their relationship. They had also worked together in assisting the authorities to unravel the causes of several crimes and nasty incidents.

The coffee-time chatter faded away as they turned two corners on their way to the pastor's office. Arthur left the door open in anticipation of Irma's arrival. He gestured for Peter to sit at the conference table and then turned to get a mug of coffee from his personal pot before joining him. As Arthur sat down, Irma entered and, seeing his signal, closed the door behind her.

"Hello, Peter, it has been quite a while since you last visited us. It's great to see you again."

"Hi, Irma, I asked Arthur to invite you to this confab, because I trust your viewpoint and your discretion."

Irma heard the tension in Peter's tone and sat down, prepared for something significant and serious.

"Dad, why don't you start at the beginning? When I saw your expression in the congregation, I knew something was bothering you. Take a deep breath, and tell us about it."

Peter arched his back and stretched his legs as he leaned back in his chair. "You're right as usual, Arthur. Something is tearing me apart, and I don't know how to handle it.

3

"Irma, the background for my problem is the recent death of my best friend. Albert Dandrich and I go way back together. We've been fishing buddies and hobbyists in local archeology and even partners in the county horseshoe tournaments. We've spent vacations together along with our wives, touring as a foursome all over the country. We even dragged Arthur along on some of those trips. I was really close to him, and his sudden death in an automobile accident was a shock."

"Was he your age?"

"No, Irma, he was quite a bit older...I'd guess that he was in his low eighties, but he was vigorous, and most people thought he was much younger."

"Dad, it's always a shock when a close friend dies, but there must be more to the story, or you wouldn't be here seeking our help and wanting to keep Mother from knowing about it."

"You're right, Arthur. The problem developed when Al's wife, Mandy, gave me his antique smoking table as a memorial keepsake. Al hadn't smoked for years, but he cherished that table and kept it next to his desk. He still had some old pipes and pouches of tobacco inside it. As soon as it arrived, Janice told me that I would have to clean it up in the garage and get rid of the remaining mixture of smells if I wanted to keep it in the house."

"Were you able to deodorize it completely?"

"I came close to that goal, Irma, and Janice even let me move it to our basement for further work, but that effort became less important when I discovered a secret compartment in the back of the pipe storage cabinet section. Lots of pieces of antique furniture have secret compartments, but this one was particularly well hidden. Being a lover of antiques, I was impressed by the craftsmanship that made the extra space behind the cabinet wall so difficult to detect. I was amazed to find that the craftsman had been able to match the wood

4

grains on the inner and outer carved walls. The grains looked identical from both sides. Anyway, when I examined the contents of that cavity, I found some disturbing papers and other items that are the reason for my coming."

"It sounds as though you found a skeleton in Al's closet, Dad."

Peter shifted in his seat and stared at his son. "I wish you hadn't chosen those particular words, Arthur, because they are exactly correct. I found an old photograph of Al in a Nazi SS uniform complete with the grinning skull and bones insignia. There were even two embroidered skull badges in a small envelope. Penciled on the back of the photograph was the inscription *Obersturmfuhrer Wilhelm Schnacht*. I looked up the rank, and it would be the equivalent of a First Lieutenant. My best friend was a Nazi officer during World War II. I sat and stared at what I'd discovered for about an hour before I forced myself to believe it."

Irma reached over and touched Peter on the shoulder. "Are you absolutely sure that it was Albert in the picture and that he wasn't simply collecting war relics?"

Peter straightened up from his hunched position. His eyes squinted as he glared at them. His voice grew louder despite his clenched teeth. "It was Albert, all right. He had the same small scar on his right cheek, and he held his chin thrust out with pride. I've been best friends for decades with a war criminal. He wasn't an ordinary German soldier; he was an officer in the Waffen SS. He must have had all kinds of blood on his hands."

Peter's appearance softened again, and he sagged back down in his chair. "Arthur, I've considered Albert and Mandy friends for longer than you've been alive. I don't know what to do about this."

Arthur frowned as he finished his first mug of black coffee. He went over to the pot to get a refill. As he returned to the table he had a distant look in his eyes. "Irma, I remember how gentle Albert was when he would pick me up and carry me on his shoulders. If he was a Nazi, he must have been adept at varying his personality to suit his audience. I suppose that even Nazis had their gentle moments, but this second identity is a shocker to me too, Dad. I'd never guess that he could have been that person in the photograph. How can we help you cope with this discovery?"

"I know how you get involved in investigations all the time. It would mean a lot to me if you could find out how he got from Germany to here and how rotten an apple he was. I'm going to have to share this information someday. I can't keep it bottled up forever, and I want to know more facts before I take it public."

"Are you talking about sharing the alternate identity story with Mother, or with Albert's wife, or with the press?"

"All of the above, Son, how else can I live with the aftermath of this mess? The realization of his true identity makes me feel dirty for having been his friend. We've been contaminated."

"Dad, tread carefully when you talk with his wife, Mandy. This is hard for me to swallow, and I've been exposed to all kinds of shocking things. She'll be a complete basket case if you spring this on her without warning.

"You'll have to give us his artifacts and papers so that we can have experts look at them."

"No problem, Arthur, they're in my van. I didn't want to pollute your church by bringing them in with me."

An hour later, after a brief lunch at Marbury's Parkville Pub, the three of them adjourned to Arthur's parsonage home in recognition of Peter's sensitivities about bringing Nazi relics into the church. Peter carried an old manila shipping envelope from the van into the house and emptied its contents onto the kitchen table. They spread everything out to make each item visible.

"You mentioned a few things, Dad, but there's quite an assortment here. That must have been a sizable secret compartment to hold this envelope."

"Albert, or Wilhelm, folded the envelope and wedged it into the cavity so that individual items wouldn't rattle or shift when the table was moved. Whoever made that smoking table was a genius with wood. Arthur, I would definitely like to acquire more of his furniture. The table is pretty old and probably American made, so it's a safe bet that the woodworker wasn't a Nazi too. The next time you come to visit, I'll show it to you, and I mean both of you. It's about time for you to bring Irma home so that she can appreciate your upbringing."

"I already value it from having spent time here with you and Janice, Peter. Even so, I agree that he'd better include me in his family reunion plans."

Arthur heard their conversation in the background as he concentrated on the items spread out before him. "Pardon my not being part of the social chatter, but I think you were right to be disturbed by this stuff. I can hardly believe he carried off the impersonation for so long without slipping up somewhere."

Irma said, "The hard part of being an impostor comes early, Arthur. After a while, you start believing it, and then it becomes natural to be your new self. It's similar to learning to drive a car. At first you have to concentrate on every action and device, but after a while the mechanics of driving become natural, and you can concentrate on traffic and conversations with passengers."

"Well, this *new self* helped guide me through my early years. He could have filled me with dangerous ideas. I was always a little bothered about your having me call him an uncle when he really wasn't one. Calling him or anyone else who wasn't part of the family an aunt or an uncle seemed dishonest to me."

Peter said, "From what we know now, it was more than dishonest; it was criminal. He used us to legitimate his new persona, and we fell for it."

"Getting back to the stuff on the table, I get the impression that you didn't go through everything, Dad. Is that correct?"

"I realized what I had found after examining a few things, and I left the rest until we could get together. I needed your support. I was hurt and in shock after realizing that my best friend had been a Nazi SS officer. I needed time to digest that information. I was also afraid that your mother would walk in and discover me looking at this stuff."

Arthur placed the photograph and the insignias that Peter had already described on the left side of the table; he stacked several folded sheets of paper and three photographs in the middle; and he positioned six small envelopes on the right side.

"Let's start with the papers. This one is a birth certificate for Albert Dandrich, born January 16, 1925 in Mt. Kisco, New York. It's marked *Copy*, so your friend must have ordered it after he arrived here. There are also discharge papers for a Sergeant with that name."

"Arthur, don't call him my friend any more. From now on he should be Wilhelm Schnacht when we discuss him. The Albert I thought I knew so well never existed."

"That's the point, Dad. The copy of the birth certificate proves that Albert Dandrich did exist, but he wasn't the one you knew. How did Wilhelm become an existing person?"

Irma had been looking at the photographs in the middle pile while the others talked. "I'll answer that one, Arthur. One of these photographs shows a group of American soldiers in a compound surrounded by barbed wire and guarded by German soldiers. They must have been prisoners of war. A second photo shows a close-up of an American Army Sergeant. He slightly resembles the man in the third picture with the SS uniform. My guess is that Wilhelm took the place of a captured American soldier and then headed for Allied lines masquerading as an escapee from a German prison camp."

Peter's hand shook as he took the American's photograph from Irma. "If you're right, then Wilhelm must have killed the man he replaced. I'll bet he thought no more of it than swatting a fly - so much for abiding by the rules of the Geneva Convention."

"Dad, governments talk about things like that. Individual soldiers and civilians in a war only try to survive. Schnacht had been trained to be ruthless. The Allies were about to win the war, and this was Wilhelm's escape route. I'm sure he would have planned this strategy well in advance. He was a smart bastard."

Irma picked up one of the small sealed envelopes, opened the flap, and looked inside. Then she squeezed the other envelopes to get a feel for their contents without opening them. "Peter, I think you discovered an even bigger problem than Wilhelm Schnacht. There are six American Soldiers in that concentration camp picture including that sergeant in the second photo. These six envelopes contain six sets of identification dog tags. I'm sure one of them belonged to Albert Dandrich. It appears that all of those soldiers were replaced by SS impostors."

CHAPTER 2 – DOG TAGS

Peter had gone home feeling relieved that he had shared his burden with Arthur and Irma. When he had found that picture and the other stuff, he had lost his ability to focus objectively on anything; he had become a bundle of raw emotions. His meeting with Arthur and Irma had restored some of his logical abilities. His agony of isolation had passed. He felt supported..

Renee Andrews, Arthur Blake, and Irma Custis functioned together as the three associates in ABC Consultants, an investigative enterprise created by Irma. Now they had gathered in Irma's apartment to analyze Peter's evidence from the smoking table compartment and to decide how to determine its significance. Renee tabulated details of the items Peter had found while Arthur searched through internet historical files about the SS organization.

Irma straightened up from having been hunched over her laptop computer. She stood, arched her back, and did a few stretching exercises. Then she walked over to the printer and stood there, removing four sheets of paper as they emerged from the bowels of the mechanism.

She raised her voice above the noise of the printer. "Arthur, I've done some research on the evolution of dog tags, and you're not going to like the results."

"Is there anything special about these?"

"What's significant is that the Army changed the layout of their dog tags in July of 1943. The ones from the table compartment are examples of the newer version that was issued during the latter part of the war. That means that the American prisoners in that picture received their dog tags after that date, and they weren't prisoners of the Germans for long."

Renee, a former Parkville Police Officer and the wife of Police Chief Bobby Andrews said, "Irma, that's good news that they weren't captives for long. Why do you think the newer vintage dog tags are bad news?"

"Dog tags issued prior to July of 1943 included the name and address of the soldier's next-of-kin. Those issued after that date did not. The later vintage of these tags will make it harder to trace their families."

Arthur looked up from his examination of the actual medallions. "We still have the minor problem that all of this took place more than sixty-five years ago. Even if we had the addresses of the soldiers' next-of-kin, we couldn't expect to find them there."

"I agree, it wouldn't be simple, but at least we'd have starting points for tracking each soldier's family. We have no family information at all with these newer style tags.

"Renee, have you recorded all the dog tag information?"

"I wrote down everything except the tetanus immunization details. I didn't think that would help us. I labeled and included blood type and religious codes as potentially valuable."

Arthur and Irma looked at the data on Renee's pad of paper:

Albert R. Dandrich, 36725431, Type O, Religion P
Maxwell P. Griggins, 35827262, Type B, Religion C
Peter M. Rodwin, 35972361, Type O, Religion P
Samuel L. Spincus, 37291043, Type A, Religion H
Warren D. Handley, 36452891, Type B, Religion P
Joseph G. Mantini, 32491263, Type A, Religion C

Arthur pointed at one name on the list. "It's interesting to me that one of the soldiers they picked for their operation was Jewish. See, his religion code is H for

Hebrew. I would have thought that SS Troops would have had an aversion to anyone who was Jewish."

"Maybe the German impostor who took his place thought that the Jewish label would give his true background better camouflage. Besides, who knows whether any of these men were outwardly religious once they adopted their new identities?"

"You're right, Irma, I'll have to check with Dad as to whether Albert went to church and if so, which one. I don't remember him going to our church. It might be a little awkward for Dad to inquire about Albert's blood type, but it would be interesting to know whether the American identities were selected because these people matched their lifestyles or other characteristics.

"Renee, would you search the available federal government databases for last known addresses and relatives of these individuals? That's diligent police work. The German replacements would have had to worry about inquiries from relatives and friends of their American counterparts. How do you suppose they approached that problem, Irma?"

"If I were in such a position, I'd do my best to stay away from home. I'd only correspond by typed letter, and I'd say that a war injury affected the way I signed my name. I might even say that my service obligation had been extended so that I wouldn't be expected to go home."

"That all sounds textbook logical, but I'll bet that it would be hard to avoid unexpected glitches. There would always be the possibility of someone showing up spontaneously or insisting on a personal contact. If six people were all trying to avoid inquiries and recognition as being impostors, the odds are that at least one of them would be discovered due to something unpredictable. I wonder what happened as these *doppelgangers* moved into American society and took the places of existing people."

CHAPTER 3 – ABC CONSULTANTS

Pastor Arthur Blake had naturally fallen into his investigation sideline during his first months at Parkville United Methodist Church about two years earlier. He had received an emergency assignment to this northwest Illinois village church following the sudden death of the unusual and mysterious Pastor William Middlemiss. Arthur's previous experience as a NASA engineer had equipped him to analyze many aspects of his predecessor's background and the church's history. During the Middlemiss investigation, he had worked closely with Parkville Police Chief Bobby Andrews and with Irma Custis, who was then the County Medical Examiner. Irma and Arthur became close friends and confidants. After Irma left her CME post, she had continued to work with Arthur on inquiring into unusual and criminal events involving the church, and she had created the ABC Consultants entity to separate their joint investigative efforts from Arthur's pastoral duties. When ABC Consultants was first formed, ABC stood for Arthur Blake and Custis. Later, after Chief Bobby Andrews married one of his officers, Renee Weems, ABC became a three-person affair with Renee joining the fledgling agency. The result was a modification of the abbreviation so that ABC now stood for Andrews, Blake, and Custis. The group operated out of Irma's apartment, but they posted their sign and met with outsiders and clients in the local Chinese restaurant, House of Ming.

ABC Consultants appeared to be too small and unofficial to accomplish very much, but the talents of its members were augmented by many outside connections. During the investigation of the death of Pastor

Middlemiss, Arthur had developed a close relationship with Penny and Joe Gonzalez, senior members of a covert government investigative agency. He also had social and professional connections through the church structure and technical connections at NASA. Renee could tap into Bobby's contacts within the Illinois Association of Chiefs of Police, and Irma added extensive forensic medicine connections to the mix.

They would need to use all of their contacts and skills to solve the case that Peter Blake had brought them.

CHAPTER 4 – DETAILS

Arthur felt his calf muscles cramping as he climbed the stairs to the parsonage front door. He had jogged the trail around Mallard Lake, located across Jeffers Street from the church. His exercise regime had suffered over the past year due to sedentary activities. To get back into shape he had extended his hikes and runs during the month since Labor Day until today he had made it completely around the lake. At the age of forty-four his stamina and flexibility were declining, but he was determined to maintain his physical fitness at the highest practical level. Today's outing had convinced him that he could still achieve his physical goals, even though the process required more preparation and effort than even a few years ago. Arthur showered, changed his clothes, and was tying his shoes when the telephone rang. He glanced at the caller ID screen and picked up the handset.

"Hi, Irma, I'm back in normal mode after my exercise run, and my church meetings are done for the day. What would you think about going out for dinner tonight?"

"Hold that thought, Arthur. First you should head for my place. Renee brought data from the records of the soldiers whose dog tags we found. If you're not too starved we can review her results and go for dinner later. Based on Renee's excitement over her findings, I think we'll have some progress to celebrate."

"That sounds good to me. It's time for this project to move beyond theories. I'll be right over."

Arthur grabbed a light jacket and drove to Irma's apartment in his Saturn Vue, stopping on the way to buy some pretzels and grapes to appease their appetites until the deferred dinner outing. By the time he arrived, Renee had transferred summaries of her data to flip chart sheets. Irma and Arthur each grabbed a yellow legal pad of paper for notes. Irma sat on the couch while Arthur tilted backward on a sturdy but ancient kitchen chair with a flat seat and an arched backrest supported by parallel dowel rods.

Irma reacted to his comfortable perch. "Don't tilt that old chair, or you'll break it and your back too. I don't want to have to, pardon the expression, minister to your health needs."

"OK, Doctor, I'll be more safety conscious." Arthur reversed the chair and sat on it backward, leaning his folded arms on its backrest.

Renee turned over the blank cover sheet of her flip chart pad. "I searched every source I could find – accessible Army files, government records, and the Internet. What I found surprised me. There are no records of any of these soldiers having any relatives during or immediately after the War. They may have added relatives by getting married and having children later, but they had no known relatives while they were in the Army."

Arthur stood up and approached the chart on the easel. "You show the dog tag information we saw before but with addresses included."

"These are the last known addresses that I found. They all date back to the period following World War II. For some reason the files I searched show no updates after that period.

Albert R. Dandrich, 36725431, Type O, 840 Millwood Road, Mt. Kisco, New York, Religion P

Maxwell P. Griggins, 35827262, Type B, 723 Hurley Street, Waycross, Georgia, Religion C

Peter M. Rodwin, 35972361, Type O, 8129 County Road 7140, Wolfforth, Texas, Religion P

Samuel L. Spincus, 37291043, Type A, 324 Old Glenns Creek Road, Frankfort, Kentucky, Religion H

Warren D. Handley, 36452891, Type B, 341 South Clinton Avenue, Bradley, Illinois, Religion P

Joseph G. Mantini, 32491263, Type A, 254 North Clermont Avenue, Atlantic City, New Jersey, Religion C

"Are you saying that each of these people lived in the listed communities at one time, but you don't believe that any of these addresses are recent?"

"That's right, Arthur. I wouldn't even know that Albert was married and that his wife's name was Mandy except for the information obtained from your father. I show no relatives, even by marriage for them. My conclusion is that this is old data, because most of them probably married at some point."

Irma had been making notes on her pad. She looked up. "Renee, did you locate anyone who actually knew them? I realize such people would be pretty old by now, but I'd feel better if I had records of human contact rather than only documentary evidence."

"Joseph Mantini worked with the YMCA in Atlantic City after the war, and one of the younger volunteer coordinators from that time remembers him. That person is now a high-ranking member of the Atlantic City Police Department, so I consider his statement a strong confirmation. An elderly librarian in Waycross, Georgia said that she remembers Max Griggins because he was always requesting books on tractors and how to do your own engine repairs. That lady had an amazing memory. I even found a woman in Frankfort, Kentucky who claims that she dated Samuel Spincus in 1946. My conclusion is that these veterans did live at the indicated addresses, at least for a while."

Arthur stopped doodling interlaced swastikas and crosses on his pad. "This information suggests that the German impostors replaced American soldiers who were selected because they had no relatives to disprove their assumed identities. What do you think, Irma?"

"That would have been the safest approach for them to have taken. Or, the impostors may have pretended to have no relatives after they assumed their new roles."

Arthur sat on the couch and bowed his head. "I pray that the American soldiers didn't have relatives who were murdered so that they couldn't identify their German replacements. If some were killed to avoid detection, I pray that God has given their souls special blessings to offset their suffering."

Irma leaned over and patted Arthur on the shoulder. She knew how divided he felt at times like this when objective analysis collided with his faith that God is loving and kind. She felt divided herself as she gravitated toward being Arthur's partner in multiple ways. Did he sense her tensions as well? Did he think it would happen, or was he avoiding all thoughts about commitment? Most men avoided the long term in favor of the *now*. Aloud, she suggested that it was time to break off their official work for the evening and share their thoughts about the case over dinner.

CHAPTER 5 – FIELD TRIP

At their meeting the next morning, Irma suggested that they should split their efforts in a dual approach.

"Let's start by studying the case with the most likely success rather than studying all six people at once. We can find a lot of information about the family of Albert Dandrich through Albert's wife, Mandy, plus Peter and Janice Blake. Arthur and I should visit his family in keeping with Peter's earlier invitation. While we're doing that, Renee, you should continue to check on the returned soldiers and their family information through legal records and the memories of people they may have contacted along the way."

Arthur and Renee agreed. He headed for his church office to arrange for a substitute preacher for the following Sunday and to call his parents about their visit. Renee went to the Parkville Police Department to get Bobby's suggestions for tracking long-missing persons.

By noon, Arthur had returned with his car packed for a week's visit. This meant a small soft-sided suitcase and his shaving kit. Irma was ready for him, and together they loaded her three suitcases and her forensics gear into his car. As they drove away, Arthur said, "You appear to be prepared for absolutely anything."

Irma turned a deadpan expression toward him. "I hope you still have clothes at your folks' house. One pair of jeans plus two shirt changes won't cut it with me for a week."

"If you think this is going to be a high society trip, you must be thinking of Richmond, Virginia. Richmond, Illinois is small and about as informal as it gets around

19

here – antique shops, candy stores, and little folksy restaurants."

"Yes, but this is that serious time when you first take me home to meet your family. I have to be prepared for anything."

They both laughed, and Arthur said, "First, you've already met them, even though it wasn't on their turf. Second, we'll have to keep things light and informal, at least until the time when Dad thinks it's necessary to tell Mother why we're really there."

"Watch out, Arthur, my reasons for going home with you might include more than investigations."

They traveled without further conversation for about ten minutes while each of them pondered their relationship. Then Arthur said, "You were completely honest with me last year, and it meant turning your back on your career as a County Medical Examiner. I'm afraid I haven't been as honest with you."

"What do you mean?"

"Not only didn't I give you details about my marriage to Cindy, but also I avoided telling you about the woman I lived with for two years before I married Cindy."

"Arthur, we both have histories, and we're long out of our teen years or even twenties. What happened back then shouldn't make a difference, although the news of your earlier roommate might tarnish your halo a bit. I was afraid to even hint at such an arrangement for us."

"Well, I wasn't in the ministry then. We were both NASA engineers, and the long hours we spent solving problems before and during space shots led us to a mutual need for release when we had those few hours away from the job."

"Next thing you'll say is that it was the logical thing to do. Right, Mr. Spock?"

"There were plenty of emotions involved then, and it wasn't so much that it was logical, but that our moving in together seemed natural and comfortable at the time."

"It must have been if it lasted for two years. Did you ever think or talk about getting married?"

"If we did, I can't remember it."

"How did Cindy enter the picture?"

"The old fashioned way – we met at the supermarket. I was picking out some fruit, and she told me that the melon I was about to buy wasn't ripe. She said that she had picked up the same one and that it didn't have any *give* at the stem end when she pressed it with her thumbs."

"That's an original pickup line."

"The attractive thing was that I saw that she thought like an engineer."

"Is that what we have going for us, logical thinking?"

"It doesn't hurt, but you have a lot more to offer. You make my life special, even when we're involved in a death investigation."

"Watch it, Holy Man; you just stole my line about how you make me feel. It's hard to get close to someone when you're doing autopsies all the time. You walked in and gave me back the magical part of life. It stopped being a mechanical thing about body parts and whether they're functioning or not."

"Thanks, Irma; I guess we don't have to autopsy our sins and our souls. What we are when we're together is the key...That being said, do you have any additional confessions you'd like to make?"

"Nope, I'm satisfied; we're both OK enough for me. Sometime I would like you to talk about your married life with Cindy. You've told me that she walked out because you spent too much time working at NASA, but I'd like to know a bit more about your married life experience. I've never been married, and I've never had married siblings...Hold that thought for another time. I know it's my turn to expose more of my personal history, but not right now. It's time for me to comb my hair. You just passed the *Welcome to Richmond* sign."

"OK, but you're not off the hook. I have the feeling that your background has some interesting details that might make me blush."

He came close to losing control of the car when she punched his right shoulder.

CHAPTER 6 – JANICE

They pulled into the driveway of a small white two story frame house. It had a blue shingled roof and bright blue shutters enhancing each window. The garage was a matching stand-alone two car affair with two separate one car doors. They had barely stepped out of the car when Arthur's parents charged at them from the back door of the house. Irma experienced an instant flashback to the time a year and a half ago when the Blakes had visited Parkville UMC and had run from their van toward Arthur and Irma, standing near the church steps. Irma shook her head to clear the flashback and return to the present.

"Hello, Janice, hello Peter; thank you for inviting me to join Arthur on his visit home."

Arthur and Peter shook hands while Janice responded by hugging Irma. "It's about time you got down here. I was afraid that Arthur would whisk you off to some other part of the country without ever bringing you home with him. Now we can officially bless the two of you."

Arthur did an awkward combination jump and spin move to face his mother. He had a shocked look on his face. "Mother, please don't be presumptuous. Irma and I are working out our relationship. If and when there's something significant to announce, we'll let you know in plenty of time for you to trumpet it to the world. Please don't put pressure on us."

Peter patted Janice on the shoulder in confirmation of Arthur's words.

Janice looked hurt and pouted. "I fixed up your old room for the two of you. I guess this means you won't both be using it."

Arthur said, "Irma can use my room and I'll sleep on the couch downstairs."

Janice slouched and turned to walk back into the house. Irma caught up with her and gave her a hug.

"Your preparations are fine, Janice. We'll use the room the way you planned it. Now, Arthur, if you'll bring the luggage, we'll be able to settle in and see the house instead of the driveway. How about giving me a tour, Janice?"

Janice beamed as she took Irma's hand and led her into the house through the kitchen entrance. Arthur looked at Peter, shrugged his shoulders, and picked up two of Irma's suitcases plus his own bag. Peter hoisted the rest of Irma's gear, and they followed the women into the house. The men headed upstairs with their burdens, while the women walked through the first floor rooms.

It was obvious from the arrangement of the displayed art that Janice was particularly proud of her collection of Italian sketches, so Irma made sure she spent sufficient time examining them to give them proper deference.

"Janice, these are beautiful. They remind me of some famous paintings I've seen in museums and art books."

"That's the point, Irma. These are preliminary sketches made by famous artists of details in those paintings that you saw. They made a series of sketches before they tackled the final work. There's no way I could afford to own or even have a chance to bid on their finished paintings, but the market tends to overlook sketches, and they are sometimes quite reasonable."

"They also help you understand what the artist thought were the most important details in his painting. You know, Janice, some people walk through a museum gallery getting an overall impression of the paintings, but never looking at the details. My training in forensics and your art historian's eye both emphasize the value of the

24

fine points. I'll bet our interests are similar in other regards as well."

"Well, Irma, I appreciate your saying that. Both Peter and I are detail people. You can't tell a valuable antique from a modern reproduction if you don't examine it very carefully. I really think that Arthur picked up his engineering and investigative skills by growing up with our discussions about the fine points of antiques and art."

"Arthur mentioned that while growing up he did a lot of things with his Uncle Albert and Aunt Mandy. Are they from Peter's side of the family or yours?"

"Neither, actually; Albert and Mandy are very close friends of ours that we treat as part of the family. I should say that Albert *was* a very close friend. He died recently in an automobile accident. It was an awful shock."

"That is sad. Was he in the antiques business too?"

"Albert was quite a bit older than us, and he retired a long time ago. I never knew his exact business, but I think it might have been sporting goods. He did a lot of traveling before he retired. We used to spend extra time with Mandy while he was gone so that she wouldn't get lonely. He may have been an athlete when he was young. He was a soldier in the Second World War, but he never talked about his wartime experiences."

"I know that a lot of the returning veterans avoided discussions because they wanted to put the war behind them. Was his family from this area?"

"No, Irma, I think they were from somewhere in New York. Now that you mention his relatives, I can't remember them ever having visited Albert and Mandy. It must have been due to the distance. They celebrated all of their family occasions with Mandy's relatives. She grew up in New England, but her parents moved to be near her sister in Milwaukee, so they weren't very far away. While you're out here, we should visit Mandy so that you'll get a feeling for that part of our almost-family. Peter and I grew up in New Hampshire, and we're the last survivors of our families. Do you have brothers and sisters?"

"I had an older brother who died in a helicopter crash during the Viet Nam War. He was almost twelve years older than me, and twelve was my age when he died. Ever since then I've considered twelve my unlucky number. Irrational, isn't it?"

"No, Irma, traumatic events scar us for life in many ways. I fell down a long flight of stairs when I was nine years old, and to this day I cling to banisters on staircases. Are your parents still living?"

"My mother died a couple of years after my brother. I've always wondered whether his death hastened hers. My father died a few years after I got out of medical school."

"Well, Irma, you'll be a welcome addition to this family."

"Whoa, Janice; Arthur and I aren't anywhere near that prospect in our relationship."

Janice blushed and grasped the edge of a shelf for support. "I'm sorry, Irma; that's the second time I did that. I'm sometimes too enthusiastic, and I rush ahead of myself. We'd better go find the men before I get into any more trouble."

After a few fruitless checks of rooms on the first floor, Janice and Irma located the men in the basement. As they went down the stairs, Janice said, "I should have thought of this right away. The basement is Peter's favorite hangout. He's probably showing Arthur some of his newly acquired antiques for the shop."

Arthur had been in the midst of examining an old smoking table when he heard the door at the top of the stairs open. He turned toward Peter's workbench and switched his attention to some old tools leaning against it before the women had descended enough stairs to see what he was doing.

26

"Where did you get these tools, Dad, I saw an old two-handled log saw like this one when I visited the reconstructed Plimoth Plantation in Plymouth, Massachusetts. Does this tool actually date back to Pilgrim days?"

Peter grasped the reason for Arthur's sudden change of focus and made a smooth transition. "It's not quite that old. That style of saw was in continued use for clearing forest land and in saw pits for at least another hundred years before they came up with improved models and introduced powered sawmills. This one was made by hand before the industrial revolution started.

"Hello ladies; welcome to my pack rat's nest. Everything I accumulate goes through this little processing center for repair and cleanup before it moves to the shop for sale or to a spot of honor upstairs if we choose to keep it for ourselves."

Irma looked around at the many random objects and pieces of furniture. "You must have to be very selective about what you keep for the house. I see a lot of things that would be fun to have, but how would you make room for them?"

Janice said, "It's not hard because we long ago agreed that if we added something to the house, we would have to transfer an existing item of equal size from the house to the shop. We love living among the antiques, but we don't want to turn this house into a museum, right Peter?"

"Absolutely, and I have to keep reminding myself that I'm in the business of selling antiques, not collecting them. By the way, Irma, take a good look around. Before you leave, I want you to select an item for your apartment as our gift to you."

"Wow, Peter, most of these things are valuable. You shouldn't be so free to part with them. I feel honored by your generosity. It does make me wonder, though, why

Arthur doesn't have antiques at the parsonage. Doesn't he love them too?"

"I'll speak for myself on that one, Dad. I do love to have antiques around, but I'm waiting until I have a real home again. I live in the parsonage, but it's a dwelling place, not a home. I had antiques when I was married to Cindy, but she took all of them when she divorced me in favor of that stay-at-home weatherman. We have all kinds of meetings at the parsonage, and antiques might get damaged there; it's an extension of the church. I'd rather be patient and wait until I have a home before I install antiques again."

Irma smiled. "He's made a bunch of rules and regulations for himself, but I detect a slight romantic outlook in this one. I'll be more than happy to make one of your antiques the center of attention in my apartment."

Janice stood between Arthur and Irma and put one hand on each of their shoulders. "That's enough playing with the clutter for now. You two get settled in, and we'll all go out for dinner. Then we'll come back here, kick off our shoes, and have a nice long rambling conversation."

CHAPTER 7 - MANDY

She had never realized how large their old country house was until Albert died and left her to roam its echoing rooms alone. They had moved here forty-six years ago in what had been the smartest business transaction of their lives. They had purchased the old Dankers farm, moved into the farmhouse, and gradually sold off land for the housing developments that now surrounded them. Because of the nest egg from that real estate, Mandy knew that she would never again have economic worries despite Albert's passing.

She and Albert had spent a good long life together. They had been married in 1947, about one year after he had returned from Europe and been discharged from the Army. She remembered that it had taken him a couple of years to get fully in tune with civilian life, but that had to be natural after such a long and bitter war. Albert had wanted to avoid conversations about his wartime experiences, and she had honored his wishes. Nevertheless, she knew from many of his little comments and occasional nightmares over the years that he had been through great stress in the Army. She had always felt that her job was to bring him back to a normal peaceful life, and she had succeeded. He had gone back to college shortly before they met, and she had enjoyed their year on campus after their wedding. By the time they'd completed six years of marriage, he had become a different person, completely relaxed and closer to her than ever, even though his business trips sometimes kept him away from home for extended periods. She had been a good wife to him, and Albert had fulfilled all of her childhood hopes for a husband. He had been a leader among his peers, humorous in all his conversations, romantic, and oh so handsome. Even in his eighties he had been the handsomest man in all of their groups of friends and contemporaries.

Mandy hustled about the house, flicking her feather duster at every surface with even a suspicion of a dust layer. She telescoped its handle whenever she spotted a spider web on the ceiling or a high shelf. It was a brief cleaning touch-up, but it would have to suffice. Janice had said that she and Peter would be dropping by for a quick visit, along with Arthur and his friend Irma. It would be a good break from the isolation she had felt with Albert gone. Mandy looked forward to meeting Irma. Arthur needed to make another attempt to settle down. His earlier marriage had been a failure, and he deserved another opportunity. Mandy had heard the proud mother excitement in Janice's voice when she said that all four of them would be coming.

She and Albert had never had any children of their own. That had been the one flaw in their otherwise ideal marriage. They had treated Arthur as their surrogate child, and they had fussed over him throughout his growing-up years. This visit would be special for her too.

CHAPTER 8 – ALBERT

Mandy opened her front door to greet her visitors and refresh her outlook on life. Janice and Peter had been so good to her and Albert in the past, and Arthur had been an important ingredient in their lives. She had heard about Irma, but this sophisticated yet open-armed woman who approached her exceeded all of Mandy's expectations. A round robin of hugging and cheek kissing ensued.

"Welcome to all of you. Come on in, and help me remember the lively times this house has seen. I've been a bit down because of loneliness without Albert here."

Janice led the parade into the living room, and brought Mandy and Irma together with one arm around each of them. "You two are so similar that you are bound to hit it off. Mandy, you won't believe it, but Irma was looking at my Italian sketches with me, and she made the same comment you once did about people who enjoyed the ambiance of a museum without ever studying the art in detail."

Irma said, "Well, some artists are impressionists, and some museum-goers go to get impressions too. What do you think, Mandy?"

"It's partly that, and partly a question of being so awed by the famous paintings that they don't want to get too close to them. Actually, some of the oil painting techniques don't lend themselves to close study. The best overall appreciation of some paintings is done at a distance. It's hard for me to comprehend how those artists learned how to paint a crude detail so that it looked sharp and focused when viewed from afar. Anyway, I'm glad you're here, Irma. Help yourself to some coffee and cookies."

Janice said, "One thing about Mandy, she always has coffee ready when we visit. Coffee is a central ingredient of her hospitality. Do you enjoy coffee, Irma?"

"I do, and I'm beginning to see how much Mandy and Albert influenced Arthur. He requires coffee to be at all functional."

Arthur emphasized her comment by smiling and helping himself to a cup of black coffee. Peter remained by the entrance to the room, looking glum.

Mandy spotted his frown. She went over and grasped his hand. "Don't hesitate to come in because Albert has left us, Peter. This place can still be upbeat; I feel his spirit in every room of the house."

Peter walked in, still holding Mandy's hand. He started to say something but thought better of it when he saw Arthur shake his head. Instead, he walked over to the tray and took two cookies. If he kept something in his mouth, he wouldn't say anything that he'd later regret. It would be difficult, but he would have to avoid announcing his revised attitude toward Albert until Arthur and Irma could learn more.

Irma winked at Peter and turned to Mandy. "How did you and Albert meet?"

"It always sounds like fiction when I talk about it, but we met at an ice cream parlor. I slipped on an ice cube that had fallen, and he helped me up. They don't have very many ice cream parlors with soda fountains anymore."

Irma laughed. "Did you by any chance slip on purpose so that he would notice you?"

"I think it was more a case of him dropping ice cubes on the floor so that he could rescue me after I fell. He always was clever and creative in his approach to people."

Peter raised his eyebrow at Arthur and Irma. "That sounds a bit manipulative to me."

Mandy said, "I prefer to think of it as having been chivalrous with a slight roguish touch. We were young then, and he was very handsome. Did you and Arthur meet in a romantic way, Irma?"

"Not exactly, he discovered a dead body in his church attic, and I came to determine the cause of death. There was nothing romantic in that scene...Was that ice cream parlor in your home town?"

"No, I grew up in Bedford, Massachusetts, and the ice cream parlor scene took place on the Canadian side of Niagara Falls during a vacation. Albert was there on vacation from Ohio State University, where he had enrolled under the G.I. Bill. The returning vets were a bit older than the other students."

"What happened next? Was it: *love at first sight?*"

"I thought that I had made a complete fool of myself, but we did have hamburgers together the next day and exchanged contact information. I didn't expect to ever hear from him again. Two weeks later he called me and said he was in Boston doing a research project and would like to visit me in Bedford. We got together for pizza and a movie, and then kept things going on a correspondence basis for most of a year before things turned serious. Then we got married."

"It sounds as though you were the research project that took him to Boston. Did he have a lot of family members at the wedding?"

"No, Irma, we were very naughty for that time. We eloped, and told our families about it later. They weren't too happy, but our marriage worked for sixty-three years, so that wasn't too bad at all."

Peter asked, "Did Albert push you to elope?"

"Nope, it was my idea from the start. I was afraid that his family wouldn't like me, so I didn't give them a chance to object. Albert had told me how difficult his mother, father, and sister were, so I sidestepped the issue. It turned out to have been a good decision. They caused trouble for us later, so we moved far enough away from them to avoid any unpleasantness."

Arthur had been listening quietly up to this point. "What kind of trouble did they cause, Mandy?"

"They said that Albert had changed during the war and that he had come back with mental problems. They said he wasn't fit to live independently, and they tried unsuccessfully to have our marriage annulled. We ended up turning our backs on them. After their legal attack on us we only dealt with my side of the family. Albert accepted that arrangement and never expressed any regrets about it later."

"How many times did you get together with his family before the trouble started?"

"Actually, Irma, I don't remember any formal gatherings with them, but it was a long time ago. As I recall, most of our dealings were by correspondence. They at least wrote letters to us at first, but then it degenerated into name-calling and legal actions. I'd rather not talk about it if you don't mind. I was upset at the time." Mandy noticed motion out of the corner of her eye and reacted to it.

"Peter, don't worry about that cookie you just dropped. Throw it out, and take some fresh ones. Are you nervous about having Arthur and Irma here?"

While Peter picked up the broken cookie, Irma took Mandy's arm and asked her one more question in a stage whisper voice. "I don't want to seem insensitive, Mandy, but the pathologist side of me has to ask you something. Is Albert buried in or near Richmond?"

"No, Dear, Albert told me many times that he wanted to be cremated when he died, so I followed his wishes. His ashes are in an urn on a shelf in the library."

This time it was Arthur who dropped a cookie.

CHAPTER 9 – CONSPIRACY

Renee reviewed the results of her search for facts about the five returned soldiers and their families. There were too many coincidences in her findings for there not to be a conspiracy at some level.

First, she had found that none of the soldiers had family members listed for the period when they were in the Army. Then she had discovered that all six returned soldiers had attended Ohio State University on the G.I. Bill for the same two academic years, from September of 1947 until June of 1949. It was also strange that none of them had continued studying to finish a four year degree. She had not yet discovered recent addresses for the five men she was tracking, so she hoped some of them would be revealed from Arthur and Irma's research on Albert Dandrich.

Renee snapped back to the present when she heard the garage door open. She glanced at her watch and realized that it was time for Bobby to arrive home, and she had given no thought at all to preparing dinner. She might be in trouble. It wasn't the first time she hadn't planned ahead. The garage door motor sounded again as the door closed, and Bobby entered through the connecting door.

"Hi, Bobby, how were things at the department today?"

"This was one of those calm days when I could actually plan to be home on time. What have you been up to?" Bobby put down his briefcase, kissed Renee, and draped his uniform jacket over the back of a chair.

"I'm still tracking some of those World War II soldiers from the case with Irma and Arthur. I'm getting interesting but confusing results. How would you go about finding current addresses for people whose last known locations dated back to the late 1940's?"

"The easiest approach is to work through the National Crime Information Center within their Missing Persons category. They have a huge database, but you need authorization to use it. I wouldn't be able to gain access for your project, because it's all outside of my jurisdiction. You also require special software and a secure computer with documentation of users and tight access control. They do everything practical to document need-to-know and to protect privacy rights, but there are ways around it if you have the right connections."

"Do you or I have those connections, Bobby?"

"You were on pretty good terms with Penny Gonzalez during that poisoning case."

"Good thinking, Bobby. As a reward, I'll let you take Momma and me out to dinner tonight. After dinner you can take me to Irma's apartment so that I can look up Penny's direct telephone number. I'll go downstairs to Momma's apartment and let her know."

"Fair enough, Renee, but you're going to have to let me get unofficially involved in this missing persons case of yours."

"You're in, but I haven't told you the whole story. It goes way beyond missing persons. I'll fill you in after we get back from dinner and Irma's place."

After a tasty but filling Italian meal, they drove to Irma's apartment, otherwise known as the ABC Consultants headquarters. Renee went up to find Penny's phone number while Bobby sat in the car with Momma. He and Momma had become great friends since she had moved into the basement apartment he had built for her. He'd never expected to feel close to his mother-in-law, but she was someone special. Her sense of humor, her personal experience of milestones in civil rights history, and her street smarts gleaned from her Chicago inner city years, were all impressive. On several occasions he had even consulted her on Police matters when he wanted to understand how people of the older generation thought. Add to that the fact that his parents had long since died, and it was only natural that he treated Momma as his own adopted mother. They were in the midst of a lively discussion of how soul food helped to remind upwardly mobile African-Americans of their past lean times, when Renee came out of the building and climbed into the right front seat.

"I have Penny's office number and her cell phone number also. It's too late to call tonight, but I'll make contact first thing in the morning. Let's stop for ice cream on the way, and then we can go home and play cards for a while until you're ready for bed, Momma."

"I'll take butter pecan ice cream; that was our favorite when you were small. I'll pass on the cards so that Bobby can get right to learning about your case and anything else he wants to learn from you. You can't keep this boy dangling on a string, Renee."

Bobby laughed and reached over the front seatback to give Momma a high-five hand slap. "It's nice to have one of the women in my house on my side." He felt Renee's playful jab in his ribs as he started the car engine.

CHAPTER 10 – COMPLICATIONS

Penny Gonzalez finished printing out several sheets displaying tabular data and walked into her husband's office. She and Joe were principals in a covert government agency that handled a variety of sensitive assignments while remaining invisible to the press and others who monitored the larger and more well-known agencies. The papers stacked on Joe's table for filing told her that he was bored.

"Here we go again. I have what appears to be an intriguing case with nasty implications, and it comes from our ABC friends in Parkville, Illinois."

"Did something happen at Arthur's church again?"

"Not this time, but it does involve Arthur and his family. Renee Andrews called to ask whether we could track down the current addresses of some World War II veterans. That seemed like a simple enough request for our assistance. She then said that these veterans had all served with one of Arthur's father's friends who died recently and that they all may have been former German soldiers masquerading as Americans."

"That German impostor possibility is intriguing. Was she looking for contact information in order to notify them of their friend's death?"

"That's what I assumed as I went through the usual procedures. I was able to get recent addresses without much trouble. Then I discovered something disturbing. The five people she was tracking all died within weeks of Arthur's father's friend."

"What were the listed causes of death?"

"Three died in automobile accidents, and two took accidental overdoses of their medications. In every case the authorities attributed the death to old age related frailties. The automobile accidents were attributed to slow reflexes and lack of concentration, while the drug overdoses were said to be due to lapses of memory."

"Did all five of these guys live in the same area as Arthur's Father's friend?"

"That's what makes these events even less likely to be coincidences. They lived in five different states. There's no doubt in my mind that some individual or organization hastened their departure from our midst."

"Somebody had a grudge against these people. Why would someone want to eliminate them when they all had to be at least eighty years old? I think it's time for us to abandon Washington for the Midwest again."

CHAPTER 11 – MOMMA

Bobby was in the midst of shining his shoes when Momma came up from her basement apartment and sat in the wooden rocking chair next to the fireplace.

"Hi, Momma, did you come up to see how policemen make their shoes so shiny?"

"No, Bobby, I came up because I'm disturbed by Renee's case. She filled me in on most of the facts this morning, telling me to keep it confidential. You already know about it, so it shouldn't be a problem if I talk to you."

"That's fine; I'll listen and shine shoes at the same time."

"This business about a close friend turning out to have been a Nazi impostor is a pretty terrible thing, but it raises the question of how well we know any of our friends. All we know is what people choose to tell us."

"Are you saying that you have questions about my background, Momma?"

"No, but I might have some surprises for you and Renee about my own. I feel a little guilty about not having told my own daughter everything she has a right to know. I guess it comes from wanting to have people always think the best of you."

Bobby stopped polishing his shoes and set them aside. "We all have secrets of some kind. Do you want to share yours with me?"

"I think I'd better, although Renee would be mad if I told you before I told her. Maybe we should wait until she gets back from the store."

"You're sounding mysterious, but that's fine with me. Besides, I think I heard her car door slam. I'll help her with the bundles, and then we'll both come back to hear what you have to say."

Bobby headed out the back door to the driveway. A few minutes later he and Renee returned carrying bags and packages. After putting them down, Renee approached her mother.

"Momma, Bobby tells me you want to tell us something you've never shared with me before. Is this something serious? Is it a health problem?"

"If you two will sit down, and be patient, I'll try to make the words come out. There are some things that you tuck away in the back of your mind and expect that you'll never have to revisit them.

"Here I am, happily living with my police chief son-in-law, and my daughter and her best friends are all investigators of one sort or another. I love you dearly, but I've been more and more bothered by the fact that my conscience isn't entirely clear."

"Momma, you always kept me on the straight and narrow way. I can't believe that you strayed."

"Keep quiet, girl. Don't make this confession any harder than it already is."

"Sorry, Momma, go ahead."

"I have to tell you the truth, even though I planned to keep it a forever secret, because everyone is so bothered that Mandy Dandrich may have been married to a disguised Nazi soldier."

"You're not going to say that you had Nazi connections, Momma. You've never even been out of the country."

Momma glared at her daughter, and Renee settled back in her chair, shaking her head.

"It's almost as bad as that. I thought I'd be able to keep secret the fact that your father was a street gang member. He never told me in so many words, but I'm pretty sure he was involved in at least a couple of murders

41

on the streets of Chicago. I never married him, and he was all too happy to get out of my life as soon as you were born, but he was a bad one."

Bobby asked, "How did you get involved with him in the first place?"

"I was young, and I got mixed up with a bad crowd. With all of the wild parties, I ended up pregnant and had to make up my mind to be responsible and become a parent. Renee, I'm guilty of letting you grow up with a fictional background to protect you from nasty rumors and accusations. That's also why my family moved to a better neighborhood where nobody knew me. We lived with Mother and Dad until you were old enough for school, and then I got a part-time job. My folks loved and supported me even though I had a street child, and that made me love them even more."

Bobby touched Renee's arm in sympathy. "Did Renee's father ever go to jail for his gang activities?"

"He was killed in a turf war between his gang and another one when Renee was two years old. I didn't even go to his funeral, because I had put that part of my life behind me."

"You told me my father died in combat during the last few weeks of the Viet Nam War."

"That's when he did die, but the combat that killed him was on the south side of Chicago. I didn't exactly lie, but I hedged a bit so that you would think well of him and would grow up unscarred by his troubles."

"Did you love him, Momma?"

"Let's say that he was an exciting guy, and I willingly had sex with him. He didn't have to force himself on me. I didn't want to get pregnant, but I accepted my status and cherished my baby – you."

Bobby reached out and grasped his wife's two hands. "Renee, does this information make you feel any different, and will it affect our family life?"

"It will take a while to get used to it, but I've had enough street and police background to know how these things happen. I've often wondered how those street gang killers go on to live anything like a normal life.

"Momma, did you change his name when you talked to me about Dad?"

"I told you his name was William. It wasn't, but his true name is one thing I'll continue to keep secret. When you were born, I was all by myself at the hospital because my preacher father wanted to make me understand his official church position. He kept my mother from coming by herself, even though she wanted to support me. I told the doctors the father's name was William Simmons, and that's what they put on the birth certificate. I wasn't married, so nobody saw anything unusual in my choosing to raise you under my family name.

"I'm telling you this now because I can understand how hard it would be for the wife of that disguised Nazi to tell her children the whole truth."

"They didn't have any children and we don't think she even knew about her husband's past, but now I know how their children would have felt."

CHAPTER 12 – MEETING IN PARKVILLE

Penny and Joe Gonzalez left their motel after a quick continental breakfast and headed over to the Parkville Police Station for a meeting with Bobby and Renee Andrews. Arthur Blake and Irma Custis were still at the Blake home in Richmond, but they would sit in on the conference by speakerphone. It was time for the several pieces of the puzzle to be combined. At the Police Station, Sergeant Al Gomez greeted them at the front desk and ushered them into the conference room. There they found Bobby and Renee testing the speakerphone connection to Arthur and Irma. Penny & Joe sat down and placed a file of papers on the table. Al Gomez left and returned to the front desk to handle any new visitors and calls.

Bobby, as the host, started the discussion. "I'm only acting as an individual and supplying this meeting room because the Parkville Police have no jurisdiction in this case, but I do have a couple of observations. First, this Nazi impostor business sounds bizarre, but we know there have been cases of Germans coming to this country and applying for U.S. citizenship under assumed names to hide their wartime backgrounds. We have to take it seriously. Second, there must be a conspiracy because there are coincidences involving six different people, and six-way coincidences are virtually impossible. Those are my initial points. Who wants to discuss some of the specifics of this case?"

The speakerphone emitted Arthur's echoing voice. "The team has formed again, and you folks are making good progress. We've discovered one way for an impostor to avoid detection by family members and some old friends. Albert Dandrich had a fight with his family in connection with the woman he wanted to marry. Consequently, once Albert and Mandy were married, they moved away and no longer had anything to do with Albert's relatives."

Irma's voice crackled through the speaker. "Albert's family became convinced he had developed mental problems due to his wartime experiences, so they were content to let Mandy take responsibility for him while they went on with their own lives."

Joe nodded and loudly said, "That makes sense. There always tended to be a gap between families and their returning soldiers. The relatives knew that they couldn't grasp what the soldiers had experienced, so they kept their distance and avoided discussing it."

Arthur cleared his throat and chuckled. "Good thought, Joe, but you don't have to speak loudly. This contraption works well enough for you to speak as though we're right there with you. Let's review some of the coincidences we've found. Bobby is right in saying that coincidences confirm a conspiracy. Why don't you start, Renee?"

"While you were speaking, I was sitting here shaking my head in disagreement. I'm going to start by questioning what you and Irma have reported. You said that Albert had a fight with his family and stayed away from them. I'm going to go out on a limb based on what I've found out about the other returned soldiers. I think Albert staged that fight, because none of the other soldiers had any family members, at least while the war was going on. That was my first big coincidence. If these men were Nazis taking the place of American soldiers, they simplified things by assuming the identities of soldiers who had no families. My second big coincidence was my discovery that all five of my people went to Ohio State University between 1947 and 1949 on G.I. Bill funding. My third coincidence was that none of my five stayed beyond that period to complete a degree program and graduate. How does Albert fit into this picture?"

Irma's voice echoed through the speaker. "That's a Bingo, Renee. Albert was at Ohio State University at the same time and also did not stay to graduate."

Arthur said, "I thought the story of that fight with his family didn't ring true. Mandy never even met them. All communications were in the form of letters and legal documents. If none of the American soldiers had families, the Nazi impostors would minimize the probability of detection, especially if they moved away from the soldiers' home towns. Do you have anything else for us, Renee?"

"I couldn't find current addresses for Albert Dandrich's five companions, so I asked Penny and Joe if they would use their connections to assist us. I told them that you have been talking with Albert's widow and know his address. Penny, what did you folks find?"

"We found enough to believe that this has gone beyond a postwar conspiracy and has become a federal felony case. Albert died about two months ago, but all five of the others died within the few weeks preceding him. Albert was the last to die. Including him, four died due to automobile crashes, and two others died from drug overdoses. Individually, these events were all taken to have been accidents."

Arthur's whistle came through the speaker. "Coincidences in both life and death: We're no longer simply trying to help my father with the trauma of finding his friend's Nazi connections."

Joe spoke in a voice only slightly more subdued than before. "We'll check on the four automobile accident cases for tampering and witness observations. The two drug overdose events should be your area of inquiry, Irma."

"I'll take charge of those, Joe. I'm sure that if you give me the contact information for the medical examiners, I'll be able to get them to cooperate. Arthur has something to add."

"Joe, we're already here in Richmond. Albert crashed between here and Lake Geneva, Wisconsin. If Bobby will contact the Richmond Police Chief and recommend us as being qualified, Irma and I will do the preliminary work to check out the wrecked car. Dad told me that it's being stored in Richmond, awaiting a visit by insurance company people. Does arranging a contact get in the way of jurisdiction questions, Bobby?"

"That won't be a problem, Arthur. Coordination between police departments is a major Homeland Security goal, and we've all bought into it in order to detect potential terrorist plots."

"What about you, Joe? Do you have a problem with our checking out the local vehicle and accident circumstances?"

"That should work out, Arthur. Put on your engineer hat, and work with Irma on the forensics end of it. You two may be better suited to checking a crashed car than we are. Anyway, we should get earlier results if we split up the work. What do you think, Penny?"

"I'm on board. I'll get Irma the location and contact information for the drug overdose incidents. The three car accidents that we'll be investigating occurred in Florida and Texas, so we'll be heading south. Keep in touch on a daily basis. There's somebody or some group out there behind all of this, and we'll want to get after them quickly. Renee, would you coordinate the information received from both of our groups? Depending on what we find, you might have to join us or go to a new investigation site."

"That sounds good to me, Penny. While you're doing field investigations, I'll look into the provisions of their insurance policies and wills if you give me all of their personal information. We might find unusual patterns in those areas also."

CHAPTER 13 – FAMILY MATTERS

Bobby pretended to read the newspaper while he watched Renee talking on the telephone. When she pushed her chair back and stretched, he knew it would be safe to distract her with his concerns.

"Hey there, partner, I'd like to talk with you if you can tear yourself away from work."

"OK, Bobby, I need a break anyway. I'm having trouble locating the insurance and legal contacts for those old soldiers. What's up?"

"When Momma told us about your father, you appeared to take it all in stride, but I have a feeling that you're bothered about it, and I'm worried that this news about your origins might hurt our relationship."

"What's not going to hurt anything is the fact that you care about my feelings when I'm bothered. Thanks, husband. Yes, I'm unhappy that Momma didn't tell me about my roots a long time ago, and yes, I'm having trouble getting used to the fact that my father was a street thug who killed people. I don't know whether Momma didn't trust my ability to handle it, or if she thought she could get away with never telling me. I'm going to give some long hard thoughts to deciding how much I can forgive her. Wouldn't it bother you if you were in my shoes?"

"It would make me up-tight and resentful. That's why I couldn't accept your 'I'm big enough to cope with this.' comment. New information like this changes our self-images and has to be a burden. I want you to know that I love you and that I want to share any emotional baggage with you. This new background doesn't affect our relationship. I married you for the person you are today, regardless of your heritage. Momma did a great job of seeing that you turned out right."

"And you do a great job of making a girl know that she's wanted. Now let me get back to work, and I'll make your favorite dinner later. We have to catch these murderers before the trail gets cold or they leave the country."

CHAPTER 14 – BATTERED CARS

Richmond Police Chief Lois Berkus met Arthur and Irma at the chain link gate of what passed for the police car pound. In addition to three wrecked and four towed cars, the fenced-in area contained two snowplow blades, a float trailer for the Fourth of July parade, an old and inoperable John Deere tractor, and a pile of road salt covered with a blue plastic tarp.

Arthur extended his arm for a handshake. "Lois, I'm Arthur Blake. You know my parents, Peter and Janice. I'd like you to meet Irma Custis. We're partners in a private group, ABC Consultants, and we're working with a federal agency on some missing persons investigations."

"I'm glad to meet the two of you. Your dad bragged about your investigation work when I saw him at the Bear's Den restaurant last month. According to him, you're a man of many hats and talents. Are you still in the ministry?"

"Absolutely, Lois, I do the Lord's work in the church and wherever He leads me through this kind of project."

"I understand from your call that you want to see the car from the crash that killed Albert Dandrich. It's that blue one back in the corner. He was a nice old gent. Sometimes I wondered how he could remember so many jokes. He'd tell them all the time at the American Legion functions. We were both Legion members."

They walked over to the smashed blue 2009 Buick LaCrosse, and started to examine it. Arthur opened the crumpled hood as far as possible and used his flashlight to peer into the engine compartment. While he examined the scrambled engine wiring, piping, and belts, Irma asked Lois for details about the accident.

"Was this a single vehicle accident, or did he collide with one of these other cars?"

"I didn't visit the accident site that day, but my records show that this car smashed into a concrete column supporting an overhead bridge. It was set back from the road and had a protective railing in front of it, but he still managed to hit the column pretty hard. His car must have gone over the railing. The troopers assumed that he had a heart attack, either before the accident or as the result of it. He was quite elderly."

"You said *assumed*. That would mean that there was no autopsy, correct?"

"The accident took place just across the Wisconsin line, so it wasn't my decision, but the facts were so clear-cut that they didn't feel that an autopsy was needed. We ended up with the wrecked car because we were so close and convenient for the towing company and because Albert's home was here."

"Lois, waiving the autopsy might have been logical when you were looking at this accident by itself, but we suspect foul play because several of his friends in other states died in similar accidents within one month of this one."

"Wow, that knowledge would shake up any cop's thinking. Maybe we'd better exhume the body and have an autopsy after all."

"Unfortunately, the body was cremated, so we'll have to look for other evidence."

Arthur stopped his examination of the engine compartment and wriggled his way out from under the crumpled inclined hood. "Irma, Lois, nothing looks unusual under the hood. I don't think anyone tampered with the car in advance."

Irma beckoned for him to join her. "Take a look at the driver's side of the car with me. Lois, I see that almost all of the side window glass is missing. Did you bring the broken glass back or simply dispose of it?"

"Sorry, Irma, the glass was swept up and thrown away to avoid flat tires, but we do have photographs that show it on the ground next to the car."

"Good, I'll want to examine those photos. Arthur, look at these scrapes along the driver's side of the car. They have streaks of maroon paint in them."

"That's consistent with the car having been sideswiped and forced off the road. Make a mental note that we should mention that to Penny and Joe. They can look for sideswiping evidence on the other accident cars. That action would let an assailant determine where the accident would take place. The problem is that it might only result in minor damage. Do you think that someone wanting to be sure Albert died could count on slight sideswiping to do the trick?"

"I'm with you on that one, Arthur. That's why I asked Lois about the glass. I'd guess that the person who sideswiped the car would have increased the fatality odds by shooting a small caliber bullet through Albert's driver-side window. If they did that, the broken glass would show cracks radiating from the spot of the bullet hole. Even broken glass on the ground would show some triangular and pointed polygonal pieces."

"Lois, can you remember from the photographs whether Albert had any bleeding on the left side of his head?"

"I don't have to remember. I thought you would want to see them, so I brought the photos in this file folder...Let's see; blood on the left side of his head is affirmative, aft of the left temple and in front of the ear. You're pretty good at this, Irma. I'll have to give you another affirmative for triangular shards of glass on the ground near the car and back on the road. There were probably pieces inside the car as well. I'll call my colleagues in Wisconsin and tell them that this case should be treated as an active murder investigation."

CHAPTER 15 – CORRELATIONS

"Hi, Penny, this is Irma checking in. Arthur and I found some interesting and disturbing information in examining the Albert Dandrich car. We've confirmed that it was murder, and we know how it was done."

"We've checked out one crashed vehicle in Florida, and we had similar results. We found that a following vehicle on a lonely road through the Everglades smashed into Max Griggins' rear bumper. Our theory is that Max pulled over to discuss the accident with the other driver and exchange information. The following driver probably knocked him unconscious. Then he put Max back into his car and pushed the car off the road into the swamp with the windows open. Max drowned as the car filled with water. The original write-up concluded that he fell asleep at the wheel and swerved off the road into the swamp."

"That's similar to our case, but a bit different to suit local conditions. Are you going to exhume the body?"

"We're in the process of getting a court order right now, Irma. We want to see if there is evidence of blunt force trauma to the head that can't be explained by the car rolling off the road shoulder into the water."

"You might find more than blunt force trauma. Look for a small caliber bullet wound. We found photographic evidence that Albert had been shot in the head; my guess is a .22 caliber bullet; and car body evidence that his vehicle had been sideswiped to force him into colliding with a bridge column. The local police are going to request that the Wisconsin cops look for an abandoned damaged maroon car with paint that matches the scrapings on Albert's Buick."

"You're making good progress, Irma. Stolen cars used in the crashes, would likely be dumped somewhere. I'll have the Florida police put out a bulletin on an abandoned car with a damaged front bumper. We can check again to see whether we can pinpoint the color from paint scrapings."

"I wish I could supply a bullet for ballistics comparison, but Albert's body was cremated, along with the bullet. It would have melted. All we have is a photo of the wound."

"If we find a bullet when we dig up Max's body, we'll save it to compare in case the other two accident cases are similar. We have people looking at those events, and we'll give them your information. You should move on to looking at the drug overdose cases once your visit with Arthur's family is concluded. It certainly looks as though somebody else knew about these Nazi impostors and decided to eliminate them."

"Watch it, Penny, you're jumping to conclusions. We haven't proved they were Nazis yet, although they were definitely targets for somebody."

CHAPTER 16 – CHANGES

Arthur sat on the edge of their bed rereading his accumulated notes on the case. Irma draped her sweatshirt on the chair and gave him a kiss on the cheek.

"You look troubled, Arthur."

"Did you ever have the feeling that you missed something, but you're not quite sure what? That's how I feel now. There's something about what we've already learned regarding this case that bothers me. If I read these notes enough times, maybe it will jump out at me."

"If you keep sitting on that bed, maybe I'll jump out at you."

"Well, that's an interesting prospect. I'll have to find a way to thank my mother for engineering this sleeping arrangement. Maybe the reason I can't figure out what's bothering me on this case is that you distract me too much."

"Are you saying that you don't like my kind of distraction?"

"Oh, I like it all right, but I'll have to upgrade my thinking processes so that I can concentrate on two things at the same time. Not to change the subject, but what did you think of Mandy? Do you think she knew about her husband's background?"

"No, I think she saw him as her hero and built their family life around him. Your mother told me that she worried about Mandy being able to have a stable life on her own."

"Becoming a widow when you are old and dependent is difficult for any woman, or for that matter, any man."

"I agree, and I think Mandy will get through this transition period without many problems, but your mother views Mandy's status differently. Those two couples spent a lot of time together over the years, and Janice saw Mandy as a very dependent follower. From my brief exposure to Mandy, I get the feeling that she catered to her husband to make him feel that he was the prime mover. In his absence, I see strength in her that she may have hidden in the past."

"That's an interesting insight. This whole case is about people and situations not being what they seem. We react to the images that people create for themselves, without knowing whether they are masks or their true personalities. Sometimes I don't even know myself completely."

"Welcome to the club, partner. How do you let someone new into your life when you haven't even learned everything about yourself?"

"It's called faith, Irma. That's one support to my life that I've learned to trust. Sometimes I have doubts and misgivings, but I get through by having faith that God will come through for me when I'm in a terrible bind and willing to admit it."

"Hold it, Parson. Are you saying that letting me into your life has put you in a terrible bind?"

"I was referring to the serious side of life, Doctor. With regard to you, I've had some strange symptoms affecting my stability and fantasies since we met. You may have something that's contagious."

"It's a rare social disease that's contagious only toward you."

"I do like that line of thought, Irma, but one of the other things you do to me when we talk, is that you sharpen my thinking process. I know now what it was that was bothering me. I have to call Mandy."

Arthur reached into his pocket and retrieved a folded note his father had given him earlier with Mandy's address and telephone number. He checked his watch to be sure it was a reasonable time and keyed the number into his cell phone. The third ring was truncated as Mandy picked up her receiver.

Irma concentrated on Arthur's side of the conversation, hoping to detect the nature of his analytical breakthrough before he announced it.

"Hi, Mandy, this is Arthur Blake calling. I wanted to let you know that we thoroughly enjoyed our visit with you yesterday. I also wanted to let you know how impressed I was with the craftsmanship on that smoking table that you gave Dad as a remembrance of Albert. It's a real delight. Are you sure that you don't mind parting with such a fine piece? I'm sure Dad would take a different item if you wanted to change your mind."

"Oh, is that so? Well, that certainly makes a difference. No, we'll be here for a few more days. If you have the time and it fits the folks' schedule, I'd like to take all of you out for lunch tomorrow. Great! I'll talk with them and then one of us will get back to you to let you know whether the adventure is on, and to give you all the details."

"That sounds good. Hopefully, we'll see you soon. Goodbye for now."

Arthur put his phone back into his pocket. He raised his right eyebrow as he looked at Irma.

"The things that bothered me were the question of why Albert would keep that incriminating Nazi material in his table compartment all this time, and why Mandy had chosen that particular piece to give Dad. Did this whole case come out of Mandy's random decision to give him that table when she could have given him any one of Albert's possessions? When we were at their house, I looked into Albert's library. He had some beautiful old furniture pieces and decorative accessories in there.

"Anyway, the mystery of Albert's identity has moved to a new level. Mandy told me that she gave Dad the smoking table because Albert left written instructions for her to do so."

Irma's earlier playful smile had been replaced by her professional's thoughtful expression. "This was no accident. Albert wanted your Dad to find that secret compartment and its contents."

"We'd better study that table some more. Whatever we find may affect our conversation with Mandy at lunch tomorrow."

CHAPTER 17 – REVISITING THE TABLE

Janice had gone to the supermarket, so Irma and Arthur were able to talk openly with Peter. They explained Arthur's lunch invitation to Mandy and the need to take a closer look at the smoking table. The three of them headed for the basement. On the way, Peter stopped to get a few special tools and a magnifying glass from his desk in the den. When Peter descended the basement stairs, he found Irma and Arthur waiting for him. He noticed an unusual expression on Arthur's face.

"What is it, son? Why are you looking at me like that?"

"I don't know if you realize it, Dad, but your tension and irritation on matters related to Albert have diffused. You're looking much more relaxed."

"I still have uncertainties, and I don't know what we're about to discover, but the information that Albert wanted me to have that table gives me hope that he wasn't as monstrous as his proud Nazi photograph suggested. Anyway, I think I know what to look for."

Irma greeted Peter with a sweep of her arm through an arc aimed at the table, suggesting that he should take the lead in this reassessment. "What do you expect to find?"

"The old master furniture makers were extremely clever. When I found that hidden compartment, I assumed that I had revealed the table's secrets. I overlooked the fact that antique furniture may have more than one secret to divulge. I once read an article about a desk with twenty-one separate secret compartments. When some of these old pieces were made there were no such things as safe deposit boxes at banks. People stored their valuables in these specialized articles of furniture. Arthur, let's turn it over and work from the bottom up toward the top. If we look at it from a different angle, we might see something more."

"Good thinking, Dad. I see that three of the legs have their square top sections flush to the bottom of the table with all edges parallel, but one leg appears to be slightly rotated. It may be a little loose."

"Ordinarily, I would agree that the leg needs a bit of tightening, but given our feeling that this table has remaining secrets, let's unscrew all of the legs and see what happens. There's a fine line structure on the bottom of the table that suggest that it was made from several boards joined together."

They unscrewed each leg and handed it to Irma to set aside. Then they tapped and gently pried at the split lines between adjacent boards. Arthur signaled his father to move back so that he could try something by himself.

"I think I have something, Dad. There's a fine square outline of a separate board in the middle. Prying at three sides of that square has no effect. The fourth side moves a little bit. I think that the central square board is actually attached to one of the edge sections so that the central square plus that edge section slide out like a drawer." He pulled on the indicated edge piece while holding back on the opposite edge.

"Keep trying, Arthur, that parting line is widening into a slot. There, it's opening wider. There is a hidden space."

Arthur had to exert a lot of force, but gradually the board slid out on hidden tongue ribs fitted into side edge grooves. "The neat thing about this design is that it won't move at all if the legs are screwed onto the table. Each leg screws through a matching hole in a bottom board to lock it. Two legs have to be removed to allow that movable board to slide. It's a tedious but secure process."

Irma looked over their shoulders. "OK, woodworkers and engineers, let's ask the next question, do you see anything inside that recess?"

Peter probed inside the cavity with a long, angled pair of tweezers. "There's something in there that feels like paper and flexes when I touch it. I'm trying to grab an edge of it, but I don't want to take a chance on tearing it. I think I have it, but it feels like it's snagged or caught on something. Give me the flashlight, Arthur."

Irma picked up the flashlight before Arthur could reach it and handed it to Peter. She noted that Peter gave the probing of the inside of a piece of furniture the same reverence that she devoted to examining the organs inside a dead person's abdominal cavity. She had always felt that the sanctity of the human body did not end with death.

Peter gave a running commentary on his effort. "I can see the problem now. There's another one of Albert's manila envelopes in there. This one looks much newer than the one with that damned picture in it. The envelope was folded to make it fit into the recess, and I've been pulling on the open end of one of the folds so that it expands as I pull on it. The more I pull, the more it jams. I'll try to rotate the folded envelope. There, it's moving. Now it's turned so that I can grab the folded edge. When I pull on that edge, the envelope will tend to fold smaller rather than get larger and jam. One more pull...I have it out! Wow, this one is bigger than the other envelope. I thought it would be smaller. That's a sizable compartment in there."

He placed the envelope on the workbench, and carefully unfolded it. As Peter prepared to undo the clasp, Arthur checked to be sure that nothing remained in the table compartment. "I think you have everything, Dad. He put it all in one packet so that nothing would rattle when the table was moved. Spread the contents on the bench the way we laid out the batch from the first secret compartment."

"Not quite yet, Arthur; I think you should see what he printed on the envelope. It's marked: *Highly confidential –*

to be opened only by Peter or Arthur Blake after my death...Albert Dandrich.

CHAPTER 18 – DIFFERENCES

Joe and Penny Gonzalez sat outside their motel alongside Interstate Ten near Tallahassee, Florida. They had spread their notes regarding the two Florida car crashes on the bench between them.

"Penny, you said that when you talked with Irma on the telephone, she cautioned you that we have yet to prove that Dandrich and his Army buddies were definitely Nazi impostors, even though she and the Blakes had evidence from that smoking table compartment to suggest they were."

"Irma was using her pathologist's training to indicate that the evidence suggested they were impostors, but that we had not yet reached the level of proving it. Why are you focusing on that point?"

"My problem is that we all agree that these six men were murdered in a coordinated set of assassinations that were made to look like accidents due to old age. If we accept the *suggestion* that they were concealed Nazis, then I can think of at least two capable organizations that would want to eliminate them. I could see the Nazi hunters or Israel's Mossad intelligence group closing in on them as part of their continuing mopping-up of hidden Nazis. If our six victims turned out to be innocent elderly Americans, who would want to kill them?"

"Hold it, Joe. Nobody is suggesting that these guys were innocent. They were definitely involved in something devious, and they probably were Nazis. Irma was only making a technical point."

"I'll buy that, but I'm making the technical point that this case will be a lot easier to investigate and solve if they were Nazis than if they were part of any other group.

Anyway, let's get back to the Tallahassee car wreck. It was a little different from any of the others."

"It wasn't that much different."

"The Dandrich wreck in Wisconsin was caused by sideswiping the car and shooting the driver. The Griggins accident in the Everglades was a minor rear-ender followed by someone clubbing Griggins' head and pushing the car into the water, so that he drowned. Joe Mantini died on an Interstate highway near Dallas when he crashed into a piece of factory shop equipment that fell off of a truck in front of him. That one killed two other people in addition to Mantini. In all three of these cases there was no other driver to interview. The first two were obviously premeditated actions by the other driver, and even the driver who lost his shop equipment kept going and disappeared in traffic. We may never know whether the equipment dump was accidental or deliberately triggered."

"Joe, with all of these other so-called accidents, it's a pretty sure bet that the dump was deliberate. Witnesses said it had been the only machine on the truck. How could he not have noticed the weight shift and loss of it?"

"Anyway, the Tallahassee accident was different because Warren Handley's car was run over by an eighteen wheel semi-trailer truck. That driver stopped and tried to give aid, but Handley's car had been crushed beyond hope of assisting him. The truck driver swore that both vehicles had been doing 70 miles per hour and that the car suddenly applied its brakes and slowed down right in front of him. He said he saw the brake lights, but that he couldn't even move into the next lane to avoid the collision because of other traffic there. If his statement was correct, either Handley committed suicide, or someone sabotaged his car. The other crashes didn't require any tampering, but this one did. We may be able to have experts check out the wreck and prove it."

"If somebody did sabotage the car, they're counting on it being too smashed up to find anything. That's good thinking, Joe. We'll have to put some crime scene specialists onto checking that wreck."

"Have we heard anything about the two prescription drug overdose cases?"

"Not yet. I emailed the reports and contact information to Irma, but she and Arthur are still staying with his folks, so she hasn't been free to pursue those cases. Even without that information, we have murder conclusions in four out of six incidents, so we should start looking for the culprits without waiting for more results."

"I doubt that we'll find only one assassin. This has been too well organized, and there have been a variety of techniques used."

"What group would want to assassinate a bunch of old men? Their victims probably didn't have that much longer to live anyway."

"Penny, I'd guess that they hoped to have the deaths dismissed as accidents, but they're sending a message to anyone who sees through the accident smokescreen."

"What's the message?"

"These guys did something too bad to allow them to die natural deaths."

CHAPTER 19 – MESSAGE FROM THE DEAD

Peter Blake undid the clasp on the envelope he had found in the second smoking table hidden compartment. He reached into it and withdrew a stapled set of printed sheets. After removing the papers, he shook the remaining contents of the envelope onto the top of his workbench. As he did so, he noticed an expression of surprise on Irma's face. Peter watched as she reached forward and sorted fourteen small items into a separate pile. He then spread out four remaining small sheets of paper so that all of them could be examined at the same time. Arthur was the first to speak.

"There aren't any photographs this time, but those small envelopes that Irma set aside sure look familiar."

"Yes, Arthur, and they feel familiar too. Without opening them I can feel the embossed dog tags inside."

"Dad, Albert or Wilhelm was your friend, at least at one time. Let's hold the smaller items for examination until after you read his stapled papers. The envelope notation suggests that he intended them for you - or for me if you weren't available."

Peter smoothed out the yellowing sheets of paper and adjusted the swing-arm light on his workbench for best illumination. Then he began to read the document that he expected to determine his future attitude toward his former friend.

Peter and/or Arthur, if you are reading these papers I am no longer with you. I preserved my story for you because I felt that I owed you the truth, but even now I will have to trust your judgment as to whether it is safe to share it with anyone else. Even Mandy knows nothing of these matters, although she has at times suspected that I had not told her everything. I congratulate you for having found this material. I assumed that if anyone could discover the secret compartments in this smoking table, it would be you.

Peter shrugged his shoulders. Then he went back to reading the document.

Many things happened during World War II that did not find their way into the history books. Some events remain unrecorded because of the lack of surviving witnesses, and some were too sensitive to record on paper at all.

I'll assume that you found the photographs in the other compartment, and accordingly, I will admit to having been Obersturmfuhrer Wilhelm Schnacht, at least for a while. Before you rush to judge me, allow me to give you the background story behind that picture.

I was born American of German ancestry, and in 1943 I was serving in England as a U.S. Army Sergeant. I was on my own because I had no brothers and sisters, and my parents had died due to illnesses during the Depression years. Later on, I invented some family so that Mandy would think I had a more normal background, but I was really an orphan when I met her. Anyway, my company commander told me that the Office of Strategic Services, OSS, was looking for volunteers for a special mission. They had to speak German and have no family. As soon as I heard that last part, I knew that it would be dangerous, but I was somewhat of a daredevil so I said I would consider it.

The mission turned out to be a very hush-hush thing prior to the Normandy invasion. The planners wanted the German High Command to think that the invasion was going to take place in the south of France so that they would pay less attention to Normandy. Somebody had come up with a crazy idea, and that's where we came in. Germany had temporary prison camps in France and the other occupied countries. Our job would be to infiltrate the German forces and influence the staff of one of those camps. They figured that many individual soldiers would get separated from their units and that small groups of soldiers could get accepted by those in command at such a camp.

We parachuted into France four months ahead of the invasion, and we pretended to have been separated and wandering around on our own. Twenty of us went in, fourteen dressed as Waffen SS soldiers and six pretending to be captured American airmen. The camp we contacted was run by a local unit of the Wehrmacht Heer, the regular German Army which would not be likely to question an SS unit coming in with additional prisoners. Because of the uneasy relationship between the Wehrmacht and the SS, it was easy to avoid mingling too closely with our hosts at the camp. After several staged prisoner interrogation sessions, we gave the camp commander the information we had obtained, and he passed it up the chain of command. The story was, of course, concocted to convince Germany that the invasion would come from the south of France.

In order to give our misinformation time to percolate up through the system, we stayed at the temporary camp for about a week. Then we sent a coded radio message that triggered an RAF air raid on the camp, during which we hoped to disappear. Unfortunately, the Wehrmacht troops saw our prisoners trying to leave and fired on them. We had to come to their rescue by taking on the real German troops. We managed to kill all of them, but we lost six of our group, three prisoners and three SS guards.

Afterwards, we released the Wehrmacht's prisoners to fend for themselves, and our remaining group of fourteen infiltrators headed for the coast where we would be picked up by a submarine. Along the way, we had a few more run-ins with the Germans, and lost eight additional brave men. Fourteen sets of dog tags are enclosed with this message. Only six of us made it to the coast and managed to get our inflated boat safely out to that submarine. Our mission had been a success, and we could only hope that the misinformation would eventually save many more Allied troops than the fourteen daring men we had lost. We who had survived vowed that we would stay in contact forever.

That's my story. It has been highly classified, and OSS made us swear to keep it secret for the rest of our lives, but I'm telling you after my death so that you will know the truth about me. Mandy knows none of this, but if my death was not from natural causes, you will have to guard and protect her. Hopefully, you won't have to tell her anything that will alter her understanding of me and our relationship.

Goodbye, my friends. You have been family to me...Albert.

CHAPTER 20 – TALLAHASSEE

Penny Gonzalez whistled as she stored assorted travel gear in their Alexandria apartment. The bad news was that she and Joe spent too much time pursuing field investigations all over the country. The good news was that an unoccupied apartment tended to stay clean and neat. As she stowed the last plastic under-bed container, she mused about someday having children and a home of their own. Biological clocks being what they are, she realized that any children would have to be adopted. Penny continued to speculate about the prospect of children until Joe's slamming of the front door shook her out of her reverie.

"I'm home, and I have news. The forensic team in Tallahassee found what we suspected. There was a wireless remote-controlled brake actuator installed on Handley's car. It was a custom variation on one of those units they sell for use when you are towing a trailer. Because of the compression of the wreck by that eighteen-wheeler, it was badly damaged and hard to spot, but it was there, just as we thought. The killer must have been driving nearby. He waited until the truck was right behind Handley and then slammed on the brakes. There was enough of the device left to clean it up and examine it, but it was a job shop unit that had no brand or serial number. They won't be able to trace it."

"That's too bad...Joe, I've been thinking about us instead of the case for the last few minutes."

"What about us?"

"How would you feel about buying a house, and maybe even moving a little farther away from the office?"

"Are you thinking about that conversation we had a while back with Arthur and Irma?"

"They were kind of right when they said we could live almost anywhere. We spend most of our time on the road, so why couldn't home be somewhere else?"

"Does the home you're conjuring up have kids in it?"

"It would eventually, but not right away. First we get used to a home, and then we move up to kids."

"If I agree that it's something we should consider and discuss soon, would you agree that we have to concentrate on our current case now?"

"Absolutely, Joe, so long as you're not trying to buy me off with a vague promise."

"I'd never do that, Penny. What's our next step?"

"I'd answer that, but I don't know if you mean the next step toward solving the case or toward getting a house."

"Focus, Penny. First we solve the case."

"I was afraid you meant that. OK, we're back to our good old diligent normal selves. I think we'll have to check on what Arthur and Irma are doing. Hopefully, we can free Irma up to work on the two drug overdose cases. We know that they must have been murders too, but analyzing them may give us new leads."

"Thanks, Penny; I promise to talk houses with you after we get this one out of the way."

CHAPTER 21 - RETHINKING

"Arthur, please put on your pastor hat, and accept my confession."

"Hold it, Dad. Protestants don't do individual confessions, but what's bothering you?"

"I took one look at that SS photo when I discovered it, and I felt that it offset every good thing Albert ever did, and then some. I completely condemned him and felt dirty because I'd treated him as a friend. Now we have evidence that the picture was taken while he was acting as an undercover patriot, and I have to reverse all of my thinking. I don't know what to feel now."

"*Judge not, lest ye be judged.* That's how Jesus put it in the Gospel of Matthew. He also said that we have to forgive the misdeeds of others if we want ours to be forgiven. The problem is that we tend to reach conclusions with incomplete or faulty information. You're a good man, Dad. You were judging what he appeared to represent when we saw that photo. Albert never changed. What we understood him to represent changed when we found this new evidence. Assuming it's true, he's back on the good side of the balance, and I have my sermon for next Sunday."

Irma studied the items on the workbench. "I'd say that Albert has been redeemed, and you may get several sermons out of this. The fourteen dog tags in these envelopes have red, white, and blue ribbons wrapped around them. The four small pieces of paper are: the Twenty-third Psalm with *Yea, though I walk through the valley of the shadow of death* underlined, the Lord's Prayer, Lincoln's Gettysburg Address, and the Pledge of

73

Allegiance. They must have carried these papers with them on that mission as good luck charms."

Peter picked up the four aged sheets of paper and held them like a hand of playing cards. "I'm convinced. These proofs are like four aces in a poker hand. They're an awesome set...Thanks, Albert; I'm sorry I doubted you."

"Before we get too serene, Dad, let's think about who would have wanted to kill Albert and the other five survivors of that mission. We don't even know whether the motive was based on events in that German prison camp or activities of our six stalwarts in later years. There was a gap of more than sixty-five years between the prison camp infiltration and their deaths. Any number of activities could have motivated the murderers."

Irma grabbed a pad of paper from Peter's shelf over the workbench. "Arthur, I think it's time for us to do some preliminary analysis work on paper. Sometimes it's easier to think after you summarize things.

"First, we can agree that our six survivors – Albert Dandrich, Maxwell Griggins, Peter Rodwin, Samuel Spincus, Warren Handley, and Joseph Mantini – came out of World War II on the good guys' side of the ledger. Second, we can be pretty sure that they vowed to keep working on things together. I say that because based on Renee's studies, they all attended Ohio State University between 1947 and 1949."

Out of habit from his engineering days, Arthur rolled up his sleeves two cuff widths. "Good start, Irma, we'll have to check, but I'll bet that they were all enrolled in the same course at OSU. These guys were a team."

Peter joined in with a question. "Your logic sounds reasonable, but if they were a team, why didn't Albert ever mention any of the others during the many years we were friends?"

Arthur smiled and turned to Irma. "Do you want to answer that one, or should I? I'm pretty sure we're thinking the same thing."

"Have fun, Arthur, you can carry the ball on this one."

"The answer, Dad, comes from their OSS mission. They were a covert team. They worked undercover. My guess is that they continued to be a covert team during all the years that you knew Albert. Tell me; was he frequently out of town for long periods?"

"He was gone quite a bit. He told us that he marketed sporting equipment, and he had to spend time with teams all over the world trying to get them to use the brands that he represented."

Irma said, "That's two points for Arthur. It's likely that these folks never stopped working for OSS, except for the fact that the organization's name changed in 1947 to CIA."

Peter said, "OK, analysts, it's my turn. Isn't it a bit of a coincidence that the CIA and our group's time at Ohio State University both started in 1947?"

"It's a coincidence if they played by the rules, Dad. The CIA wasn't supposed to do any domestic spying or information analysis."

"And do you believe they always played by those rules?"

"I'm not that naïve. Their first assignment, or perhaps training placement, was to be college students."

Irma added a note to her pad. "I like your thinking, Arthur. Maybe the college period was for training. Where would be a better place for that? So many veterans were going back to college under the G.I. Bill payment plan that our team of six would never have been thought unusual."

"When we get back to Parkville, let's spend some time looking at that OSU period. It may have been training, but I'm keeping my mind open to the possibility that it was their first civilian mission. Speaking of missions, weren't you supposed to check the facts on the two cases of death by accidental overdoses of medicines?"

"You're right...Peter, I'm afraid we'll have to leave the idyllic surroundings in Richmond for our home base. We'll go first thing tomorrow, but I'll be looking forward to coming back again. You and Janice have been wonderful hosts."

"Thanks, Irma, but make sure that Arthur keeps me advised and involved on this case. I'm not too old to feel the appeal of this investigation business."

CHAPTER 22 – BOBBY AND RENEE

Arthur and Irma parked in front of the Police Station as their first stop in Parkville. They had promised Renee and Bobby that they would keep in touch during their stay in Richmond, but with all the unforeseen developments they had failed to do so. They felt better when they saw Renee's car in the parking lot. At least they would all be together to compare notes.

They entered the Police Station, walked through the empty front lobby into the office section. They found Bobby and Renee in Bobby's office studying a satellite view of Parkville on their computer monitor.

Arthur knocked on the doorpost as they entered. "Where is everyone? What's happening?"

Bobby nodded and stood up. "While you two have been away, we've been looking for a lost Alzheimer's patient who wandered away from home and couldn't find his way back. Bruce Higgins is his name. He's been missing for a day and a half. He's in pretty good physical shape and is only sixty-two, so we think he'll be OK if we get to him soon. He's from Father McGraw's parish. He walked away from their rummage sale and disappeared. You church folks always manage to keep us cops busy. Renee's been helping me out *ex officio*, so neither one of us has had time to do much on your Nazi investigation. I hope you don't mind."

"No problem Bobby; Irma and I just got back into town. We haven't even taken our luggage out of the car. We'll get settled, and then I'll find some folks from our church to help with the search."

"Sorry, Arthur, I didn't mean to be abrupt. It has been a bit frustrating. We already have a big contingent from your church looking for Bruce. Wally Sanborn organized it. They've been searching the wetlands off the far end of Mallard Lake. We want to be sure we find Bruce before he wanders into the lake or some other water and gets into real trouble. Renee has been enlarging satellite photos, looking for places he might be hiding or seeking shelter if he's scared."

Renee blinked as she looked away from her computer screen. "It has been fun working with Bobby again. I get to see how much he cares about people. I'm afraid I haven't been doing much data searching for ABC Consultants while you two have been gone."

Irma took off her jacket and sat down. "You're doing the right thing, Renee. Hopefully, you'll find him before he gets hurt. Sometimes we forget that our current case isn't the only problem that needs attention."

Arthur said, "Is this the same Bruce Higgins who used to help Bill Martin with his carpentry projects? The last job they worked on together before Bruce got sick was a storage shed behind the firehouse. Did anyone look over there? He might be looking for a place that feels familiar."

"If he were there, he'd be all by himself, because the Fire Department people are all looking for him in the open space sections of town. I'll give Chief Johnson a call and ask him to check the shed in case Bruce headed that way."

"Thanks, Bobby. We'll be back to help out as soon as we drop off our stuff."

"I'll keep you posted on the status of our search, but plan on coming to our house for dinner and catching-up time. Make it seven o'clock this evening."

"Will do...see you then."

Arthur and Irma went back to the car and drove to Irma's apartment. There they unloaded all of her luggage plus her newly acquired antique cabinet from Peter's collection. Arthur stayed for one cup of coffee and then headed back to the parsonage. When he arrived, the telephone was ringing.

"Hello, Pastor Blake here, may I help you?"

He heard a familiar voice. "We're not going to let you out of town any more. You seem to have the answers to all our problems."

"What do you mean, Bobby? Was he actually in that shed?"

"Not exactly, but the fireman who checked your theory found a trail of wet footprints leading from the shed to the firehouse. Apparently Bruce fell into some water somewhere and went to the shed for shelter, but he was so chilled that he went into the firehouse and curled up with a blanket on one of the cots in the sleeping quarters. He was lying there, shaking from the chill when Sam entered the firehouse. They would have found Bruce when the fire trucks headed home later, but it's likely that he would have been in much worse shape by then. Thanks for the suggestion, Arthur."

"I'm glad it worked out. His family will be relieved to get him back. Now I can grab a nap before getting together with you folks."

"Good. While you nap, we'll fix dinner at our house. I'm going to call Irma with the information about Bruce. When I do, I'll tell her that we'll pick her up on our way home. She wanted to spend some time getting to know Momma. Set your alarm to get to our place by seven o'clock."

When Arthur woke up, he sat up for a moment and rubbed his eyes. It took a few seconds for him to realize where he was. His mother's innocent manipulation of him and Irma into joint quarters had been like a pleasant dream interval. He had yet to consider when they might recreate that experience in the future. As he thought back to his teenage years, Arthur wondered when he had managed to become more straight-laced than his mother. He also realized that she had become a lot mellower in her attitudes than he remembered. Dad was a comfortable constant, but Mother was morphing into a significantly different person. He would have to spend some extended one-on-one time with her in order to appreciate the extent of her changes.

Arthur forced himself to get off the bed, performed an abbreviated exercise routine to regain alertness, and washed up. He had slept longer than expected, and he would have to hustle to make his seven o'clock dinner deadline. As he changed his clothes he realized that this was the first time he had been away from Irma in more than a week.

After ringing the front doorbell, Arthur listened to the sounds emanating from the Andrews house and realized that there was a true party atmosphere inside. Renee answered the door after what seemed like a long delay, but probably wasn't. He could use some relaxation time to readjust his biological clock.

"Greetings, Arthur, come on in and join us. We were laughing so hard that I almost didn't hear the bell."

"What's happening? What's so funny?"

"Momma was doing her Oprah Winfrey imitation. She's interviewing Irma as a young Hollywood starlet. Come on in and enjoy it."

Arthur watched as Momma not only conducted a lucid and hilarious interview but also changed her posture and walk to something younger and fairly reminiscent of the television star. Soon he was laughing and applauding with the rest of them.

"Mrs. Weems, you should have been a TV star yourself."

"Now, Arthur, you do the same as everyone else, and call me Momma. Then you might remember your history, and you'll know why I didn't get on television. When I was in the right age range, they weren't hiring any black folks for television. Oprah came along at the right time."

Arthur said, "That's a good point, Momma. Timing is going to be a big key to our current case, too. Finding the group that was responsible for six murders will depend on the timing of the event that triggered this rampage."

Irma gave Arthur a hard stare. "I thought we were relaxing tonight. We were going to put off shop talk until tomorrow."

"Maybe you can compartmentalize things, but my mind is working on leads and analysis all the time, at least in background mode. And, yes, I'm also thinking about my next sermon and catching up with anything I missed at the church. Vacations and relaxation periods work for me because I still have my mind in gear. I can't shut it down entirely."

"I guess you are a Sherlock, because that's the way he was. Nothing bugged him more than when there were no cases to analyze."

"What about you, Irma? Can you turn off your forensic studies of everything around you?"

"I can keep it in the background better than you, Arthur, but I can also understand how it drives you. As a matter of fact, that difference between the ways we approach things is one of your attractions for me."

Bobby laughed and put his hand on Arthur's left shoulder. "I do believe the pastor is blushing. He's not used to being called attractive in public. Well, Mr. Blake, I think you're a pretty cool cat too, even if I do stop short of saying that you're attractive."

Momma did her Oprah walk toward Arthur. "Renee's afraid to say anything in front of Bobby, but I think you're attractive too. I'll even back up my words with action. I'm going to start going to your church so that you can help me find God's way."

81

"Momma, I suspect that God's been walking with you and keeping an eye on you for some time. When you come to our church, you'll be teaching us a thing or two."

Renee had gone out to the kitchen during this exchange. She stood in the kitchen door and clanked a cowbell. "Enough socialization, dinner is ready. Afterwards we'll have some sweet liqueurs and toast our return to investigations tomorrow – not tonight. This kind of fun with company in my own home has always been my dream."

CHAPTER 23 – OVERDOSES

Irma prepared herself for action early the next day. She had awakened before her alarm clock could rouse her, and now she sat at her laptop, sorting and responding to the many emails that had accumulated during her trip to Richmond. Among them was one from Penny Gonzalez that included the information about the two prescription drug overdose deaths that Irma was charged with investigating.

She opened Penny's email, and found a summary of the known facts about Peter Rodwin and Samuel Spincus and the circumstances surrounding their deaths. These had been cataloged by investigators from the local police departments following the unlikely revelation that six friends had died within a short period in separate apparent accidents. Three facts immediately caught her attention. Both men had been living in nursing homes, one in Evansville, Indiana and one in Lexington, Kentucky. They hadn't been very far from each other. Both had been forced by their families to give up their driving privileges.

The pattern of coincidences suggested that Rodwin and Spincus had been murdered within their nursing home environments because they could no longer be eliminated through car accidents. At least they would have been examined by the staff physician at each nursing home, and that meant that she could interview two people with medical expertise who had actually examined the men after they died. If she called the doctors at the two facilities, she would be able to compare their independent stories.

She placed the first call to Dr. Fenton Velner of Ripplestream Nursing Home in Evansville, Indiana, and was connected to him after a brief wait.

"Dr. Velner, this is Irma Custis. I'm a former Illinois County Medical Examiner, and I'm calling on behalf of a federal investigative agency. I need to ask you, as the certifying physician, whether you noticed anything unusual when you examined Peter Rodwin after his death. We have reason to suspect that his death was not accidental as it originally appeared."

"I'm glad you called, Dr. Custis. The Evansville Police visited me last week, and told me that Peter's death was one in a series including several of his friends. That obviously made me suspicious, so I reviewed my notes. I had found signs of an injection in his left arm, but given the fact that he had overdosed on his sleeping pills, I didn't take it to be important. I also observed some redness on his left wrist that I took to be due to a tight watchband, but in hindsight, it might have been caused by some form of restraint. I didn't note down any redness on the other wrist, but I can't say for sure that it wasn't there. I do admit that I wasn't looking for signs of foul play."

"Do you remember anything unusual about his face or mouth?"

"I thought this was a typical case of one of our seniors saving up his pills to deliberately hasten his demise, but I wanted to be charitable to his memory by indicating accidental death. He would have had to save up individual pills, because we never let residents have a bulk quantity of medications. I did notice some abrasions inside his mouth, but I took that to mean that he panicked after taking the pills, and that he tried to make himself vomit them back up by sticking his finger down his throat. I've seen a number of cases where seniors try to commit suicide but change their minds at the last moment. The retinas in his eyes also showed inflammation."

"That's useful information, Doctor. Thank you for being candid with me. I have one final question, did you find a glass next to his bed, and did it have any water in it?"

"That's exactly what bothered me. When I was called in, I noticed a full glass of water next to his bed. The night nurse said that he always slept with a glass of water next to him for sipping during the night. She said that she hadn't refilled it after she found him. How did he take an overdose of pills without any water?"

"Thank you, Dr. Velner. I'll send you a copy of my preliminary report after I check on his friend who died under similar circumstances."

Irma spent a few minutes neatening up her notes. Then she placed a call to Dr. Selma Dawkins at the Pleasant Pasture Nursing Home in Lexington, Kentucky. Dr. Dawkins answered on the second ring from the switchboard operator. "Selma Dawkins here..."

"Dr. Dawkins, I'm Dr. Irma Custis, and I'm following up for a federal agency on the details of the death of Samuel Spincus. You may have been advised that his death was unlikely to have been due to natural causes because five of his close friends also died at about the same time."

"Hello, Dr. Custis; I had heard that from the Lexington Police. I can't argue with the logic that so many simultaneous deaths are not likely to have been independent random events or natural. How can I help you?"

"I've spoken with the doctor at another nursing home where one of Samuel's friends died. If you would describe the details of Samuel's appearance and conditions when you first found him, I'll be able to compare the two events."

"I still have his file on my desk. Once I heard that there were questions, I set it aside to review it. Let's see if I noted anything unusual. Here's something; he was found with his watch on the floor beside him, and it had a broken watchband. That bothered me at the time because Samuel was found in a relaxed position on the bed, but the watchband looked as though it had been mangled."

"What about marks on the body?"

"I saw what could have been an injection needle mark on the left side of his neck, but I didn't examine him closely enough to confirm that. Samuel was a little nervous and tended to pick at pimples and scabs, so I took it to be a mark from his scratching. I may have been wrong."

"The police report indicates that he had visitors on his final day. Can you tell me anything about them and when they left?"

"I did hear that two men visited him, and that they stayed fairly late. I couldn't identify them, but there was a lot of visitor traffic that day, and I might have passed them in the hall. I had the impression that they were social workers. You'd have to check with the Lexington Police about them."

"Getting back to the body, did you notice anything unusual?"

"Sam normally had a somewhat florid complexion, but I did notice that his skin was pinker than usual, even right after death. I assumed that he would shortly lose that coloring, but with all the other things I had to do, I didn't follow up on that."

"Did you examine his eyes?"

"I did, and there was some unusual redness, but at the time I concluded that it might have been due to his rubbing his eyes because of itching or from the assumed overdose of medications."

"Were you close friends with him, Selma?"

86

"As a matter of fact we were pretty close. Why do you ask?"

"Just a hunch because I've always heard him referred to as Samuel, and you used the more familiar version, Sam."

"That was a humor thing between us. He was the only one who ever called me Sel, so I reciprocated. Based on our conversations, I would never have expected Sam to horde medications for a deliberate overdose. He enjoyed life too much. He'd keep telling me, 'You wouldn't believe all the things I've done along the way.'"

"I understand, Doctor. Hopefully, we'll soon catch those who were responsible for your friend's death. Thanks so much for your help."

Irma said goodbye, touched the *END* button on her cell phone, and set it down. She realized that in this last conversation she had finally started to see the personality of one of Albert's friends. They would have to stop treating them as victims and learn more about them as individuals before they would be able to determine why they had all been assassinated.

In the meantime, she had a pretty good understanding of how these two were killed.

CHAPTER 24 – COMPARING NOTES

Arthur could hardly believe that this was only the second Sunday since his father brought his dismay about Albert to church. Today, Arthur had used a disguised variation on this experience to preach about forgiving others because you can't see the world from their point of view, and because they may have hidden circumstances affecting their actions. He remembered a particularly cranky and difficult accounting manager at NASA whom he had tried to avoid for years. Jack Mariston had been rigid and nitpicking every time Arthur had been required to generate project budgets and justify expenditures. Then Arthur had discovered through a mutual friend that Jack had lost his oldest son in a drowning accident, and that he was spending every bit of his off-duty time sitting with his comatose wife in a long term care facility. Once Arthur had learned these facts, he realized that this man was more of a saint than a curmudgeon. He had found it hard to comprehend how Jack could concentrate on his professional duties under the circumstances. Arthur recalled that by the time he had left NASA to redirect his career path toward the ministry he and Jack had even started to become friends.

Arthur's thoughts returned to how neither he nor his father had been able to see the true nature of Albert Dandrich during all the years they had known him. He was sure that they hadn't unraveled all the strands of Albert's mystery even now. How many more versions of this person would they find? Arthur felt that he was an open book to people, but he knew others wouldn't share his self-understanding. Aloud he said, "We're all hiding in plain sight."

Admonishing himself to avoid voicing his thoughts, especially when others were present, Arthur grabbed his jacket and headed for Irma's apartment and their planned summary of the facts of this case. He saw it as a jigsaw puzzle with alternate pictures on both sides of each piece. Which side was the correct one?

Upon arrival, Arthur found that Irma and Renee had set up the dining room table with pads of paper and pens to add formality to their discussions. To show that they wanted him to take the lead, they had given him the only chair with arms and had set a carafe of coffee and a mug at his place. He couldn't avoid smiling at the arrangement.

"Wow, I guess ABC Consultants is a bigger organization than I thought it was. Are we going to be formal all the time now?"

Renee said, "No, but we wanted you to have one time when you could feel that you were our fearless leader."

"I don't know about the fearless part. Let's sort out our thoughts and findings, and then we can have a conference call with Joe and Penny to get their contributions. Maybe the patterns will start to become obvious. Irma, what did you learn about the two nursing home deaths?"

"They were definitely murders. They were initially called overdoses because that's what the medical staff members had seen in the past, and they thought these were more of the same. Once the residence doctors learned that six friends had died almost simultaneously, they gave more credit to secondary observations that pointed at murder."

"What can you deduce about the circumstances?"

"Quite a bit, but if you don't mind, I'll save that part for when we're talking with Penny and Joe. I'd rather not assemble my theories and facts twice, and I'd like to see the reaction I get from our professional friends."

Arthur raised an eyebrow at Irma's comment, but kept on going. "We have six deaths that we agree must have been murders because of their very close timing. Renee, would you please tabulate the exact dates and places of these events. We may be able to infer the number of killers who were involved and their priorities by the sequence of the deaths."

Irma said, "There were at least two killers involved, because the Lexington nursing home victim, Samuel Spincus, had been visited by two men shortly before he died. The police have been unsuccessful in tracking those visitors. All I can tell you was that they were less than fifty years old and physically fit. These same men may have visited Peter Rodwin on his last day because of similarities in the appearances of the two victims, but I don't have a definite confirmation of visitors in that instance."

Arthur made a few notes on his pad. "That's important information. It suggests that our victims died due to an organized conspiracy and that they were not killed by any of their contemporaries. These men were quite a bit younger.

"I'm thinking that the killers weren't very particular about legal ethics, so my first inclination is to guess that they weren't part of a group from our government, because they stole cars and deliberately crashed them in at least two cases."

Irma shook her head. "I think you're going too far with your logic on that one, Arthur. Covert government hit groups wouldn't follow normal guidelines, especially if they were trying to make things look accidental."

"I'd like to think you're wrong on that one, but I won't argue the point. One thing that bothers me is that we've been treating these six friends like anonymous statistics. Albert Dandrich was the only one we knew much about. We should get to know the others. How do you feel about that, Irma?"

"I had planned to bring that point up if you hadn't. While I was checking on the so-called overdose cases, I discovered a little bit about Samuel Spincus, and he came across as an interesting and friendly person. When you think about it, they all had to have strong and unusual personalities to achieve what they did during World War II. I think that the solution to what happened to them lies in reconstructing their postwar civilian histories. We don't even know what Albert was doing when he went off on his business trips, and he was one of your father's closest friends."

"Sometimes you know less about a close friend than you do about a stranger because you don't question what a friend tells you, while you're suspicious and curious about a stranger. What do you think, Renee?"

"I'll give that an *Amen*. So many times people try to get close to you and snow you with their stories. If you have street smarts, you don't accept anyone's story at face value. That's something it takes a while to learn. Momma gave me a made-up story about my father when I was a kid, and I took it as Gospel because it came from her. Only recently did she tell me and Bobby the truth."

Irma stared out the window as she said, "Do you resent Momma because of all the years she had you believing her made-up story?"

"No, Irma, I can't resent Momma. She's been my guardian angel for all of my life. I can even see how she used that story to protect me from falling in with the wrong crowd. I'm saying that you have to look for inconsistencies in people's stories and to be suspicious if you find them. Did you get taken in by someone's story?"

"Not exactly, Renee, I'm afraid I was the one giving people an exaggerated story about my background. Does that admission make you look at me any differently?"

"Hell, no, Irma; we've worked together long enough for me to appreciate you for who you are. Right here and now you're my friend, and I know that I can learn a lot from you and rely on you. Anything that happened a long time ago only contributed to your becoming the person you are now. None of us is perfect."

Arthur gave a thumbs-up sign. "Irma, do you realize that Renee just gave you an applied version of this morning's sermon in four sentences. It was probably easier to understand than my opus, too.

"Now, I think it's time to consult with Penny and Joe. I'll call them in speaker phone mode so that we can all exchange what we've learned."

CHAPTER 25 – UNOFFICIAL INVESTIGATIONS

Peter Blake had set down the telephone with a smile on his face. Sometimes the direct approach was the best tactic. Arthur and his associates were being meticulous in their investigations, but he might be on the road to the first breakthrough. He had called Mandy and asked whether he might rummage through Albert's files in the hope of finding something that would lead to identifying Albert's killer. Arthur and company weren't saying much about Albert's death having been a murder, but Mandy had sensed it ever since she had lost him. Mandy had agreed and asked for an hour's delay so that she could make sure the house was clean. Peter had always gotten along well with Mandy, and now he would have full access to all of Albert's stuff.

He stocked his canvas gym bag with a digital camera, a head-mounted flashlight, and several file folders. He would photograph items that Mandy didn't want taken and sort key removable papers for study later. Before he closed the bag, he added a box of candy that Irma had left in appreciation of the Blakes' hospitality. It would put Mandy in a good mood and make her more receptive to his taking some of Albert's papers and other objects. Then he headed for his van.

Mandy opened the front door before Peter could ring the doorbell. She appeared to be agitated, and her hands were shaking.

"Peter, I opened Albert's office for you and turned on the lights. There's something wrong in there. He was always so meticulous about putting everything away, and now it's messy enough to tell me that someone else has been in there."

"Was the office door locked when you entered?"

"Absolutely – I had to get the key from the special place where Albert kept it. He and I were the only ones who knew about it. The key was hidden in an old tool box."

"Why did Albert keep the key hidden?"

"He told me that for some of his international dealings he had to have more currency than it was safe to carry, so he always had a small cache of diamonds in there to use in bargaining."

"Didn't that seem unusual to you, and did you check whether they were taken?"

"I trusted my husband. Even though I didn't know much about his business, I knew he had negotiated some large contracts. When I saw that things were messier than usual, I shut and locked the door without touching anything. I'll check on the diamonds when we go in there together."

Peter was surprised that she would know where to look for the jewels, but he kept a calm expression on his face. "Let's take a look. After you unlock the door, I'll go in first so that I can see and photograph the condition of the office before we move anything." Peter removed the camera from his bag and nodded to Mandy that he was ready.

Mandy's stealthy movements as they approached the office door belied her eighty-one years. She removed a string from around her neck to reveal a key hanging from it. Peter noticed that the key had smooth sides and an intricate series of fine notches along the edges. It reminded him of his safe deposit box key from the bank.

Mandy unlocked the door and stepped aside. Peter turned the handle and eased the door open. As it swung into the room, he noticed a piece of paper folded like a *V* flutter down to the floor, but he didn't mention it to Mandy. He stepped into the office and scanned his eyes over the whole room.

"The room looks empty now. Is this the only entrance?"

"This is the only way in or out. If someone was in here, he or she would have had to come right through the house. It makes me feel violated."

"The office looks a lot neater than my workspace, but you said it's messier than Albert kept it. Are you sure it hasn't been disturbed since his death?"

"Peter, I haven't felt ready to go through his things yet. When I opened the office to prepare it for you, it was my very first look since the car crash. Albert would never leave files and piles of papers on his desk like that."

Peter looked at the stacks of documents on the desk and visualized his previous visits with Albert in the library, family room, and other areas of the house. He had to agree with Mandy that Albert had been careful to keep all of his papers out of sight. This was unusual.

"Mandy, are you sure that you haven't had any lawyers or financial analysts over, going through Albert's papers for estate settlement purposes?"

"I'd been putting that off. I felt that I needed at least a couple of months to let the dust settle before I suffered the intrusion of strangers into his life and estate."

"But you're OK with my looking things over now?"

"That's different, Peter, you're practically family. It's having prying strangers underfoot that bothers me. Having you going through things in the office will almost make me feel as though Albert is in there again."

"Let me take some pictures of this place, and then I'll go at the papers. I promise I'll be neat with them, and that I'll put everything back in its original location. In the meantime, you should check to see whether the diamonds are still here."

Mandy brightened. "I already checked. They are."

Peter made a mental note that the diamonds were hidden somewhere that could be seen. He opened the first file drawer as Mandy left the room.

CHAPTER 26 – CONFERENCE CALL

"Can you folks in Washington hear me? Joe? Penny?"

Joe's slightly crackling voice erupted from the speaker. "Penny and I can hear you loud and clear, Arthur. I assume that Irma and Renee are with you there?"

Irma said, "You have the whole A, B, and C of ABC Consultants on this end, Joe. We'll let Arthur be our spokesperson for now, and we'll jump in to correct him."

Joe laughed. "That sounds like such a good tactic that I'll let Penny take the lead from our side."

Penny's familiar soft tones set them at ease. "We're sure now that all of the car accidents were really murders. Not only that, but we know that they must have been arranged by a sophisticated group with significant resources. A special truck and a piece of heavy shop equipment were used in one incident, and a custom electronic device was used in another. What did you conclude from investigating the so-called overdose cases, Irma?"

"They were murders, too. I interviewed the house physicians in both cases, and I found that the killers used almost identical procedures in both events. It's not definite for Peter Rodwin, but Samuel Spincus was visited by two unidentified men shortly before he died. Both victims displayed initially-ignored needle punctures, and they were probably killed with the same injected toxin. Because I investigated by telephone interviews only, and the bodies were no longer available, I can't be too specific about the injected compound, but both doctors described cherry-red skin color and eye examinations that revealed bright red retinal arteries and veins. These symptoms suggest that both Peter Rodwin and Samuel Spincus had been injected with some compound of cyanide. Cyanide poisoning causes death quickly, affecting virtually all body tissues, but having the most adverse effects on the brain and the heart which require the most oxygen. The blood vessels and skin become unusually red because cyanide limits the ability of tissues to extract oxygen from the blood."

Joe's voice over the speaker had a tone of awe. "Irma, I am completely impressed by your diagnosis. You made two telephone calls and determined the cause of death in two murders in different states. Were you as impressed when she told you, Arthur?"

"I'm as impressed, but Irma didn't tell Renee or me her conclusions in advance of this telephone conference. She wanted us all to get the information at the same time. However, our exchanges about these deaths suggest something even more awesome to me."

Penny said, "What's that, Arthur?"

"There's a sixth person involved in this investigation, and he's guided all of our analysis up to this point. Albert Dandrich has been directing our thoughts from the grave."

Renee stared at Arthur. "You're a Christian pastor, and you're telling us you communicate with the dead?"

"No, I said that Albert has been communicating with us. If he hadn't put the photographs and dog tags and other documents in the hidden compartments of that smoking table and left instructions for it to be given to my father, would we even be sitting here? The only reason we know that the six deaths were murders is because they all occurred at about the same time. The only thing that made that remarkable is that Albert left us evidence that these six people had been affiliated for a very long time. Following her husband's instructions, Mandy gave Dad that table right after Albert died. Albert knew that as an antiques dealer, Dad would examine the workmanship of that table and find the hidden compartments. He also knew my background and that I would pursue the mystery, and we would get involved. There would be no mystery to investigate if we didn't know that all six of these men were connected."

Penny whistled through the telephone speaker. "You're right. That old man has been in control. Not only that, but his detailed planning suggests that he was a professional intelligence operative. These men served together under OSS during World War II, and they most likely continued to serve as an intelligence team in later life."

Renee said, "Do we assume that because they were in OSS, they would have continued on to the CIA? That's not the only intelligence agency in our government. Even your agency fits that description, Joe."

"Right you are, Renee, but I can state that they weren't working with us. If they were an undercover team, it may take some serious work to discover their sponsorship. The value of such teams lies in their remaining undetected and unacknowledged."

"Don't look now, Joe, but they were detected and assassinated."

"Yes, Arthur, but that fact will only make their agency less likely to claim them. No group wants to admit a failure."

"What about contacting groups with the mission of plugging security leaks and getting revenge on those who did this?"

"We'll call in all the favors we've accumulated and try that approach, but there's a circumstance under which it might not work."

Irma said, "What do you mean, Joe?"

"It's conceivable that their own agency had them eliminated because of something they did, or because they were no longer valuable assets."

CHAPTER 27 – FEEDBACK

After wrapping up their conference call, Arthur, Irma and Renee adjourned to their favorite restaurant, House of Ming. The proprietor, Tony Fleming met them at the door and announced that he would seat them at the large round table in the back corner so that they would have privacy when they were joined by the fourth member of their party. He wouldn't give them any more information following this cryptic announcement, but he did say he would compensate them for the delay with a complimentary round of drinks.

While they awaited their unknown guest, the three of them decided to each make one guess at his or her identity.

Renee said, "It has to be someone that Tony knows, so I'll say it will be my favorite associate and husband, Bobby."

Irma said, "That's too obvious a guess. Tony was being mysterious, so I suspect that we will soon see Arthur's clerical colleague, Father McGraw. Your turn, Arthur; who do you think is coming?"

"I think you both made good guesses. As a matter of fact, I did receive an email from Father McGraw, a thank you note for assisting in finding Bruce Higgins, the Alzheimer's patient who was lost. I'm going to assume that our visitor will be someone unexpected enough to amuse Tony to the point of buying us drinks. It will be either Jack Hendron from our residence for homeless veterans, or it will be Wally Sanborn."

Renee said, "That's unfair, Arthur. You can only guess once."

"If that's the way you feel, Renee, I'll select only one name. I'll say it's my father."

Irma said, "Why the sudden switch?"

"Because he just came in the front door and is talking with Tony."

They all watched as Peter approached carrying a large corrugated file storage box. He set it onto the next table and draped his jacket over a chair.

"Greetings co-conspirators; you folks have so much fun with solving problems that I thought I'd try it too. I've been doing some prying on my own, and I found quite a few interesting things. By the way, order anything you want. Tony has instructions that lunch is on me."

"Wow, Dad, you look as though you have answers to all of our questions."

"Let's say I have a few answers and a lot of additional questions that may add new directions to our inquiries.

"Hi, Irma; Janice and I have been missing your upbeat attitude already. This must be Renee – I don't think we've met, but I've heard many positive things about you."

"Same here, Peter; someday I want to talk with you about a couple of antique gifts for my momma."

"Dad, before we get too folksy and hungry, show us what's in your treasure chest."

"That's exactly what I had in mind. I've already asked Tony to let us talk until I signal him that we're ready for food.

"The reason for my having materials and information for you is that I used my long friendship with Mandy to get access to the contents of Albert's home office. In the process, I've learned that there are secrets in that house and family that I never imagined."

"Dad, we've already collectively concluded that Albert worked for a government intelligence agency. Penny and Joe are trying to learn which one."

"Well, Number One Son, how would you react if I told you that I suspect that Mandy might have secrets of her own?"

"OK, Dad, it's time for me to listen instead of talk."

"For starters, Mandy told me that she had gone into Albert's locked office for the first time since he died and found papers and files out of place. She said that she had opened the office for me, but that she had locked it again when she saw files out of place."

Irma said, "That's natural enough for an older woman. She was probably nervous."

"She even opened the front door with shaky hands, but I think it was a sham. She stood with more erect posture than I have seen before, and she walked with alertness and stealth when we went into the office. She also gave me a story about the office being kept locked because Albert had diamonds in there for international trading use. I was skeptical of that one, although I couldn't be sure. While I was going through Albert's things, I found no sign of them."

"They may have been hidden too well."

"That's possible, Renee, but the whole idea of a diamond cache sounded a bit far-fetched. And why would she tell me if they were there? Having known diamonds around would make most women of her age nervous."

"You're reading a lot into a few of her actions and comments, Dad. Why do you think she might be hiding things from people around her?"

"She gave me the key, and I unlocked the office and opened the door. As I did so, I saw a hidden tell-tale paper that Albert had inserted above the door from inside the room, flutter to the floor. I asked Mandy if there was another entrance to the room, and she said, "No." Because the tell-tale marker was still in place, Albert must have left the room through another exit; and Mandy must have entered by a different way when she found the messy files.

102

While I was alone in there going through papers, I did some exploring and found a trapdoor to the basement hidden underneath a rug. I climbed down the wooden steps beneath it, and behind a partition I found a staircase that led to the kitchen via another trapdoor. This was an old farmhouse, and the basement was probably used as a root cellar for cool storage of fresh vegetables and preserves in jars. They've lived there for many years. Mandy had to know about the kitchen trapdoor and stairs and the office trapdoor too."

Irma frowned. "I can't argue with your logic. Mandy entered through the trapdoor when she said she had entered through the office door."

"What did you find among his papers, Dad?"

"I found that these six old men had been quite remarkable when they were younger. The papers I uncovered made me wish I had known them all in their prime. Albert was the only one I did know, and he was middle-aged by the time he and Mandy moved to Richmond."

"Did you find their complete histories, Peter?"

"No, Irma, I learned enough to appreciate them as individuals and as members of a team, but I learned very little about that team's activities. We may never know much about what they did. They appear to have been quite disciplined about not writing down anything about assignments or organizations. I don't even know whether they worked for a single agency or for several."

"Dad, show or tell us what you found about each of them. We've already concluded that we won't be able to solve these murders until we know more about the victims."

"Albert Dandrich appears to have been the leader of the group, and his files show talents for organization and communication. Some of his papers were written in shorthand or code that I haven't been able to decipher. In most documents he referred to himself and the others by numbers rather than by names. Albert's number was 31.

"Max Griggins was designated by number as 10, and his special skill was artwork and printing. He seems to have been in charge of creating identification and legal documents for the team when they were traveling incognito or needed access to a place that required permits. The few samples of his work that I found look authentic.

"Peter Rodwin, known as 01, was the language expert. Based on what we know about their OSS episode, all of these men had to speak English and German. Rodwin also spoke fluent French, Spanish, and Russian. He could also read Japanese, but he couldn't speak it.

"Samuel Spincus, code 77, was the scientist of the outfit. He had gone back to graduate school and had earned a Ph.D. in Physics. From the documents I found, he had ongoing correspondence relationships with many of the world's top scientists. He used several pseudonyms in the course of this correspondence, so that his pen pals thought he was several different people.

"Warren Handley, designation 13, was the computer specialist. He had been in on the beginnings of the computer revolution and had kept himself up on the state of the art until very recently, when his age had started to affect his skill level. He anticipated this skill deterioration and had recruited a much younger partner to assist him. I was not able to find the identity of that associate.

"Joseph Mantini, code 04, was a weapons expert. He knew the specifications and operational requirements of most of the world's weapons systems, including some of the most highly classified ones. He was a pilot with fighter jet and multi-engine ratings. I found a few documents that suggested he had high-level contacts within the air forces of several major countries.

"After going through Albert's files, I came away with the feeling that in their prime, these six men could have tackled virtually any sensitive intelligence job."

Arthur raised his glass in a toast salute to his father. "Dad, I'm impressed. You did a remarkable intelligence job yourself. Do you know what Mandy was doing while you were analyzing the contents of Albert's office?"

"She never came in on me, but I did my best to look casual, deliberate, and unemotional in case she was watching me on video. Nowadays, video cameras are tiny and easy to hide. I actually assumed that she was watching me. I felt immune during my searches, because she couldn't interfere without admitting that she had been watching. I don't know how Mandy fits into Albert's hidden profession, but I think she is more than an elderly housewife."

Irma nodded her assent. "In a few days, I'll contact her to see if I can get more information out of her."

Peter put the cover back on his file box. Then he sat down and faced the others. "You have some great analytical talents, Irma, but I don't think that would be the best way to use them. Mandy would be suspicious of you pumping her for information. I'm sure she only let me into the house because of our past social relationships. At this point she'll only open up to someone she feels she can trust. Let Janice talk with her. Janice would be accepted by Mandy as her folksy friend."

"Dad, I'm amazed by the information you've obtained. The idea of Mother doing an investigative interview is astounding. Have you two been going to spy school?"

"Arthur, there is something to heredity, you know. You had to get your analytical inclinations from somewhere. Once you started to play this game, we thought it would be fun too. For some time we've been monitoring everything our Police Chief, Lois Berkus, has been doing and saying, and she hasn't even realized we were interested. Irma, when you quit as County Medical Examiner a while ago, we did some online research and figured out why – no problems, we love you just the way you are. All of this has been our way of sharpening our skills for the time when you might need our assistance. We think we're ready to help, and remember that I brought the mystery of Albert to you in the first place."

Irma said, "Well, there goes my sense of privacy. Peter, I can't get peeved at what you and Janice did, but we are checking on some very dangerous people, and I wouldn't want to see either of you get hurt."

"I'll speak for Janice in saying that we promise not to get involved beyond our local area. We simply want a taste of your action. We'll appreciate you all the more for it. Right now it feels like we're the children asking you parents if we can do what you do. Renee, are you on our side?"

"I'll support you, Peter. You demonstrated with all of these documents that you can be effective; and as a former police officer, I know that a suspect will talk openly to someone perceived as a friend while refusing to talk to anyone official. That's why police try to get a cooperating gang member to wear a wire and record or broadcast his conversations."

Arthur shrugged. "OK, nobody would believe Mother was hiding anything anyway. If she can gather information without altering her personality, she'll do well. Let's ask Chief Berkus to have someone in plain clothes following her in case she needs assistance."

CHAPTER 28 – AGENCIES

"Penny, none of this makes any sense. I've contacted all of my friends at the sixteen official Intelligence Community agencies and at the tactical agencies we know about as insiders, and I found zero leads to this group's connections."

"That's not completely surprising. If they had been working for us, would someone checking the official agency listings have been able to find them? There are small agencies that aren't what they appear to be and other agencies that don't show up on anyone's list. Intelligence is supposed to be covert."

"I realize that, but it's deflating to my ego. I'm even supposed to have contacts in the agencies that don't have names...I suppose they could have been working for another government."

"That's not likely, but I suppose it's possible. It would be more likely that they were working undercover in a way that was not revealed to official members of their agency. They might have been a self-contained group that their agency did not want to acknowledge so that they could disavow them in case they screwed up. Such a group would not be officially recorded anywhere."

"Your suggestion makes sense, Penny, and it fits the profile that Arthur generated through his father's research, but that kind of arrangement should have resulted in several of my agency contacts knowing about them."

"Some may have known about them but couldn't claim them because this group had been responsible for off-the-record black ops."

"What else might they have been doing?"

"They could have been acting as an intelligence agency for hire by large corporations."

"That kind of outfit might have been employed by either a domestic or a foreign corporation."

"It's definitely worth considering, Joe. There's lots of industrial espionage going on. Companies are looking for each other's trade secrets and technical data. They even try to get information on classified government contracts so that they might be in position to generate the winning proposal next time."

"Our government assists them on the last point. If your company is a Defense Department contractor, even on an unrelated project, you can usually justify receiving copies of other contractors' reports on the grounds of their making your efforts more efficient. It's a loophole that I'd like to close."

"I agree with you on that one, Joe. Our problem now is that we don't know who these six guys worked for or what they were doing. Were they good guys, bad guys, or impartial consultants for sale to the highest bidder? We need more information about the group, but at least we know more about them individually than we did before Peter Blake did his amateur snooping."

"He may be an amateur, but he was in the perfect position to get by Albert's wife, who was the gatekeeper for the group's information."

"Arthur has a lot of questions about Mandy's role in all of this. What do you think, Joe? Is she a nice old widow lady, or is she a player of some kind?"

"I requested some checks on her traveling history, and I learned that she seldom traveled out of the country with Albert, and except for driving trips she accompanied him domestically only once or twice per year – typical vacation travel. If she was part of this, she supported it in a staff function from home."

"How much did Albert travel?"

"He made international trips several times per year under his own name. The problem is that Peter discovered that the group generated their own good-quality phony credentials. We have no paper trail to track where any of them went when they were pretending to be other people."

"OK, Joe, let's assume that you're correct and that this was some kind of an independent group. They must have been efficient if they never attracted the attention of any of the official government agencies. That lack of visibility may also support the theory that they were working for industrial corporations, but that's a bit iffy. Our problem is that until we know what these guys were doing, it will be almost impossible to identify their assassins' motive."

"And continuing your thought, without a known motive, how do we find the assassins?"

CHAPTER 29 – TWO OLD FRIENDS

"Janice, thank you so much for suggesting this shopping event. I hadn't been at a mall since Albert last took me. I've become a complete homebody."

"Well, Mandy, you wouldn't know that from looking at what you bought. You're like the starving man who only picks at his food. I thought you'd be buying lots of things to spruce up the house and change its décor. That's why I brought Peter's van instead of my sedan. With your brief shopping and this light traffic, we'll be home ahead of schedule."

"I'm getting too old for major acquisitions or refurbishing the house. Besides, if I don't change anything, I'll feel as though Albert is still with me. After so many years together, the transition is hard."

"I understand your feelings. I think it's harder for an older woman to adjust to a lost spouse than it would be for a man. They have their hobbies and their businesses to fill their time. We immerse ourselves in relationships and the home environment. Without the relationships, the home space gets boring."

"Janice, I've lost Albert, but I still have you and Peter and my other friends. Thanks for keeping in touch with me and including me in your outings. You folks are my support team."

"When Arthur is in town, should I have him call on you as a pastor? He has a lot of experience working with families that have lost a member."

"That would be fine, Janice. It would also help me to remember the times when Arthur was with us on vacations and at outdoor events. Things that happened long ago seem all the more pleasant when you get older."

"You're not that old. You have plenty of life ahead of you. What are your plans? Are you going to take up new hobbies or run Albert's retirement business?"

"There really isn't any business to run. Albert had pretty much given up his traveling and sales work. His office is more a museum than anything else now. I might ask Peter to appraise some of our antiques, so that I would know which ones are worth selling. Without Albert or children, I'll have to do some thinking about what I should do with the house and its contents. And what will happen to everything after I've gone?"

"Mandy, you're not going anywhere yet. The nice thing about a small town like this is that we know and take care of each other. Tonight, for instance, we're going to get you out of your house-bound mood. We'll all go to the Bear's Den Restaurant for dinner."

"Thank you, Janice; that would be fun if it won't inconvenience Peter. He seemed to enjoy going through all of Albert's old papers and things when he was over."

"Mandy, there's no one happier than an antiques specialist going through attics and containers of old objects and papers. He wanted me to thank you for the opportunity. He said that Albert must have had interests and experiences that we didn't even know about."

"Some things were surprises to me too. I still have some taped-up cartons in the attic that I haven't tackled. Albert gave the impression of being very neat and a clean desk person in his office, but that was only the tip of the iceberg. He maintained his neat façade by storing most of his belongings in the attic. Usually, it's the woman who has all of the stored knickknacks, but I was no match for him. I never told him this, but I actually rummaged through two of his cartons last year, and then I threw them away. He never even noticed the two that were missing. We all save too much during our lives."

"Don't say that to the antiques dealer's wife. Saving and preserving old things is our family's mission."

"Touché, but some things are more worth saving than others." Janice noticed a far-away look in Mandy's eyes as they pulled into her driveway.

CHAPTER 30 – ALONE AT LAST

For the first time since they had returned to Parkville from Richmond, Irma and Arthur found themselves alone at the parsonage. It was a roomy old house with lots of small rooms, a typical design from the days when the richest rural family was the one with the most children. On a windy night like this, the frame house emitted a continuous symphony of creaks and groans. Arthur returned from the kitchen with two mugs of hot chocolate, each of which sported two floating marshmallows.

"Great idea Arthur...Those mugs remind me of the period when I was caring for my sick father. Hot chocolate time got rid of all the somber and scary thoughts."

"I figured it was time for us to curl up on the couch and relax for a bit. It's hard to believe that only two and a half weeks ago Dad brought us those items from the smoking table. We need a break from everything that's happening on this case."

"That sounds great to me. Working together is fine, but we have to figure out what to do in our fun time, assuming there will be some."

"Do I really come across as always being serious? I thought I was the light-hearted one and that you were the deep one."

"I'd throw one of these pillows at you, but I don't want to get hot chocolate all over your couch. I guess we're both like tall steins of beer – deep but with frothy heads; of course I'm lighter than you are, your holiness."

"I'll have you know that Jesus had a great sense of humor. The problem was that his disciples didn't know whether it would be OK to laugh. Jesus had to be amused at their reactions when he walked on water out to their boat."

"And I was equally amused at your reaction when your mother set up your old bedroom for us. Are you Mr. Propriety?"

"It was more a matter of getting the answer before the question. We hadn't discussed our relationship. We'd been playing it cool and letting things develop naturally. When Mother announced that sleeping arrangement, I thought you would feel pressured and would wonder about my family's attitudes."

"I did for about a millisecond, and then I realized that we were on the verge of hurting your sweet mother's feelings. I figured it would be better to do a little time warping and get to where we'd probably be a little later on. I also wanted to see whether you were willing to take the next step or if it would bother you. You're not complaining, are you?"

"Hardly, but you keep surprising me. Every time I think I can predict what you will say or do, I discover new facets of your personality. I have to admit that I had a longer time frame in mind for us."

"And that's the way it should be. I have to keep you off-balance so that we never take each other for granted or have a stale relationship."

CHAPTER 31 – QUESTION MARKS

"Penny, according to Arthur, Albert Dandrich left sealed cartons of materials that no one has examined. We could take legal action or make other arrangements to see those items, but before we get aggressive with Mandy, we should see what our other five members of the group left behind. We should also find out more about their families."

"I'm ahead of you on that one, Joe, but my preliminary results aren't particularly useful. These guys were all selected for that OSS World War II mission because they had no families to miss them if they were killed. It turns out that Albert was the only one of them to get married but have no children after the war. The rest of them eventually had big families. They would have had to be very discrete to work their intelligence missions in among their family obligations and schedules without being detected."

"Keeping their secret lives hidden would have been difficult, but the large family would have been an asset. There would always be some family member who would have appropriate and valuable connections."

"You would think that all of those family members would ask awkward questions about periods when they were unexpectedly away, but our society isn't what it used to be. There was a time not that long ago when people watched their neighbors and tried to find out what they were doing. Nowadays everyone values privacy and pays little attention to the neighbors. So many people travel on business on short notice, that trips for contact meetings or intelligence missions wouldn't be noticed. I know we're unusual cases because we're in the business, but do you know a lot about all the people in our development, Penny?"

"I'll admit that I don't know everyone in our apartment house or many in the other buildings, but they don't know us either. We're all traveling so much that relationships don't happen. I do know that our apartment isn't bugged, because I've done an electronic sweep every month since we've lived there."

"I didn't know that. Anyway, these five guys apparently had very low profile lives. That would be expected for anyone involved in covert operations."

"Their families and nominal occupations were quite varied. The only common characteristic I've learned about Albert's five associates is that they each moved within their local communities every few years, at least until about fifteen years ago."

"They were minimizing the chance of neighbors and others getting too close to them. Maybe the last fifteen years of not moving mark their retirement period."

"Albert lived in the same place for a long time. Why was he so different?"

"That's a good question."

CHAPTER 32 – ONWARD AND UPWARD

"Irma, what are your feelings about flying saucers?"

"That came out of nowhere. Is Mr. NASA Engineer planning to take me away on a spacecraft?"

"That would be an interesting trip, but I'm semi-serious. When you read about reports of UFO sightings, do you tend to believe them, or do you look for a mundane explanation for them?"

"As a scientist, I look for logical explanations, but I also have to keep an open mind for the unexpected result, if the evidence supports it."

"You still didn't tell me your answer to the question of UFO's and visitors from outer space."

"OK, I'll play your game; I've always felt that there are so many stars and planets out there that I'd be surprised if there weren't life forms on other worlds, but I doubt that those forms of life would be anything like humans."

"Do you think that some of those life forms have visited us?"

"I'd have to say that's not very likely except for microbes living inside meteorites that may have crashed on Earth. Is there a purpose behind this line of questioning? Is this recreational discussion, or does it have something to do with our case?"

"Among the papers that Dad retrieved from Albert's office were his notes from classes at Ohio State University. It turns out that our six people were all enrolled in the Department of Physics and Astronomy at Ohio State. The best known professor in that department was J. Allen Hynek who investigated reports of UFO sightings for the U.S. Air Force under three project names, Projects Sign, Grudge, and Blue Book. Project Sign's dates were 1947-

1949, and they changed the name to Project Grudge in 1949 in part because the findings in Project Sign had been so negative regarding the validity of UFO sightings that they needed a new name to appear more objective."

"The government wanted to play down these reports so that people wouldn't get panicked by them."

"That's right, and how better to assure that outcome than to have covert government grad students working on the project?"

"It would have been unusual for all six of our veterans to have had college degrees. Yet they were all in Physics and Astronomy graduate school."

"That makes it all the more likely that they were placed there as representatives of a government agency."

"That would also explain why none of them got degrees. They probably didn't have all the prerequisites and credits they would need. Your analysis of why they were there sounds reasonable, Arthur."

"Let me add to that the fact that 1947 marked the beginnings of Project Sign, the U.S. Air Force, and the CIA. With such a simultaneous startup, I would guess that if our former OSS soldiers were acting as government monitors on Project Sign, which was an Air Force project, they were probably doing so for the CIA."

Irma applauded. "Well done, Mr. Magician, you've woven all the strands neatly together. If we assume that they were working for the CIA on Project Sign, then they probably continued to work for them on other projects later. We should ask Penny and Joe to follow up on that lead."

"I could even speculate that the CIA would have justified their work on Project Sign as being at least international, because they were looking at the interface between our country and outer space."

"I knew you'd manage to get back to that topic. Do you believe in flying saucers?"

"Having helped NASA launch interplanetary probes, and knowing how long it would take to get them to any place outside our own solar system, I'll say that I have an open mind on the prospect. I'd want to see some very careful analysis of the observation data before I'd take my answer all the way to a yes."

CHAPTER 33 – VOIDANT

Penny stood by the stove and flipped the final pancake in her batch as Joe emerged from the bedroom. She carried the steaming platter over to the breakfast table and set it on a ceramic tile hot pad. Joe noted the cloth napkins and flowers on the table and understood that the presentation was a message for him.

"Wow, those pancakes smell good. Is this some kind of special occasion?"

"It's a little thank you for your commitment to go house hunting after we finish this case. It might even be a sample of the higher style of living you might experience when we're in that house."

"Point well taken; I do intend to live up to that promise. I'll be domestic too. Right after breakfast I'll take the garbage out for collection."

"Be even more domestic and take it out now before you miss the pickup. The food will still be warm if you hurry."

Joe saluted and headed down the hall with the white kitchen trash bag and a black bag from emptied wastepaper baskets. Maybe this family atmosphere business wouldn't be too bad. He had to admit that he was getting too used to seeing Penny as a work partner. They did need to emphasize their home life. If there were ever a lengthy time interval between cases, it would be fun to use it to refurbish a house of their own. He opened the outside door and headed for the dumpster with his two contributions. As he turned the corner, he came to an abrupt stop.

A tall man wearing a dark baseball cap, sunglasses, and black uniform jeans and shirt had pulled three plastic bags of paper trash out of the dumpster and thrown them into the back of a black pickup truck which was already laden with others. This was neither the uniform nor the vehicle of their trash collector. Joe realized that it must be someone retrieving trash for some kind of investigation. He dropped his bags and ran toward the dumpster.

"Hey, stop right there. I'm a federal agent."

His quarry saw Joe coming, and jumped into the pickup truck. He had left the engine running for a quick getaway, and he now drove it in a tight turn behind a row of parked cars so that Joe would not be able to read the license plate. By the time Joe reached the dumpster, the truck had exited the parking lot and turned right, merging into traffic. Joe examined the dumpster and saw that the only remaining bags were full of garbage rather than papers. He retrieved the bags that he had dropped, threw them into the dumpster, and then headed back to the apartment.

"Hey, slowpoke, your pancakes are getting cold. What took you so long?"

"Our domestic moment has been cut short by other members of our covert community. It looks as though someone has reacted to our inquiries about affiliations of those old veterans by investigating us. They grabbed all the paper trash from this building to sort it for significant discards."

"Did you shred everything related to this case?"

"I don't think we even had any case papers here. We'd better increase security at the office. Be sure that the computer systems don't allow wireless pickup of our data processing and internet activities."

"That's standard procedure, but no harm in checking for any lax practices. Apparently there are people who are supposed to be on our side but really aren't.

"Now we'll have to see whether we can figure out which agency is behind this. Any ideas, Joe?"

"This guy might have been from the agency that had employed our six veterans, or he may have been from another group that just wanted to know what we're investigating."

"We're part of a community of professional bloodhounds. Hopefully, their interest in our work is curiosity rather than some malicious motive."

"Arthur filled me in on his investigation of the Ohio State period in the forties. He was pretty convinced that they were working for CIA at that time. It would be logical to assume that they continued to work for the Company."

"They may have been a black unit even then. There would be few active records of them at Langley."

"I don't think we'd gain anything trying to walk in the front door of CIA headquarters looking for details of an operation from a long time ago. We'd better use some of our back-channel contacts that have some history to them."

"You sound as though you have a particular contact in mind, Joe."

"Do you remember codename Voidant? He goes way back to OSS, and he was behind the political scenes during the fifties – had access to White House insiders under Eisenhower, not to mention some of Ike's war buddies."

"That's a new codename to me, Joe. I assume the *void* part signifies someone who isn't there, meaning that he would be very hard to find, right?

"You're correct, Penny. He is virtually impossible to identify and always has been."

"Well, smart guy, how do you suggest that we contact him?"

"Every once in a while, you test my reaction to a story about some guy you went with before we ever met. It turns out that I also had a background before we met. Voidant cannot be found. He has to find you in response to a special message. The message has to be coded and placed in a continuously changing location. I've had contact with him before, and I know that code."

"I'm suitably impressed, Joe, but do you know where the contact signal has to be placed?"

"In the old days, it may have taken a lot of traveling to reach the proper physical location. Now he's older, and technology offsets the relative immobility of age by letting him select a virtual online location. I'll start at a known website and solve a series of coded problems leading to other sites until I finally find a problem with zero for its solution. At that point I click on the 'contact us' button and leave my coded identification. The response will be a new code to use for my message along with how and where to send it."

"Do you ever get to actually see this Voidant?"

"If I ever did see him, I wouldn't realize it anyway. He has never been identified by anyone. I'll do the computer work from the office. I don't think I can trust the scrambling on our wireless network here...In the meantime, I'm going to warm up your special pancakes in the microwave and appreciate your special brunch setup."

"It was supposed to have been breakfast."

CHAPTER 34 – COFFEE BUDDIES

Wally Sanborn parked in the lower lot of Parkville United Methodist Church and trudged up the stairs to the main office. The combination of allergies and a recent lack of exercise had detracted from his usual high level of physical fitness. He'd have to work on that later this week. He turned into the office and found himself facing a beaming Shirley Hadley, the church Secretary.

"What's happened, Shirley? You look as though you're about to burst with good news."

"You are so right, Wally. My son Jeremy has been accepted to the University of Wisconsin at Platteville, and he's been awarded a full tuition scholarship."

"That is great news. Does he have his major picked out already?"

"With his peripheral involvement in things that have been happening around here and his part time work for Bobby Andrews, he has only one interest, a Criminal Justice major. This is a big day for our family; here, have some pastry from Hadley's Bakery."

Mentally, Wally groaned as he took an almond crescent Danish, reminding himself that it would add that much more time to restoring his fitness, but he couldn't disappoint Shirley."

"I would have written a recommendation letter based on Jeremy's participation in the youth missions program, but I'll guess that he had plenty of support from others and wouldn't have needed my contribution."

"Pastor Blake sent a letter, as did Chief Andrews, and he was also championed by Professor Edward Middlemiss at the UW-Platteville Political Science Department. They all talked about Jeremy's assistance with inquiries around here, and that made the Department of Criminal Justice interested. Professor Middlemiss had already prepared the ground by documenting our investigations for case study use by the Department."

"Jeremy earlier talked with Blake about what it would take to get a career with NASA. Now he's decided to pursue one of Arthur's other careers. I'm pleased for all of you."

"Thanks, Wally. If it's any consolation, at one time he considered talking with you about an Army career...Did you stop into the office for anything in particular?"

"I was going to ask whether the Chief Investigator is in the church. He's been pretty hard to find over the last couple of weeks."

"You timed your visit perfectly. He's in his study. If you're heading over that way, would you mind taking this file folder to him?"

Wally took the folder and headed for Arthur's study. It had been a while since they had shared coffee and brainstormed. It was usually a worthwhile experience. He looked through the open study door and saw Arthur reading an old NASA report. Several others were piled up next to it.

"Hi, Arthur, I thought I'd stop in for a bit if you're not too busy. What are you studying?"

"Believe it or not, I'm trying to understand what NASA thinks about Unidentified Flying Objects, otherwise known as flying saucers. It's amazing how many reports have been written on the subject."

"Does NASA believe in flying saucers?"

"NASA reviewed some of the early astronaut reports of UFO sightings and concluded they were seeing the extra-vehicular-activity floodlight boom. The round light assembly on the end of the thin boom tube looked very similar to the round object the astronauts photographed from the space capsule."

"Does that analysis explain all the reported sightings?'

"Nope, but it points in the direction of rational explanations for most of them. I'm not ready to speculate about the others. Anyway, Wally, I'm tired of looking at this old paperwork. Come on in and chat for a while."

"Shirley took care of me. I brought my own pastry. Would you like to share it?"

"Thanks anyway, Wally, but she gave me my quota earlier this morning."

Arthur got up to refresh his coffee from his omnipresent pot. Wally found his favorite mug on the tray and filled it. Then Arthur pushed the reports aside and they assumed the relaxed postures of old friends at rest.

"Arthur, before I forget, here's a file folder that Shirley gave me to deliver."

"Thanks, she saves up the papers I have to sign in this folder. It's a frequent visitor to these quarters. What brings you over this way?"

"Let's start with the fact that you've hardly been around the church for the past couple of weeks. There's no problem with you visiting your parents, but this old Army guy is getting curious."

"Are people starting to say that I'm not around enough to do my job properly?"

"No, I'm starting to smell a new investigation going on, and I feel left out. Do you have anything happening that could use my kind of assistance?"

"As a matter of fact, I was going to ask you what you knew about the old OSS."

"That was a bit before my time, but I know some things about it. What are you after?"

"I know that during World War II, they tapped military people to volunteer for some of their special missions. I hope to corroborate that some of those people stayed with OSS after discharge and later stayed with the organization after it became CIA."

126

"That's an interesting theory, Arthur, but my guess is that it would have been more likely that the GI's were discharged and then later approached by the new CIA for a mission after that agency had been established. Except for top brass, OSS pretty much shut down after the end of the war. Parts of it went to the Department of War, as it was called then, and parts went to the State Department."

"You do know about this stuff, Wally. What part of OSS ended up being what part of CIA?"

"The paramilitary or what I call the skullduggery part of OSS became the Special Activities Division of the CIA. Does that answer your question?"

"It sure does, Wally. Thanks a lot. I suppose you'd like me to tell you why I'm asking these questions."

"I assume it has something to do with your latest case, and I'm drooling over the prospect of learning something about it, so please fill me in."

"OK, this is confidential, so keep it between us. My Dad's friend was involved in an OSS mission shortly before D-Day. I'm trying to find out whether he became part of the new CIA, and I can't ask him, because he was murdered recently."

"Now, there's an interesting chunk of information. Even this long after the fact, it would be hard to get personnel and mission information for the startup CIA. Most of their staff came out of World War II and were still operating in war mode. The first missions were also involved in the opening salvos of the Cold War, so there would have been lots of classic spy stuff going on. CIA has always been afraid to release information for fear that it would end up hurting or killing their contacts in other countries."

"Could I get access to some of the early information through the Freedom of Information Act?"

"They're exempt from it. In the 1990's, they let one writer in after many negotiations and secrecy agreements to write a book about four of their pioneer leaders. The process took a couple of years, and they redacted all the specific details they considered sensitive. They also said they wouldn't do another similar project again."

"How do you know about all this stuff, Wally?"

"I've told you in the past that one of my Army logistics functions was to prepare custom items for Special Forces missions. Well, I was in charge of preparing similar custom items for other agencies as well. I got to know personnel as I trained them to use my outfit's packages."

"I'm always amazed by the number of things you've done. You always have some appropriate experience or knowledge to match my current need."

"Well, Arthur, what I have for you this time is the information that there is no simple way to find out what the CIA did on an individual mission level during its early days. I doubt that I've helped you very much."

"Oh, you have. I'm now pretty sure where I need to look. I only have to solve the problem of how to retrieve my target information."

CHAPTER 35 – CONTACT

"Zero! My problem solution was zero on this site. That means I'm ready to leave my coded identification credentials in the comment box. Here goes; there, I hope he's monitoring his communications or that he at least has some kind of interface to let him know when a contact has been made."

"Joe, you sure have a lot of faith in this Voidant person. I hope he can give you the information you want or can send you to someone else who can."

"Let's put it this way, if he can't then nobody can."

"You said that he's supposed to give you a new code and directions for communicating with him. Once you have that, what are you going to ask him?"

"Arthur is convinced that our OSS people worked for CIA during the early stages of that group's existence. I think he's correct on that one. Neither one of us knows whether they continued to work for the Company in later years, but during the ensuing decades they must have been doing something sensitive enough to make someone want to kill them. I'm going to start at the beginning with Voidant. I'll ask for proof they joined CIA and for some idea of their early missions. Once we have that information, we should be able to use our own contacts to follow the sequence of events over time. We're not exactly outsiders to covert operations."

"I hope you get something useful from running this tedious maze to contact Voidant. Fortunately, it won't lose us anything except time. If it doesn't pay off, we're in no worse shape than we were before."

"It's still a gamble. We're revealing our hand. If Voidant doesn't want to help us, he could pass details of our interest in these people to the group that assassinated them. That possibility could have all sorts of nasty consequences."

CHAPTER 36 – IMPRESSIONS

Janice looked up from the art book she had been studying. She waited until Peter completed his tightening of the door hinge on an antique sewing cabinet. Then she cleared her throat.

Peter looked up and set down his tools. "You have my attention. I know enough to respond to that sound. What's happening?"

"While I've been studying art, I've been thinking about Mandy. I just realized that we should use an art technique to figure what's been going on with her.

"I had a nice outing with her when we went shopping, and nothing seemed different about her. She's always so polite and folksy when we're together. She's consistently been that way over the years. I think that's why we've never noticed anything unusual about her."

"What do you mean?"

"We always see her up close, and she comes across as a very lovable woman and friend. I'm not saying that that's an incorrect impression, but we might see something different about her if we were to use the art technique of perspective to try to be objective and look at her from a distance."

"How do we do that?"

Janice got up from her chair, went over to the desk, and picked up a pen and a yellow lined legal pad of paper. In the left-hand marginal column she wrote down the numbers one through twenty.

"Let's write down facts about her, not how we feel when we're with her, and see where it takes us."

"That's fine with me Janice, but some general impressions may have to be added too. You start."

"OK, I'll start with the fact that she didn't want to buy much of anything when we went shopping together. She used to buy lots of things and get scolded by Albert for going over their budget. Mandy said she wasn't buying because she wanted to keep everything the way it was with Albert there. It's also conceivable that she wants to pack up and leave soon."

"That's a valid entry. I'll say that she told me about the hiding place of the office key when she had that key on a string around her neck. There was no need for her to reveal the normal hiding place."

"Good one; I'll add that she rushed to have Albert's body cremated when she had once told me that she didn't believe in cremation."

"I'd call that one borderline. Put a question mark next to it. She said that Albert left instructions that she should have him cremated, so she may have simply been bowing to his wishes ... I'll add that she said she had gone into the office through the door when she must have used the hidden entrance from the basement because the tell-tale marker on the door had been set up from the inside."

"I'll go back to her story of how she met Albert. She said that she slipped on an ice cube in a soda fountain and that Albert helped her up. She also suggested that he had dropped the ice cubes to make her slip. That sounds hokey. She may have slipped on a cube, but if she did, it would have already been on the floor, and she staged the fall to meet Albert."

"Next item: When Mandy led me to Albert's office, she abandoned her old lady persona. Her posture was erect, and she displayed fitness in her stride."

"It may or may not be significant that Mandy has continued to attend the American Legion meetings after Albert's death."

"That's another question mark. Lots of widows keep their veterans' organization connections ... How about those diamonds she told me about? I'll bet that they didn't exist, and that she mentioned them to make Albert and his buddies seem more mysterious. She walked into the office and said they were still there without appearing to have looked at all."

"I'll accept that one, but it could have been a case of them having been hidden in plain sight ... Only a woman would notice it, but when we went over there with Arthur and Irma, there were visible cobwebs in several places. She was always extremely particular about not having guests unless everything was immaculate. It may have been a natural symptom of the transition to widowhood, or she may have dropped a pretense that she had always displayed in the past."

"I'm detecting a trend in these items on your list, and I'm not sure I like it."

"I see it too. You wanted to look through Albert's stuff after you discovered that he might have been hiding behind a mask and living a double life. Now we're seeing that Mandy may also have hidden her true self behind the mask that she showed us."

"Even more than that, with this mysterious setup in Albert's office, she may be putting on a new mask just for our benefit."

CHAPTER 37 – THE ORACLE SPEAKS

Joe knocked on Penny's doorpost and stood in the open doorway, awaiting her response. He looked pleased with himself.

"Since when do you knock? Are you getting formal or something?"

"I wanted to do something to get your undivided attention. I am pleased to announce that Voidant has responded. He's given me the contact code and the site address at which I am to make contact. I also have a thirty minute window in which to send the message, so I'm starting right away. You may want to join me."

"You get started. I'll be there shortly, as soon as I find something."

Due to his initial enthusiasm, Joe hadn't noticed that Penny had been going through several file drawers and had stacks of papers all over her desk and side table. He decided he had better do his job and let her finish hers. Enthusiasm always made you think your job was the only important one. He headed for his computer and entered the coded message. Then he grabbed a mug of coffee and awaited the response.

Voidant had to be almost ancient by now. Was he still as sharp as ever? Did he continue to have useful contacts, or had everyone in power forgotten about him. At least Joe was looking for old information. They say that even people in the early stages of Alzheimer's disease retain their long term memories.

He knew that his reception of the code and site address meant that Voidant would see his message promptly. The problem was that Joe had no idea how much research Voidant would require to obtain the answer. He finished his coffee, refilled his mug, and started to complete his latest travel expense report while he waited.

Penny walked into Joe's office, smiling because she had finally unearthed the document she had needed. She was surprised to see that her husband no longer looked optimistic. When he looked up at her she raised a questioning eyebrow at him.

"Maybe I expected too much, Penny. I've been sitting by this computer for longer than it should take, and nothing at all has come in. I would expect him to at least respond saying that there are no records."

"Don't worry, Joe, we're no worse off than we would have been if you didn't know about Voidant and how to contact him. I found an old report on early Cold War CIA projects that might be useful. It has only general unclassified listings, but..."

The outer office doorbell rang, and Joe jumped up from his desk. Very few people knew that they were a government agency. The sign on the outer door said *Trading Trends Newsletter*, and the staff of two women in the front office actually published that monthly periodical in between their data analysis activities for the agency. Nancy opened the door to the connecting passageway.

"Joe, I have a messenger at the front door, and he has an envelope that requires your signature. He wouldn't settle for mine."

"Thanks, Nancy, I am expecting something."

Joe headed for the front door, wondering if this was Voidant's way of telling him that the information he sought was extremely sensitive. He found a Marine Sergeant Major waiting for him with a large envelope.

"Sergeant Major, I'm Joe Gonzalez. I understand you have an envelope for me."

"I do, Sir, but I'll require two ID's with photos before I can deliver it to you."

For good measure, Joe supplied three ID's which the Marine examined in great detail.

"Thank you, Sir; please sign this sheet in the three places indicated by the letter X."

Joe signed as directed, and the Marine handed him the envelope.

"Before you go, may I ask your duty posting?"

"I'm assigned to the State Department, but this delivery originated elsewhere. It was routed through State Department Security, but I have no idea about the originating source. That information is above my pay grade, Sir."

"Thank you for your promptness, Sergeant Major. I understand the security aspects."

The Marine left, and Joe headed for his office with the packet of documents that had been too sensitive for electronic transmission.

CHAPTER 38 – IRMA

When Arthur visited Irma's apartment Wednesday afternoon, he received an unexpected response.

"What are you doing here?"

"It's a sunny afternoon, so I thought I would drop in to see you. Aren't you glad to see me?"

"Arthur, I'd be a lot happier if you were over at the church being the Pastor. It's your job, and you should pay more attention to it."

"Everything is under control there. I've signed all the papers that Shirley had for me. I've met with Wally Sanborn, and I've reviewed the trustees' budget and project list with Bill Martin. Things are going smoothly."

"I'll grant that you have Parkville UMC organized than a lot better than it was under Pastor Middlemiss, but part of your job is to be visible over there for substantial parts of the week. You're supposed to prepare plans for the future of the church, and to visit the sick."

"Well, coach, nobody is sick right now, I've finished preparing my sermon for Sunday, and I was there long enough to meet with Shirley and two other folks today. I'm simply efficient at my church work."

"OK, Arthur, you may come in, but I'm worried that you're giving a lot more time to the investigation side of things than you are to your pastoral duties. This isn't the first time we've had this conversation. Coffee's ready in the kitchen. Help yourself."

Arthur headed out of the front room and returned with a steaming mug. "See, you must have expected me today. You have my coffee."

"I know you well enough to always have coffee ready for you. I don't think you can tie your shoes without a mug of coffee nearby. Now, sit down at the table, and don't change the subject."

"Irma, I appreciate your concern, but most of the time the investigation work is part of my pastoral duties, or it grows out of them. Don't forget that even our present case was brought to me at church by Dad. If someone comes to me at church and says he has a problem, I'm supposed to help him work his way through his dilemma."

"I'd say that this case is a borderline example. Your father is not a member or even a frequent attendee at Parkville UMC."

"Outreach is one of the church's major duties. When he came for help, I saw that he needed top priority attention."

"You have lots of glib answers, but I still think that you're dividing yourself into too many pieces and slighting your church congregation."

"Watch out, Irma; you're starting to sound like Angela King, the District Superintendant, and I could never get close to someone with her outlook."

"Drink your coffee, and stop talking about your other girlfriends. I'm not the jealous type. I'm also not trying to mother you, but I would like some answers to my questions about where your career is likely to go."

"Can I help it if I'm good at many things?"

Arthur set down the mug. He removed his hand from it one second before the couch pillow hit him. A second pillow hit him before he could throw the first one back.

"OK, I give up. I'll have to call Bobby and press charges against you for assault with a fluffy pillow. I understand your concern and your arguments, but I'm sure I can handle more than one career. I'll deny it if you quote me, but I find that being a pastor in a small town, in the absence of a traumatic congregational problem, is not a full time job."

"You're saying that you turned to doing things with me out of boredom?"

"Hardly, but you are good at twisting my words against me. I'm saying that, with your assistance, I can be a good pastor, and a good investigator, and a whole lot more. I also think that you are completely without limitations as far as being able to tackle any goal you wish."

"OK, Preacher, you've talked your way out of the doghouse. Now, did you come over here for more than sweet talk?"

Arthur removed a folded piece of paper from his shirt pocket. He smoothed it out and handed it to Irma. This is one of the many articles I found online about the supposed UFO crash in Roswell, New Mexico in July of 1947. I hadn't realized that the Roswell incident occurred while our six veterans were at Ohio State University involved in the department that was studying UFO's. Americans were really taken by the many reports of visits by extraterrestrials at that time. If as we speculated, our group was part of a CIA effort to have the Ohio State study say that we had nothing to fear from space invaders, then Albert Dandrich and his friends may have also worked to suppress the news of supposed spacecraft wreckage and alien bodies at Roswell."

"If they were working for a government agency like CIA, they certainly were in position to do something in connection with all of these reports of visitors from outer space. I hadn't realized that so much of this UFO sensitivity occurred in such a narrow time window."

"The intriguing thing to me is that the intensity of reports went way down after the 1947 to 1949 period when they were at Ohio State. Either there was little merit to the space sightings, or our group was instrumental in helping the government calm people down."

"There is another explanation that you may have overlooked, Arthur."

"What's that?"

"As a population, Americans are easily distracted in their attention to different news areas. People may have become more concerned about the Cold War, reports of Russian spies attempting to steal atomic secrets, United Nations debates, and eventually, the Korean War. Most people have enough problems on their own world, without worrying about the question of visitors from other worlds."

"I agree. You forgot to mention that people were still getting used to affluence and peace after the country's worst depression and biggest war. I brought the Roswell thing up because of the coincidence of subject matter and timing to the Ohio State effort."

"If you want to call this a brainstorming session, I will remain non-negative and say that you were right to have been impressed by those facts. I'd like to know what this group's next assignment from CIA or whomever would have been after the UFO questions died down. I'm sure they would have moved on to something else."

"I agree, Irma, and that something else probably would have been international in nature and higher immediate priority than UFO sightings if these guys worked for the CIA."

"I think we've taken this line of thought far enough. We need input from official people like Joe and Penny and their government agency."

"I've already told them that we at ABC Consultants think they worked on UFO's for the CIA."

"Thanks for the hint. I'll have alphabet soup ready for lunch in ten minutes."

CHAPTER 39 – MESSAGE

Joe Gonzalez opened the padded outer envelope of the packet the Marine had delivered and found a second envelope inside. That envelope had no markings on it: no classification or for your eyes only indication. He was surprised when he handled the envelope to feel a lumpy object inside it instead of papers. Joe opened the envelope with a knife, and found a small box in it. He walked over to Penny's office to show her what his coded interactions with Voidant had yielded. As he entered, she looked up at him with an expression of anticipation.

"Penny, all of our mysterious exchanges of messages have resulted in the delivery of a commercial pack of playing cards by a marine sergeant major."

"They must be significant, or they wouldn't have been hand-delivered by that sergeant major. If they answer our questions, I'll say that Voidant is a genius."

"Why do you say that?"

"He may have communicated highly classified information to us without violating any secrecy laws whatsoever. He sent us a simple innocuous item. Neither he nor we are handling a single classified document. Our job is to discover the significance of the deck of cards."

"Well, they look old-fashioned, and there's no writing on the outside of the box."

"Sit down at my table, and we'll examine them together. I'll get the desk lamp with the built-in magnifying glass."

Joe opened the flap of the box and spread the cards face-up on the table.

"This isn't a normal American poker deck. They look strange. I've never seen cards like these."

"I may have seen such cards once. Count the number of cards in the deck. I'll guess the answer is thirty-two."

"...28, 29, 30, 31, 32. Penny, I'd say that was a very good guess. What do you know about these cards?"

"It's a traditional German skat deck. Skat is a three player game, and it's the most traditional and popular game in Germany. I saw cards like these at a tournament in Milwaukee during one of their Summerfest celebrations. They used the old-time card decks and the players all wore traditional Bavarian outfits. The suits are different from ours. Instead of clubs, spades, hearts, and diamonds, they have acorns, leaves, hearts, and bells. They also use combinations of yellow, green and red for the suit markings."

"Well, at least both deck styles use hearts. Is this skat an easy game, and is playing it with these cards supposed to tell us something?"

"It looked pretty difficult to me, but I suppose experience would make it easier. Let's get on the computers to see what we can find. I'll look up facts about the deck, and you look up details about the game, OK. Joe?"

"That's as good a way to start as any. Voidant is definitely telling us this deck has a message, and we already know that it has something to do with Germany."

Joe returned to his office and began to retrieve the rules for Skat. It appeared to be a pretty interesting but somewhat complicated game, somewhat similar to pinochle, which he had played with his dad. The number of cards in the deck came from the fact that it was played with sevens up through aces: Eight different numbers times four suits equals thirty-two cards. The old-style German decks, like the one they had received, had slight variations on the picture cards and aces. He still didn't get the full significance of the old deck. The game could be played just as well with a modern deck. Were they supposed to determine a specific historic date from this delivery? The rules said that the cards were dealt three at a time, like pinochle. He had thought pinochle was unique in that dealing technique, but apparently, he had been wrong. Could the importance of this deck lie in the relationship of skat to pinochle?

Joe started to let his hands explore the deck. Although the cards were old, they shuffled and dealt like a deck that had been used only a few times so as to remove its original stiffness. Was that important? There were too many variables to this puzzle. He admitted to himself that he was stumped. Voidant might be so smart that things he expected to be obvious sailed right over Joe's head. He felt stressed as he continued to stare at the deck of cards, wanting them to talk to him. Joe suddenly realized that Penny was standing in his office doorway staring at him.

"I give up. Either I'm a dunce, or Voidant is a lot smarter than I am, or there isn't anything to be learned from these cards."

"Joe, does that mean that you would consider your wife the most brilliant person you know if she tells you she has solved the puzzle and understands the message?"

"Absolutely, you are both beautiful and smart, and I'll grant you three wishes if you tell me what the cards reveal to you."

"Good phrasing; I feel like a fortune teller now. I went online, and I discovered that the Iron Curtain boundary dividing Europe following World War II created cultural differences between East Germany and West Germany. One of those differences involved the game of skat. It seems that card-players in West Germany changed over to the French-style deck with the clubs, diamonds, hearts, and spades suits, while the East Germans stayed with the old traditional decks like the one we have here."

Joe interrupted. "You're saying that Voidant told us that our group of six veterans worked in East Germany.

That would make sense. We know they were all German speakers. Do your fortune-telling cards tell you who they worked for?"

"Let's use backtracking and deduction to find an answer to that one. From what Arthur worked out about this group's earlier Ohio State assignment debunking UFO sighting reports, they would have been either connected with the CIA or the Air Force at that time. We can probably assume that they continued to work for the same organization. If they were assigned some mission or missions in East Germany, they probably wouldn't have been working for the Air Force. They had bases in West Germany but had no way of operating in the East. Therefore, I'll agree with Arthur that it's likely they were working for the CIA."

"They may have even continued to use German contacts they made while working for the OSS during the war."

"Assuming that we are correct, do we have to find out what they were assigned to do in East Germany, and how well they did it?"

"No, Penny, I don't think we meet the need-to-know criterion for that one. At least we have some sense of what they were doing."

"I think we can also guess that they were pretty efficient to have been entrusted with East German missions. Anyone who was a bungler would have been caught or at least lost his usefulness over there. OK, we have a reliable group of six people working for the CIA in East Germany during the Cold War. The Berlin Wall came down in November of 1989, so that would have been about the latest time period when they would have been useful over there."

"Not to mention the fact that by then they would have been pretty old for field operations. Albert Dandrich would

144

have been sixty-four in 1989. They may have stopped doing field work earlier than that."

"I don't think that really matters, Joe. The important things are that we now have a feeling for where they worked, who they worked for, and the fact that they had been retired for a long time before they were murdered."

"You might have to amend that last point. They may have been retired from the CIA but working on projects of their own. That would jibe with the materials that Peter Blake found at the Dandrich home."

"Frankly, Joe, I don't know what to make of Peter's findings."

CHAPTER 40 – FAMILY VALUES AND BENEFITS

Renee Andrews had spent several frustrating days trying to learn more about the six elderly veterans who had been murdered. On paper, they all appeared to have lived normal and very different lives, but she had been sure that she would discover some common patterns if she looked long and hard at their personal histories and data. All had been married, and all but Albert had raised families. Albert and Mandy had not had any children at all. Max Griggins, Warren Handley, and Joseph Mantini had each been fathers of two children, while Peter Rodwin and Samuel Spincus had each had three. Because of the veterans' ages, their grandchildren had already started to have children, so their collective families were large. Apparently, the families had loved their patriarchs, because the various obituaries and eulogies had glowed with the importance of the departed vets to their offspring. Renee wondered how many, if any, of the family members knew that their eldest members had been very special people. She had to say that about them, even though she could not yet certify the exact details of that uniqueness.

All six of the veterans had received Veterans Administration death benefits and some of them had received insurance benefits as well. She didn't know the details of Albert's benefits. Renee had found that while each of the five men she studied had worked in significantly different fields and for companies varying in size from three to two hundred employees, they all had health and life insurance policies from a company called Prosaic Insurance, Inc.

Renee knew that she would find little more useful information within a reasonable time, so she called Arthur

146

and asked for an ABC Consultants meeting to compare notes. Arthur agreed that it was time to assess their findings. He suggested she meet with him and Irma at his office in the church. He offered to pick up some sandwiches before they all gathered.

CHAPTER 41 – CORRELATIONS

Shirley had converted the simple sandwich lunch into a catered buffet supplied by her husband. Walter. Hadley's Bakery had expanded to become Hadley's Bakery and Catering, and Shirley grabbed every opportunity to demonstrate the quality of the catered food. Even Walter had been surprised by the popularity of his cuisine. Arthur's office table displayed several varieties of deli sandwiches on small delicate rolls plus a tray of egg strata and a platter of cookies and pastry. The various food items surrounded a silver urn with a spigot that dispensed coffee with French vanilla flavoring.

Irma and Renee arrived together, having met in the parking lot, and they both exhibited pleasant surprise at the lunch spread. Renee spoke first. "You do throw a classy party, Arthur."

"It's to show my appreciation of Walter Hadley's talents. If I ate this food all the time, I'd gain a lot of weight. At least I convinced him to make the sandwiches on small rolls."

Irma nibbled a sugar cookie. "I could get used to this fare at our meetings. I might have to request Walter's assistance when we meet at my place also. Should we eat first, or commute to the table during our discussions."

Arthur moved the chairs within easy reach of the food. "No commuting required. Let's have everything within reach while we talk." He filled his coffee mug and sat down. "That French vanilla taste is pretty good...Renee requested this session, so she should start. Are we getting any closer to understanding them and what they were doing?"

"To tell you the truth, my research showed that all but Albert had such big happy families that I was almost jealous of them. They had long marriages, with children, grandchildren, and even great-grandchildren who obviously loved them. I'm sure that part of this impression was enhanced by the fact that they've been virtually retired for quite a few years so that they no longer disappeared from their homes for long periods of time."

Arthur gestured with his coffee mug toward Irma, who quickly finished off her last bite of a small roast beef sandwich. "What's your viewpoint on these men?"

"I can understand Renee's impression of them. The doctors who treated the ones who died while in retirement homes gave me the definite feeling that our veterans had been sociable men who made a big impact on those around them. People enjoyed their presence and their participation in group activities."

"Do you think their sociable nature was genuine, or was it due to skills they had picked up as covert operatives?"

"Well, Arthur, it may have been due to some of each. Family life would require developing sensitivities to the needs and desires of others, but it wouldn't hurt that they had been trained to get along among strangers."

"To fill you in, Renee, we think that these men worked for the CIA at Ohio State with the mission to minimize public acceptance and belief in the many reports of UFO's during the late 1940's. The government was looking to avoid panics or hysterics while they tried to get society back to normal after World War II. We also suspect that they continued to work for the CIA in later years, but Penny and Joe are trying to confirm this and figure out what they went on to do. I have to admit that our preliminary conclusions have to be classed as speculation so far."

Irma finished off her egg strata dish. "I think I'm enjoying this catered meeting too much. You're right about the speculation aspect. We don't really know what happened after the Ohio State years, but we're assuming that they worked for the CIA because of their OSS background and because of the coincidence of their mutual time at OSU. If it hadn't been for their all dying at about the same time, we wouldn't even be giving them much attention. Was there anything unusual about their death arrangements, Renee?"

"Not much; they had the usual VA death benefits for old soldiers, and they had some private insurance. They had worked for a variety of different firms in various fields, but all of those companies were insured by Prosaic Insurance."

Arthur laughed loudly. "Well, group, it's no longer speculation. We'll have to give ourselves an *A* for deduction skills. Split the name of that insurance company, and read it from both ends toward the middle. The result is CIA Pros."

CHAPTER 42 – JANICE AND PETER

"Peter, you told me about Albert's World War II background with the OSS when you wanted me to spend some time with Mandy, but you'd been upset and irritable for quite a while before that. Was that something to do with Albert and Mandy?"

"Janice, you were a real trooper when you took Mandy shopping to sense her outlook. I owe you a complete explanation of what's been going on. Sit down in your favorite chair, and try to understand my motives as I explain them to you."

"I'll put on my calm meditation face, and I'll try to accept whatever you say."

"It all started when Mandy gave me Albert's smoking table. While I was cleaning it up so that you'd let me have it in the house, I found a secret compartment with papers and objects in it."

"That sounds exciting. We've had several desks with hidden spaces. What was in your compartment?"

"Here's where you'll get to see why I'd been so uptight. I found photographs and other items that convinced me that Albert was not who we thought he was. According to the material I found, Albert had pretended to be an American soldier, but he was actually a German soldier in the Waffen SS, a Nazi. The papers said that his real name was Wilhelm Schnacht."

"That information upset you, and you thought that I wouldn't be able to handle it if you shared it with me?"

"Not exactly, Janice...I simply wanted to be absolutely sure before I said anything, so I took the stuff I found to Arthur because he investigates these kinds of things. If my first conclusion wasn't correct, I didn't want to spread false rumors about Albert."

"So that was your father and son event. Now you're saying that you weren't sure I could handle such bad news, and you're also saying that I'm a blabbermouth who would spread a false rumor. Would you like to dig yourself in still deeper? Whatever happened to trust between us?"

"Of course I trust you, Janice, but I didn't want you to doubt Albert if it turned out not to be true."

"To show you that I can be calm in the face of something so unexpected, I'll ask whether it turned out to be true. Did it?"

"We went back and checked out the smoking table again, and we found a second hidden compartment. It held more information that said that Albert had been on a secret OSS mission where he disguised himself as a Nazi soldier to accomplish his mission. The new information said that he was a patriotic American after all."

"Did that make you feel better, and is that when you decided to tell me about Albert?"

"It took a huge load off my mind, but I have to admit that I still waited before telling you."

"Why?" •

"I really don't know why I waited. Maybe I thought the whole thing would now dissipate, and you would view Albert in the same way you did before he died."

"You blew it, Peter. Not only didn't you trust me enough to share everything with me, but you grasped at the answer you wanted to hear. I'll ask you the question that comes into my excitable, irrational, unreliable mind...How do you know which of those two sets of conflicting documents about Albert represents the truth?"

CHAPTER 43 – PHONE CALL

Renee had already left the meeting. Arthur rearranged the chairs to their normal locations. He poured the remaining French vanilla coffee from Walter Hadley's urn into his own coffee pot so that he could drink it later. Then he carried the silver urn back to Shirley in the main church office.

While Arthur was gone, Irma gathered up the remaining food in plastic bags to take back to her apartment. There was no point in letting food go to waste. She enjoyed several extra morsels during the packaging process. The telephone rang.

"Pastor Blake's office - he's not in right now; may I take a message?"

"Irma, is that you? It's Peter Blake, and I have some important input for you and Arthur."

"What is it, Peter? You sound as upset as you were when you first had questions about Albert."

"Absolutely, Irma; I am that upset. Janice and I discussed the conflicting stories from the smoking table evidence, and she pointed out that we really don't know which of those stories is correct. We wanted Wilhelm Schnacht's Nazi background to be wrong, so we jumped to accept the story of the OSS mission. What if that was his cover story, and he and his companions really were Nazis? I don't know what to think now."

"That's very astute thinking by Janice. Tell her it's definitely worth consideration. Arthur is in a different office right now, but let us explore that line of thinking, and then we'll give you a return call. You and Janice have opened up another aspect of the case for our investigation. Whether the Nazi identity is true or not, we should be diligent and consider both options. Thank you. You've been very helpful." She set down the phone as Arthur came back into his office.

"Who was on the phone, Irma? Do I have a pastoral call to make?"

"That was your father. He finally got around to telling your mother the complete story of the Albert puzzle, and she reminded him that the evidence could be correct either way. We still don't know whether Albert and company were Nazis or the OSS heroes from the second version of the story. Your dad's upset all over again."

"I had considered that possibility, but I didn't want to raise it and disturb him. I'm not sure that it makes a lot of difference so far as our learning what this group did for the CIA, but it might make a major difference in determining the motive behind the assassinations.

"Our space program got its initial thrust, pardon the pun, through the efforts of a major group of captured and transplanted German rocket scientists from their Peenemunde facilities where they developed the V-1 and V-2 weapons rockets. They were relocated to Huntsville, Alabama at the new Marshall Space Flight Center. The leader of that group was Wernher von Braun. He and many of his associated scientists and engineers had been Nazis, but we didn't care, because we needed their help. Our allies also collected German rocket scientists to help with their programs. Our first space launch rockets were based on the German V-2, and von Braun's people designed the Saturn V, which was the heavy lift rocket that got the Apollo program going. They were Nazis, but our space program owes them a huge debt of gratitude."

"You're right, Arthur; the feelings of people toward their former enemies may not be at all similar to those between countries. Now Germany and Japan are partners with the United States on many projects. Our government will work with anyone and any country to achieve our national goals."

"It all goes back to the New Testament admonition to forgive your enemies so that they will forgive us when we trespass on their goals and aspirations. It's a difficult path for many people to take, especially when the enemy has mangled their lives and those of their families."

"Getting back to the specifics of our case, it might be easier to understand what Albert's group was doing, if these men were really Nazis rather than Americans working for the OSS."

"Why do you say that, Irma?"

"It's the Wernher von Braun thing all over again. Maybe the CIA needed Germans for covert operations against other Germans."

"That would assume that they took the place of American soldiers, probably through murder, and that our OSS realized it and decided to turn them to our side rather than punish them for their treachery."

"Warfare, whether hot or cold, is usually waged by some very hardboiled people. Most of us would feel very uncomfortable if we had them in our families."

"I think we'd better present these discussion points to Joe and Penny and get their reactions."

CHAPTER 44 – COLD WAR TACTICS

"Hi, Joe, your friends here at ABC Consultants have conclusive evidence that our group of six veterans was working for the CIA."

"That fits with our thinking, Arthur, but how did you confirm it?"

"Renee found that they worked in different industries but that they all had workplace benefits from Prosaic Insurance."

"Is that significant?"

"Read the word Prosaic from the back end toward the middle and then from the front end toward the middle."

"Gotcha...CIA Pros...That outfit has used a lot of weird dummy company names like that.

"Well, we've made progress, too. We think we know where they did their covert operations work."

"May I guess before you reveal the answer?"

"I suppose that would be OK, but you have this nasty habit of sitting back in Parkville and solving problems before your paid government professionals do. You may have one guess only."

"They worked in East Germany."

"If you weren't a pastor, I'd cuss at you. It took us a lot of sophisticated spy work to get that information. How did you solve it?"

"You're not going to believe this, but my mother came up with the key point."

"Your mother isn't even involved in this investigation."

"Always respect your mother's intuition. My dad finally filled her in on the evidence found in that smoking table, and she realized that we had accepted the more palatable story that these guys were Americans on an OSS mission, when it was just as likely that they really were Nazis. Then Irma pursued that line of thought and came up with the OSS realizing who they were and offering to let them stay, but only if they worked for us. Once Germany was partitioned into East and West, where would we get a team with better credentials to send into the East for covert work?"

"It would make sense if we could trust them. Why would OSS and CIA let them loose on such sensitive assignments?"

"I'm sure they would have tested them on controlled jobs first, such as the UFO Sightings Study. CIA might have also convinced them that they were in danger and might be betrayed or eliminated if they didn't play it straight. Albert had married over here by that time, and some of the others may have also. They had come over to become Americans, and they probably wanted to prove their worth to us."

"It starts to look like an interesting chapter in the story of the Cold War. I wonder what assignments they may have had."

"Irma and I had an interesting discussion in which we compared our government's handling of the German rocket scientists under Wernher von Braun and his associates with their oversight of this group. When my father checked out the documents in Albert's office, they indicated that Samuel Spincus had credentials as a scientist. It's possible that this group was supporting the rocket science efforts by going back to get additional records of earlier work or by spiriting additional scientists out of East Germany."

"That would be hard to prove, but it does make some sense."

"My guess is that they were either murdered for what they did on these covert jobs or for what they did as Nazis in the SS. I doubt that there would be more than a few people left alive who would have records of either of those matters."

"One of those people is likely to be behind the murders."

Richard Davidson

CHAPTER 45 – FISHING TRIP

Despite the choppy water Captain Bob's deep sea fishing boat, *Random Rose*, eased away from its Miami dock with four clients, full bait and beer coolers, and a promise from the captain that he knew exactly where the fish would be today. Bob's daughter, Sara, had the wheel and she revved up the engines as they emerged from beneath the bridge and headed for open water. The dual inboards had more than adequate power to chew through the swells, but every so often they would ride up on a wave crest and come crashing down into the trough behind it. Everyone wore life vests. They gripped the handholds and braced for each successive impact. Conversation waned during this transition period as Sara navigated toward a protected cove in the lee of a horseshoe-shaped island about two miles beyond the harbor bridge.

During the open sea leg of their trip, Bob had the opportunity to assess his passengers while appearing to scan them to be sure they were safe and secure. The three who were dressed like sailors in blue jeans and white T-shirts wore assorted baseball caps, one each from the St. Louis Cardinals, New York Yankees, and Chicago Cubs. The fourth man, who had arrived at the dock separately, was decked out in a flowery pink Hawaiian shirt and red/blue plaid baggy shorts. His head was unprotected, and his blond hair surrounded a pronounced bald spot that was already glowing red. Bob knew that Mr. Bald Spot's name was John Twinings, and that he had been the one who had arranged this outing. Twinings had told him the names of the other three men, but Bob had already forgotten them. He figured that he would refer to each one by the team on the baseball cap he was wearing.

Sara brought *Random Rose* into the cove and slowed the engines. The cove was large enough that she would be able to let the boat drift while fishing rather than having to anchor or maintain their position with the engines. It was a unique location and almost always sure to hold several species of fish. Today would turn out to be even better than usual for catching fish, but Captain Bob would also catch a few surprises.

Sara and Bob tended to the baiting of the lines and the usual spread of snacks and drinks to keep their clients happy. Within two hours they had already reeled in more fish than would be typical for a complete average day. Everyone appeared happy but relatively quiet. The three men with the baseball caps had entered into a contest with each other over who would catch the most fish, and they were taking it very seriously. The one with the Chicago Cubs hat was complaining that he should receive extra points for having caught a fish that was much larger than any of the others. Captain Bob didn't think the intensity of their contest would lead to a fight, but he kept that thought in the back of his mind.

John Twinings came over and caught his attention. "Bob, this is a great boat. Do you have enough gas to do some touring as well as fishing?"

"That depends how far you want to go, and I'd have to charge you for the extra fuel I use."

"There'd be no problem with the extra charges. I'm scheduled to drop my friends off in Key West tomorrow, and it's such a beautiful day that I thought it would be fun to go there by boat. We've caught more than enough fish to give us time to do some touring."

"What about your friends' fishing contest? Will they be willing to end the competition early?"

"I'll ask them, and then I'll get back to you."

Twinings moved away and gathered the others together. Bob was surprised to see him pass money to each of the others and follow that up with a handshake. Then the three with the baseball caps reeled in their lines and sat down to drink beer and swap stories. They seemed more relaxed and talkative.

Twinings returned to Captain Bob's side. "Everything's set for the trip. I found out how much was in their betting pool, and I made them all winners. The best kind of competition is one where nobody loses. Here's an extra bonus for you too." Twinings gave Bob some folded bills and moved off to get a fresh beer from the cooler.

Bob was surprised and impressed by the amount of his bonus. He was used to strange requests from his clients and not at all unhappy at the prospect of a side trip to Key West. The fishing along the key islands was always good, and the Key West social life was special. He passed the word to Sara, and discussed the route that she should take. Bob would suggest that they stay overnight in the Key West Harbor and enjoy the nightlife. He was sure that Twinings would be more than willing to increase the charter fee for this extra sojourn. Whoever Twinings was, he had plenty of cash and didn't mind spreading it around.

CHAPTER 46 – CHALK TALK

Penny and Joe sat in their conference room preparing to analyze the case by tabulating information on their chalkboard. The board had three columns. Column one was titled *who they were*. Column two was labeled *what they did*. The last column was headed *who killed them*. At the bottom of the board crossing all three columns was the note: *All six were connected in life and death.*

Joe walked to the board and printed items in column one. "I see only three options here. They were Nazis, they were American heroes, or they were something else. So far, we have competing documentation supporting the first two prospects. We have no evidence to say they were something else, but we should list that alternative to make our analysis complete."

Penny got up and approached the board. "Give me the chalk for column two. Under what they did, I would put CIA, UFO investigation, and East Germany covert missions."

"What about Peter's suggestion from his research in Albert's office that in retirement they became industrial espionage contractors?"

"I'll accept that. They could have wanted to keep their hands in the game after retirement."

"I've been thinking that there's another explanation for Peter's findings. If they came over as Nazi impostors and couldn't talk about work they had done for the CIA, they might have set up that industrial espionage or counter-espionage thing in order to have something they could openly discuss with their families."

"That's worth considering, Joe, but they already had cover stories. Remember that Renee checked their backgrounds and found that they all had jobs with CIA dummy companies. Those companies are supposed to look like normal businesses to civilians and associates."

"I agree that they're supposed to look normal, but our group may have wanted to set up their own cover business so that they could actually talk about working with each other. They hid their interconnections during the period when they supposedly worked for the dummy companies."

"Let's get back to our chalkboard. What do we put in the third column? What are your favorite theories for who killed our group members?"

"I have some entries, and I've asked Steve to work on some as well, but before we get to that, I think that we need more information from Renee Andrews. We should have detailed histories of all of our men, so that we stop referring to them as faceless group members. These were individual human beings, and whatever their origins, they lived for a long time in this country and had stories to tell. I have the feeling that their stories may hold the key to finding their killers. Anyway, I'll ask Steve to contribute to filling in the last column on the board."

Joe left to find Steve DuBois, their senior associate in the agency. Steve had been responsible for much of the field work on past cases and served as liaison to an ad hoc brainstorming group they convened from time to time at Arthur's church in Parkville. Steve's current assignment was to gather information on groups with both motives and capabilities to have carried out the six assassinations.

While Joe was out of the room, Penny started to enter her own list of potential culprits. She wondered how many would be on Steve's list. By the time the men returned she had listed: CIA, Nazi Hunters, Mossad, and Outer Space Aliens. As she finished posting the last entry, she smiled in the hope that a little humor would help them generate more creative thinking.

Joe returned with Steve, and they halted in front of the chalkboard to read her list. Steve said, "Your list is a good start, Penny, but one item slightly disagrees with my analysis. You may have thought you were joking when you listed the Space Aliens. You're not far from one I give a significant probability to be the culprit. I'm not concerned about creatures from outer space, but I wouldn't discount the involvement of fanatical humans who believe such creatures have visited us. Those groups were unhappy when our government declared UFO sightings to be due to natural events and hoaxes. I consider them a definite possibility."

Penny erased her final entry and replaced it with UFO Fanatics. "I'm sure that your list goes well beyond mine. You've had more time to think about it."

Joe laughed. "Watch out, Steve. She's putting pressure on you now."

"That's OK, Joe. We all have to play by the brainstorming rules that no suggestion is too outrageous, and that negative comments are not allowed. I think that all of Penny's items are reasonable, and she didn't even have to erase the Space Aliens entry."

"I did that because I wasn't really serious about it. What else do you have, Steve?"

"Along with my thinking that these guys may have offended the UFO believers, I suggest that they may have made enemies in East Germany while on covert missions."

"That's a good one. I'll add that to the list. Joe, do you have a different one?"

"I'll suggest the option that one of them had the others wiped out and then committed suicide or died in an accident he was supposed to survive."

"That's intriguing." Penny added Group Self-Destruction to the list.

Steve flipped over the top sheet on the yellow legal pad he had brought with him. "You might also add Other World War II Veterans to the list. If American vets found out these guys were Nazis who took the placed of U.S. Army people, they might want one final act of revenge."

Joe had been looking out the window for several minutes. He turned to face the others. "I've been listening to the suggestions with mixed feelings. I'll be positive and add Holocaust survivors or their families, but I'll be negative in a constructive way by suggesting that maybe all the entries based on long-simmering grievances are less likely than a motive based on something reasonably current."

Penny said, "That's an interesting thought, Joe. What motive for killing them based on something current do you have in mind?"

"I have no idea; it feels right to me."

CHAPTER 47 – FAMILY TREES

Irma answered the telephone with a slight edge on her voice. She had received a letter from a distant cousin who was trying to organize a family reunion, and it had bothered her because she had never even known that side of her family existed. Her mother, who had died while Irma was a teenager, apparently had a half-brother from the remarriage of her father after he had walked out on Irma's grandmother. The reunion request letter had taken Irma by surprise, and she answered the telephone in the expectation that this would be its follow-up call.

"Hello, Irma Custis speaking..."

"Hi, Irma, this is Renee; is everything OK? You sound a little formal and hesitant."

"I'm fine, Renee. I was on edge because I thought the call would be from some distant relatives who've been pushing for a gathering. I never even knew they existed, and now they're acting as though we've known each other all our lives. Frankly, I'm working on excuses to get them off my back."

"If it's anything coming up soon, I may be your excuse. Penny and Joe have requested that I come up with detailed information on the families of our deceased veterans. I'm short on time because Momma has to go to Chicago soon for an operation, and I want to be with her throughout her trip. I'm hoping that you'll be able to work on the family details project with me so that we can complete it sooner."

"I'd be happy to pitch in. What kind of operation is Momma facing?"

"Her back has been bothering her for quite a while. She's tried home remedies, treatments from the chiropractor, and support trusses of various kinds, but none of them have helped very much. They're going to do some exploratory surgery and hopefully insert a spacer or cushion to give her some long term relief. She'll need some loving care for quite a while after the operation, so I want to free up my schedule to give it to her. I have a week or so before the trip to work with you on this research, but later on you'll have to take it over."

"That sounds like a great mother-daughter relationship plus a good job for me. I've been getting a little bored without my autopsy work. Instead of examining an individual after death, I'll work with you on examining the surviving family members. Where should we start?"

"If you don't mind, I'll head over to your apartment now. I have death notices on the five men who had children. I doubt if we have to get additional information on Albert Dandrich's family. Albert and Mandy had no children. Peter and Janice Blake know everything about them anyway."

"That sounds good to me, Renee. I'll be ready for you when you come."

After hanging up the phone, Irma cleared the dining room table and set out a bowl of fruit for snacks while they worked. Then she turned on her computer and laid out pads of paper for notes. She knew that this would be a complex project. The murdered men had been so elderly that they would have several generations of offspring. Irma paused with that thought. Whenever she referred to children, she wondered whether she would ever have any of her own. She was ready to face the prospect of adoptions, but she didn't know how long she could be patient with Arthur's ambiguous commitment uncertainties.

A few minutes later the doorbell rang. She opened the door to welcome Renee, who bounced in with a big smile on her face.

"Thanks so much for being my co-researcher, Irma. I'll feel so much more relaxed while I'm traveling with Momma and when we get back after her operation."

"Is that the only reason you asked for my help?"

"What do you mean?"

"Renee, I do have medical training, and my glance at you as you entered suggests that you have something else to announce to me."

"You are sharp, Irma; I haven't told anyone at all yet, but yes, I'm pregnant."

"Congratulations, and I suggest that you tell Bobby before some other sharp-eyed person informs him. In the meantime, come on in; we'll celebrate with some pink lemonade while we work."

They sat down at the table, and Renee removed a set of papers from an envelope. "These are the best obituary notices I found for each of them. They should give us a good start. Once we have the names of their relatives, we'll be able to check them out to add more details."

"Did Penny & Joe determine the sequence of the six murders?"

"They did, Irma. The first death was Max Griggins, followed in sequence by Joseph Mantini, Warren Handley, Peter Rodwin, Samuel Spincus, and Albert Dandrich."

"That's interesting. Albert wasn't killed until after the two who were poisoned in their assisted living facilities. My first guess was that the perpetrators would have killed everyone who still drove before they went after the two who were living in institutions. I guess their sense of order wasn't the same as mine."

"They may still have been logical. Albert was the last to be killed, but he was geographically far away from the

168

rest of them. All the others were much farther south than Albert's death site in Wisconsin."

"That's a good point, Renee. Anyway, let's study their obituary information in the same sequence as the killings. First, show me the information for Max Griggins who died by going off that remote road in the Everglades."

Maxwell "Max" Griggins, 84

Max Griggins, of West Palm Beach, Florida, went to be with the Lord and his loving wife of 40 years, Dolores, after his sudden death on Friday, August 6, 2010. He was born February 13, 1926, in Waycross, Georgia, the only child of Barbara and Tim Griggins. Max is survived by his twin children, Jennifer DeStefano (Anthony) and John Griggins (Lucy). He is also survived by four grandchildren, Casey DeStefano, Anne Denning (Robert), Dr. Mary Waters (Harold), Congressman Paul Griggins (Jill), and three great-grandchildren, Sarah Denning, William Griggins, and Cathy Griggins. Max lived in West Palm Beach for more than thirty years, where he worked for Wingly International Services Company until his retirement in 1996. Max served his country in the U.S. Army and was a proud veteran of World War II. He was deeply committed to his family and had a lifetime passion for painting and drawing cartoons. Many of his political cartoons appeared in his local newspaper. He will be sorely missed.

"That obituary seemed pretty simple to me, Irma. It went along with our theory that the OSS volunteers had been selected because they had no relatives to mourn for them if they died during their secret operation. Notice that the obituary mentions no sisters or brothers, and although it's not spelled out, Max's parents might well have died before he went into the Army."

"I agree that his details fit that theory. His wife died before him, so his survivors are two married children, four grandchildren, and three great-grandchildren plus the spouses of everyone who was married. I did notice with interest that the list of his grandchildren includes a doctor and a congressman. It sounds as though this family placed a priority on education and success. I also noticed that the information in the obituary jibes with Peter Blake's report that Max Griggins had the skills to create believable documents to support covert missions. He was both a painter and a cartoonist. I'll bet that he knew his way around specialized computer graphics programs also."

"Do you think there was any significance to the fact that he was the first one killed?"

"We'll need more information before I'd attempt to answer that one. It could be important, but it could also be random chance that set him up to be first. Let's look at the obituary for the second victim, Joseph Mantini. His car ran into a piece of shop equipment that dropped off a truck in Dallas."

Joseph Mantini, 85

Joseph A. Mantini, 85, of Dallas beloved husband of Marie, nee Fossi, died suddenly August 9, 2010. He was the loving father of Rudy (the late Susan), and Warren (Denise). He was the cherished grandfather of Helen, Cheryl, Rodney, and William. He was the son of the late Tony and Estelle Mantini of Atlantic City, New Jersey. Joseph lived for twenty-five years in Dallas, where he was retired from Hilliard Aero Systems, Inc. He attended Ohio State University, and he was a member of St. Andrew's Episcopal Church.

Joseph was a World War II veteran, having served in France following D-Day. He was awarded a Purple Heart and a Bronze Star.

The funeral was held August 13 in Highland Park. The family asks that memorial donations be given to St. Andrew's Episcopal Church of Dallas or a charity of your choosing.

Irma wrote down several notes on her pad before she spoke. "It's interesting to me that both Joseph and his wife had Italian names, but they belonged to an Episcopal church rather than a Catholic one. As I recall, Mantini's Army dog tag indicated he was Catholic."

"That's nothing, Irma, nowadays people worship in all kinds of church variations. I was raised in an older neighborhood on the south side of Chicago, and I went to a historically Swedish Lutheran Church. The neighborhood had been built when the majority of the people living there were Swedish. Over time it shifted to being primarily black, but we all stayed with the neighborhood church that was already there. It all worked out well, and I learned a lot from the few Swedish folks who still lived there.

"I was surprised to see that Mantini's son's wife had died, but then I remembered that he died at 85, so his son might be about 60 or so, and his wife would have had a reasonably long life and been near that age. Peter Blake had told us that his findings suggested that Joseph Mantini was a weapons expert and a pilot. That would fit with the listing of Hilliard Aero Systems as his employer."

171

"Right, Renee, but don't forget that we don't know whether that was a completely legitimate firm. We had concluded that our six guys worked for the CIA, and might show CIA dummy firms on their resumes. We might want to see what we can dig up on that company."

"I agree. We still don't even know for sure whether these guys were Nazis or patriotic Americans. Mantini's info would make a case for him having American roots because of his service against the Germans after D-Day and the medals he earned for it. On the other hand, he named his oldest son Rudy, a common German name."

"Let's move on to our third victim, Warren Handley. He was the one that Joe pointed out as having died in a different manner. His car had been modified to allow someone to remotely trigger his brakes when he was in front of a big truck traveling at high speed. That happened in Tallahassee, Florida, but the obituary indicates that Handley lived in southern Illinois. That says that his killers must have tracked him to Tallahassee to kill him on their schedule, rather than waiting for him to return home. It also suggests that there was a sense of urgency to this operation."

"That's a great deduction, Irma. We're starting to see inside the minds of the assassins. Let's see Handley's obituary."

Warren J. Handley, 84

Warren J. Handley, 84 of Carbondale, Illinois died suddenly on Friday, August 13, 2010, while traveling in Florida. Warren married Peggy Sue Wilson in 1972. She preceded him in death on May 12, 2009. He was a U.S. Army veteran and served from 1943 to 1946, as a Sergeant First Class in the Signal Corps during World War II. He worked for Comthrush Computer Engineering for many years, retiring in 1996. In recent years his hobby had been reconditioning discarded computers for donation to charitable organizations. He will be remembered for his devotion to the American Legion and St. George's Episcopal Church.

Those left to honor his memory include two sons Kenneth Wilson (Glenda) and Herbert Wilson (Linda), four grandchildren, Henry Wilson, Karen Lansing, Peter Wilson, and Cheryl Murphy, and one great-grandchild, Samantha Murphy. Memorials may be directed to the charity of the donor's choice.

Irma compared the obituaries they had reviewed so far. "I see that both Warren Handley and Max Griggins retired in 1996. I don't see a retirement date for Joseph Mantini, but I'll bet that it was around the same time. We'll have to find out what happened in 1996; it may have been when they severed their CIA connection."

"All three of the obituaries we've examined suggest confirmation of Peter Blake's findings as to their skills. Max Griggins was the artist. Joseph Mantini was the aerospace technician, probably including weapons knowledge and flying skills. Warren Handley was the computer expert."

"On the personal side, Handley apparently didn't have any children of his own. His two sons have his wife's prior name. They probably resulted from her previous marriage. The list of grandchildren and the one great-grandchild, suggests that the sons were already adults when Warren Handley married Peggy Sue Wilson in 1972 and that the two granddaughters were either divorced or widowed. They have different last names, but no spouses indicated."

Renee made a note on her yellow pad of paper. "We can also see that all three men we have reviewed so far had jobs that would let them take off and travel whenever necessary. Max Griggins worked for an international services company. Joseph Mantini was in aerospace work and could claim a contract anywhere. Warren Handley was involved in computer engineering, and that could require developmental or maintenance contract efforts abroad. They were all good cover jobs for a team of people in the CIA."

"I'll bet the others will have had suitable occupations also. Let's turn to the death announcement for Peter Rodwin. He was the fourth one to be killed."

"Good enough, Irma. Here it is:"

Peter Rodwin, 87

Peter K. "Pete" Rodwin, 87, of Lubbock, Texas died Monday, August 16, 2010 in Evansville, Indiana at his assisted living residence, Ripplestream Nursing Home. He was born February 7, 1923 in Wolfforth, Texas to the late Sherman Rodwin and the late Emily Martinez Rodwin. Pete was a retired consultant to Texas Tech University in Foreign Languages, and had made a name for himself as a simultaneous translator at international conferences around the world. He was a member of the Greenfields Baptist Church and a World War II Army veteran. Although never married, he is survived by his adopted children, Maria Rodriguez O'Connor (Sean), Kent Kreutzer (Lydia), and Paul Choi; plus two grandchildren, Patricia O'Connor, and John Kreutzer. Memorials may be directed to Save the Children Federation.

Irma made a few notes and underlined them. "I can see how effective this group must have been for covert international work. Not only did they have an array of key skills represented among them, but they had a simultaneous translator with a good reputation who could get into key international meetings. Most of the time, diplomats and government officials don't even know the identity of their translators. They hear disembodied voices in their headphones."

"He was probably raised bilingually. His mother was Latino and married outside her culture long before it was it was considered acceptable to do so. Then he continued the practice by adopting multicultural children. My guess is that Peter Rodwin felt at home in almost any cultural setting."

"I'll make one amendment to your comment, Renee. His mother was Latino if he really was American born. We still have that nagging prospect that all of these guys were transplanted Germans. Of course, Peter's language facility would have simplified the transplant process."

"You know, that caution is something that I'm finding harder and harder to remember. These obituaries, with their family trees and social interaction information, make it hard for me to think of these guys as anything but what they said they were."

"That would be exactly what you were supposed to think if they were impostors. Let's move on to Samuel Spincus. He was the last victim except for Albert, whom we'll review separately."

Samuel Spincus, 89

Samuel C. Spincus, 89, formerly of Frankfort, passed away peacefully at the Pleasant Pasture Nursing Home in Lexington, Kentucky on Wednesday, August 18, 2010. He was the son of the late David and Linda (Simmons) Spincus. He married Hilary (Cline) Spincus, who survives in Lexington. Samuel was a kind and joyous man who was a veteran of the U.S. Army, serving in World War II with a rank of master sergeant. After the end of World War II, Samuel attended Ohio State University and the University of Michigan, where he earned a PhD in Physics. He served as a lecturer at the University of Kentucky while consulting with many international scientific corporations for many years, until his retirement in 1996. Samuel was the author of several technical and science fiction books, the latter written under the pen name of Futurus Brown. After his retirement Samuel purchased a home in Gainesville, Florida, where he and Hilary spent their winters. In addition to his wife Hilary, he is survived by three daughters, Jessica Bloom (Raymond), Jill Wanger (Wesley), and Helen Steiner (Joseph); three grandchildren, Paul Bloom (Ellen), Kevin Wanger (Celia), and Jesse Steiner (Eleanor); and two great-grandchildren, Nancy Wanger, and Fred Steiner. He will be missed by all his family and friends.

"You were right, Irma. There's another 1996 retirement. His bio fits the information from Peter Blake that Spincus was the scientist of the outfit. Everything matches what we expected to find."

"That's what bothers me. When Peter Blake came up with the skills information for these guys and the suggestion that they had formed an independent industrial espionage group, it sounded like something out of *Mission Impossible* or some other suspense movie. The setup was too perfect for me to accept, and here we've found supporting evidence for it. These were unusual people."

CHAPTER 48 - EXPECTATIONS

Irma had a nagging feeling that she should stop in at Parkville UMC. Arthur had said he would take her to lunch, but it was now two o'clock, and she hadn't heard from him. For some reason nobody had answered the church telephones when she called, and she was starting to feel a little worried. Irma tried to be an objective thinker; she knew that worrying never helped anything. Today was different. She had convinced herself that that Arthur might be in some kind of trouble, and she decided that she had better drive over to check on him. This business of seeing someone as your destined mate saddled you with a burden you couldn't shake off. She had new obligations, and she would follow up on them.

Irma parked in her favorite corner of the church's lower lot and headed for the door. As she walked, she realized that hers was the only car there and that she hadn't noticed any cars in the upper lot as she passed it. When she reached for the door handle, she wondered if the church would be locked, but the latch released easily. She headed upstairs to the sanctuary and offices but heard nothing and encountered nobody along the way. This was definitely abnormal.

The church office was empty, as was Arthur's office and study. The sanctuary was set up for Sunday worship, with everything in a finished condition. Maybe she was overly concerned. They may have all gone out to lunch, even though they should have been back by now. Irma took a drink from the water fountain to settle her nerves. Then she went back to the church office to wait for someone to return. As she entered Shirley Hadley's office her eyes scanned the desk for anything unusual. She saw the letter-size sheet of paper with green marker letters: *Church office closed - Gone to hospital - Will return soon.* The unevenness of the letters and words suggested that the note had been a rushed afterthought on the way out the door.

Irma hurried back to her car and headed for the only local hospital, Parkville Care Center. It didn't have all the facilities of the big hospitals, but it would be the most likely source for emergency treatment. She had been there many times in her previous role as County Medical Examiner, and she knew many of the staff members there. She parked in a *Reserved for Doctors* spot and hastened into the almost-but-not-quite-certified Emergency Room. She spotted Donna Frieden, the nurse from the church's affiliated Veterans Residence in the waiting area, and rushed over to her.

"What's going on, Donna? Is one of the veterans ill? I saw the note that Shirley and others from the church had headed over here."

"No, Irma, the vets are all doing pretty well. It was a nasty fall, and his leg may be broken."

"Whose leg is broken? Is it Arthur? He was supposed to call me earlier, and I haven't heard from him."

"Arthur's fine. It was Bill Martin who got hurt, and it's mostly my fault. You know that Bill and I have been dating. Well, I occasionally ask him to make improvements and repairs at the Veterans Residence so that I can see him while I'm on duty. This time I asked him to hang some posters over the staircase for the guys to see when they come down the stairs. It's tricky rigging a ladder or platform over a flight of stairs, and Bill took more of a risk than normal to show off for me. He ended up falling off the ladder and bouncing down to the first floor. He landed in an awkward position and couldn't move without extreme pain. The Parkville paramedics were off on another call, so we loaded Bill into the back of Arthur's Saturn Vue.

179

Shirley and I kept him from bouncing around on the way over here."

"How did you get him into the car?"

"Alberto Hernandez from the Residence helped Arthur load him. Bill's left leg was bleeding a bit, so I applied a pressure pad to it during the ride. They're working on him now, but they wouldn't let me assist, so I have to wait here."

"What happened to Arthur and Shirley?"

"Shirley went down to the cafeteria for a coffee break, and Arthur's taking advantage of being here by visiting patients who might appreciate seeing a minister. They're both fine. I know how you must have worried, but it wasn't your guy who got hurt. It was my Bill."

"How are you holding up?"

"I'll be fine. I feel a little guilty and stupid for making him do dangerous things in order to have him near me. I'll have to learn to be patient and restrict his presence to off-duty time. Bill really is a great guy. I've never had anyone so willing to do things for me before. I'd better not screw things up by getting him hurt all the time."

Arthur returned to the waiting room while Donna and Irma were talking. He heard their last few exchanges but waited for a pause before making his presence obvious. When he walked forward, he was surprised at how natural it felt to greet Irma with a hug, even in this public place.

"Hi, ladies, Bill will be on crutches for a while. He won't be riding his bicycle with you right away, Donna, but I'm sure you'll be able to find some more sedentary activities that you can share."

Irma caught Donna's slight blush. Then she turned to Arthur. "I was afraid that you were going to turn out to be the patient when I saw the note about the hospital on Shirley's desk. I never know what to expect with you."

"I'll make up for my emergency change of schedule with you tonight. If you follow me back to the parsonage, we can drop off one car, and I'll change for dinner. You look great the way you are."

"I'll bet you say that to all the girls."

"Not always, but, Donna, you do look great too."

"Thanks, but you two get out of here and enjoy yourselves. Walter's going to close the bakery early and pick up Shirley. I'll stay with Bill for a while and then go home with them. I called Mark Adamowski, our overnight nurse, and he's coming in early to sub for me."

Irma gave Arthur an unsubtle nudge and winked at Donna. "Let's go, Arthur, that's our exit cue. I'll meet you at the parsonage."

When Arthur arrived he found Irma waiting in her car in the driveway. He pulled up behind her, and as they both got out he said, "I should have left my car behind for Donna to use."

"Don't worry about that right now. I need you to think about me for a while. One of the problems with getting involved with a pastor is that you end up sharing him with lots of other people. In case you didn't notice, I was worried about you, and I was pretty sure that you would be the patient in that hospital."

"Not this time, I was being the Good Samaritan for Bill. I'm smart enough to stay away from using a ladder on a staircase. Thanks for your concern though. I'd feel the same way if I thought you'd been hurt."

"Would you, or would it be the same level of concern you'd have for any member of the congregation?"

"Are you saying you don't think I consider you special?"

"Let's say that I'd like to hear a little more romance in your expressions of feelings. *Concern* and *consider* aren't exactly emotional terms. I know that I can't expect you to change to match my expectations, but sometimes my tensions boil over. Try to give me a clue about your feelings now and then."

"I didn't realize that you needed me to spell things out all the time. You know I think we have something special here. I'll try to make my feelings more obvious. Was there anything other than the hospital emergency that triggered your tensions?"

"It might have had something to do with my learning that Renee is pregnant. They're moving on with their lives. I need to see some progress in our relationship sometime."

"That's great news for Renee and Bobby. I know they both want kids. Let's take them out for dinner to celebrate."

"Maybe we should hold that thought for a while. As of lunchtime, she hadn't told him. I suggested that she had better do so right away, but we'll have to await confirmation of his knowing about her condition before we speak up and cause problems."

"We can at least toast them and say a prayer for them on our own. Are you too upset with me to go out for dinner?"

"I'm upset enough that I think it would be better if I cooked dinner for you here. We need some time by ourselves."

"That's fine with me. Am I allowed to ask how you and Renee did in looking at the background of the five murder victims you were studying?"

"No you're not, but later on I'll let you in on a new theory that I'm developing."

CHAPTER 49 - REHASHING THE EVIDENCE

Janice Blake had been helping Peter at his antiques shop for most of the day. Customers liked antiques to look old, but they didn't like the shop to be full of dust and grime. She had given herself the initial assignment of dusting most of the displayed items, especially the smaller ones, but before long she had added the task of rearranging many of the items to create more attractive displays. Peter could explain in detail the background of almost every item, but his sense of aesthetics in displaying them left something to be desired. As she made progress toward the logical and eye-catching presentation of a large assortment of medallions, utensils, and toys, she recalled Peter's report following his investigation of Albert's office and papers. She realized there was a problem.

"Peter, please come over here. I think we need a discussion."

"What's happening? Are there some items you can't identify?"

"I've been thinking about all those papers you brought back from Albert's office and your conclusions about what that group of men must have been doing."

"What about them?"

"The problem is that you found everything too easily. If I had left all of these old tools and decorations and household items in a haphazard condition, customers would have a hard time trying to find sets of matching or complementary objects. It would take quite a while, and they would probably overlook some valuable things. They would need my related item displays or your expert's knowledge to guide them in order to be successful."

"That's probably true."

"You searched Albert's office, which had been locked up after his sudden unexpected death and found detailed and matching information on all six members of their covert group without much effort. Mandy wasn't even in there to answer your questions. It was too easy."

"It was easy because Albert was a good organizer and kept neat files."

"These guys worked for decades for the CIA. When you work for that kind of agency you learn how to hide what you are doing and who you are. You don't organize it for any intruder to find without difficulty. You were meant to find all of those records."

"If that were true, then Mandy would have had to arrange everything for easy discovery. But when would she have done that. Don't forget, I called her and asked if I could visit and look at Albert's things."

"When you called, was she receptive to the idea of your visit?"

"She was, because she couldn't quite handle the idea that Albert had been murdered, and she wanted to assist anyone who was investigating what happened."

"Did you go over right after you called?"

"I waited for an hour or so because she wanted to clean the house a bit. You know how particular she is about cleanliness."

"I know that she was that way before Albert died, but her house hadn't been cleaned well when we visited along with Arthur and Irma. I think that delay for cleaning was actually used to arrange those papers and other items so that they would be easy to find."

"Why would she want to do that?"

"Before I answer that one, did you find any papers about their service during World War II, either with their regular units or with the OSS?"

"None at all; all the stuff I found was from their later work with industrial clients. They didn't even have anything describing their CIA work."

"The lack of CIA documentation is understandable. Having such documents might even be illegal. I would expect some information about their days as soldiers if they all served together. I'd also expect some papers from their days at Ohio State if they had been there as students rather than agents."

"OK, I didn't find anything on their earliest times together. They may have discarded the oldest files a long time ago. Everybody doesn't keep things forever like we do. What are you getting at? Why is this important?"

"It's important because you were meant to find information on the efficient and entrepreneurial group they had become. You were supposed to forget to look for what they were once."

"What do you mean?"

"Nazis"

"That would mean that Mandy knew about that background."

"That's right."

CHAPTER 50 - THE COMPANY

Joe counted the telephone rings. Three, four...*she must not be in the office*...five...

"Mary Byrne speaking, may I help you?"

"Hello, Mary, it's Joe Gonzalez. I was wondering if we could arrange for a contact in connection with a current case. We worked so well together last year."

"Hi, Joe, that sounds as though it would be a nice change of pace from the rat race here. I can leave a little early today. Where would you like to meet?"

"The weather's pretty nice. How about meeting at the Iwo Jima Memorial at Arlington?"

"I haven't been there for a couple of years. That's a great suggestion. I can be there by four o'clock. Will that work for your schedule?"

"That's perfect, Mary. Thanks, and I'll look forward to seeing you there."

Joe clicked the disconnect button and thought back to last year's multi-agency investigation when Mary Byrne had coordinated all of the information inputs through Communications Central at the CIA. That effort had demonstrated that the CIA was willing to share information with other agencies under certain circumstances. He hoped the successful outcome of that joint effort would be a good precedent for his request for cooperation now. Joe planned to only ask for confirmation of information he already had. He was sure that this approach had a much better chance of success than asking for new CIA information. The Company taught its personnel to be leery of volunteering any data without multiple approvals. At least he would be meeting Mary in an open area where she might feel free to talk with him.

He was the first to arrive at the Marine Corps War Memorial. It featured the Iwo Jima statue with its group of helmeted Marines raising the American flag after securing the island from its Japanese occupiers. He left the car and walked over to pay his somber respect side-by-side with several other tourists. There was something about that statue and the photograph that inspired it that grabbed your thoughtful attention. He turned toward the adjacent Arlington National Cemetery and continued his somber meditation. While he was deep in thought, Mary arrived and approached him with a similar respectful expression on her face.

"Thanks for picking this spot, Joe. It always makes me think of all those people in the military who give up everything for our country. It's not the question of whether war can be noble; it's the amazing realization that so many people will put their lives on the line when they are called to defend our nation and our way of life."

"That's one of the reasons we're here. My topic for the day, and my case, speak to that subject."

"What do you mean?"

"I'm not going to ask you to divulge anything from CIA files that might require a need to know. Let me tell you a story, and then I'll ask you to check my facts and verify its truth. I doubt that you will know about this because it happened a long time ago, but I'm sure that your sources can confirm the story or shoot it down, as the case may be.

"My story starts during World War II, about one year before the battle that's commemorated by this statue, but in Europe, rather than in the Pacific islands. Your predecessor agency, the OSS, set up a mission to infiltrate a temporary German P.O.W. camp with German-speaking soldiers and pass misinformation up the German chain of command that the invasion of Europe would come on the Mediterranean coast of France. After the information had been conveyed, the OSS team called for an airstrike on the camp so that the team members impersonating SS troops and their American Army Air Corps prisoners could escape.

"Something went wrong. Either the airstrike hit the wrong people, or the Germans got wise to the plot. Anyway, quite a few people were killed, and the six people rescued by the evacuation submarine were SS officers masquerading as the American infiltrators.

"It's not clear when the identities of the German impostors were discovered, but they were allowed to travel to the U.S. at the end of the war, go through the discharge process, and replace their American counterparts in civilian life. My guess is that they were being monitored by the OSS throughout the process. Once the CIA was established, these six individuals were gathered up and told that if they wanted to continue to live as Americans they would have to work for the CIA and infiltrate East Germany. The arrangement worked out well, and the group continued to perform CIA missions in East Germany until Germany was reunified, and perhaps even a few years longer. They all seem to have retired from any government connection in 1996.

"This whole arrangement is very reminiscent of the government's use of German rocket scientists to get our space program going, without any particular attention to the question of whether any of these individuals had been Nazis. I have some documents with specific details about these people that I will give you if you would be willing to check the actual facts and confirm the truth or partial truth of my story."

Mary took the unmarked envelope from him. "Joe, this all sounds like an interesting and intriguing story, but why is it important that it be confirmed now, so long after the end of these people's adventures?"

"It's important now because someone or some group assassinated all of them in August, trying to make their individual deaths appear to be accidents. It's important to the security of our country to find out who killed your six former agents."

"That got my attention, Joe. We don't take kindly to the assassination of our agents, especially those who have served us over a long period of time. I'll attempt to verify your facts, but I can tell you now that we frequently have used agents who had once been among our adversaries. Who is in a better position to learn what is happening on the other side? Our country is quite pragmatic in these matters."

"Thanks, Mary. I'll be waiting for your report." He looked up at the Iwo Jima statue. "I wonder what countries those Marines and their ancestors had come from. It takes an uncommon blend of backgrounds to keep our flag planted and waving proudly."

CHAPTER 51 - CAMERAS

Penny looked at her caller ID screen, saw Steve DuBois indicated, and picked up the telephone. "Hi, Steve; thanks for checking in. How are you doing on the nursing home cases?"

"The traditional response would be to say I have good news and bad news. The good news is that I contacted the Ripplestream Nursing Home in Evansville, Indiana and found that Peter Rodwin did have two male visitors on his final day, as was the case with Samuel Spincus at his nursing home in Lexington, Kentucky. The Lexington Police had already checked for surveillance camera pictures of Samuel's visitors and had come up empty. It turns out that there were functioning cameras in Evansville, where we previously had no definite indication of visitors, and we've captured a few good stills of two men."

"What's the bad news?"

"The bad news is that so far we've been unable to get identities for them. We've used facial recognition computer searches of all the files we can access, and we've had no success at all. Either these guys had a completely clean slate or never even had a driver's license."

"There's a third possibility, Steve, and it may change your bad news into good news. They may have come from another country. Send the photographs to Interpol, and see what they can discover. We're talking about the deaths of men who were involved in international espionage for the CIA. A foreign group may well be involved in their assassinations."

"That's a good suggestion, Penny. I'll get right on it. Give my best to Joe."

Penny disconnected and considered Steve's new information. It was beginning to look as though these men had been killed either because of their Nazi backgrounds or because of their CIA activities. If they could prove that the killers were foreign nationals and discover their citizenship, they would be a lot closer to finding a motive and solving the case.

She considered how she had first become involved in this affair by agreeing to check on the current addresses of old veterans for Renee Andrews. Sometimes the most significant cases came as interruptions to activities you thought were more important. She hadn't even been particularly enthusiastic about helping Renee.

Joe entered her office looking pleased. "Mary Byrne has agreed to check our theories and add some CIA backing to this case. I had thought they would be reluctant to reveal information, but when I structured the inquiry around the assassination of their agents, she became very interested and promised a priority response. That's a big step forward."

"It's a step forward if she confirms Arthur's conclusion that they were CIA agents. We've taken his logical assumption to be the truth, but the CIA may lose interest if it turns out this group was doing something else."

"My guess is that they'll remain curious about this group even if it turns out they had been working for someone else. Can you imagine how the CIA would react if they had overlooked a group that had been working here for the East Germans, for example? No matter how we resolve the group's affiliation, they were doing something significant that requires the CIA's joining us in the investigation."

"I have new information for you."

"Oh, you're cool. You let me go through my whole speech without interrupting me to announce your news. What's happened?"

"Steve has photographs of the men who carried out the nursing home killings, and they're not in any of our domestic databases. Steve's sending the pictures to Interpol for analysis against the international records."

"That is interesting. This has been a good day for this case. With both the CIA and Interpol getting involved, I see valuable feedback in our future."

CHAPTER 52 - SPECULATION

Arthur and Irma sat on their favorite rock next to the Mallard Lake parking lot across from the church. They had just completed a hike around the lake, and now they were recovering from the exertion in the coolness of the early autumn evening. Their expressions reflected mutual satisfaction with their achievement.

"Arthur, we should spend more time outdoors like this. Does it make any sense to say that I feel closer to you when we're outdoors than when we're indoors, even if we're discussing the same things?"

"I know what you mean, and I agree with you. We spend so much time indoors with office work, investigations, and church duties that it's special to venture outside. Here we're surrounded by God's creation instead of the walls of a building."

"We also pay more attention to each other when we're not distracted by our list of things we have to do."

"Your description of our indoor relationship makes us sound like an old married couple, working on tasks together or separately, while your outdoor description sounds like a couple getting to know each other for the first time. I conclude that you far prefer the early discovery relationship to one that is more committed and long range."

"Stop putting words in my mouth. I didn't say or mean that."

"I've been trained as a counselor to understand the meaning behind what you say."

"And I've trained myself to see through your teasing." She pulled him closer and kissed him...What's so bad about being an old married couple?"

193

"I'd say there's nothing wrong except for the *old* part."

"Did I hear something new in what you just said?"

"No, I've never liked to think of my parents as being old."

"That's not what I meant, and you know it. Did you say something new about our relationship?"

"I suppose that in my mildly emotional way I acknowledged what we've both known for a long time."

"Well, Your Holiness, would you mind saying it again in words that might directly appeal to me?"

"Do you suppose that you could put up with my unemotional task-centered ways for the long term and marry me?"

"Wow! That was a lot more than I expected. You do know how to surprise me, but the answer is a definite yes. I expected to have to wear you down for another couple of years before I'd hear that from you..." He curtailed her response with a kiss, followed by several more for good measure. Then they sat quietly holding each other.

After what seemed like a long time, Arthur gave Irma a final kiss. "Now we'll find out whether my saying those words changes the way we work together."

"Of course it does, but I know what you mean. If Penny and Joe can work well together, we should be able to do so too. I'm sure I'll contribute more without all those uncertainties rattling around in the back of my head."

"I don't want to put a damper on things, but from my limited experience I have to say that uncertainties don't end with marriage."

"Let's say that creative uncertainties can keep the marriage fresh and move on from there. Who will we tell first, your parents?"

"That's probably a good idea, but I'm not sure we'll survive the festivities my mother will want to throw. Speaking of my parents, they've been continuing their own investigations and discussions with an interesting result.

Dad called yesterday and said that they are convinced that Albert was a Nazi and that Mandy knew about it. They're not sure when she found out, but they think that some of her actions can only be explained by that. It's a speculation that, if true, would make us look at the whole situation differently. What's your reaction?"

"Right now, I'm wondering what I should call your parents under our new future outlook."

CHAPTER 53 - CONFIRMATION

Penny walked into Joe's office carrying two cups of coffee. She set one down on his desk and sat down in his guest chair with the other one.

"What's up, Penny, are you bringing me a peace offering or a bribe?"

"I'm convening our planning conference in anticipation of our field meeting."

"You must be several steps ahead of me. What field meeting?"

"Mary Byrne called and suggested that I join you for a meeting this afternoon. She said it would be at the same place and time. She'll be bringing someone along."

"She's getting back to us a lot sooner than I expected. It sounds as though they had good records."

"It's intriguing that she wanted both of us there. I enjoyed working with Mary on that other case, and it will be good to see her again, but I suspect that she's come up with more information than she expected. Maybe she wants to take a task force approach between us and the CIA. If so, what would you think about that?"

"I'd say that you may be reading more into her comments than are justified, but there's nothing wrong with adding their resources to the mix. Once we've identified the people who were behind the six killings, someone has to track them down. Your feedback from Steve suggests that they may be from an international group. We'd have trouble going after such people, but the CIA has resources everywhere."

"I wonder what new information she found. I detected an edge of excitement in her voice when I talked to her.

Whatever it is, I'll bet that this will be an interesting meeting."

"It's interesting enough that she's concerned about bugged offices or someone overhearing us. She wants the outdoor venue."

"You picked that spot for your first meeting, Joe."

"True, but I chose it because I was afraid that Mary's associates at CIA wouldn't want her to talk with us at all."

"Anyway, this may be a significant meeting. Review all of your facts on the case. She may ask some pointed questions. Then you can take me out for lunch on the way to the meeting. The Liberty Tavern should be a convenient choice."

"That sounds fine. We'll leave in an hour."

After they finished their break-from-the-routine lunch, Penny and Joe drove to the Iwo Jima memorial and parked next to a black van with a handicapped license plate. They got out and started to scan the area for Mary and her companion. As they walked past the van, the sliding side door opened, and Mary waved to them from the middle seat. She stepped out, and at the same time the driver got out and opened the rear doors. He activated a power lift mechanism to lower a man seated in a wheelchair to the parking lot. While the mechanism operated, Joe noticed that several maintenance workers had placed sawhorses bearing *TEMPORARILY OUT OF SERVICE* signs across the parking lot entrance and exit. The workers stood next to a truck filled with cold-patch blacktop for filling pavement holes. Joe realized that somebody had decided that this meeting required extra security.

Mary shook hands with both of them. "Joe, Penny, you're right on time. I'm glad you could make it on short notice. I brought along someone I'd like you to meet."

Joe and Penny turned to face the elderly man who had driven his motorized wheelchair into their midst. He looked as though he was in his eighties, but he had a youthful twinkle in his eyes. He extended his lean right arm to give them each a surprisingly firm handshake.

"Greetings to both of you; Mary started to inquire about your story, and I told her to come and consult with me. You see, I know quite a bit about the history of this case and these people. I've been following their activities for many years."

Penny realized that this man was old enough to have been a contemporary of the slain men. "Were you in the OSS?"

"Yes, they've kept me around as a consultant who knows about OSS missions. I also handle the odd bits of World War II leftovers that come up from time to time."

Mary Byrne intervened. "Before your conversations progress too far, we had better get you introduced. Penny and Joe Gonzalez, I'd like you to meet Albert Dandrich."

Penny and Joe stood open-mouthed as they stared at the man in the wheelchair. Joe was the first to speak. "You survived the assassination attempt in Wisconsin."

The older man smiled. "No, I'm not that Albert. You see, I'm the original, the soldier that he replaced. After the problems at that P.O.W. camp, I made my way to the French coast where I caught a boat ride across the channel from some fishermen who were members of the French underground. They had their eyes out for escaped allied soldiers, and they assisted me. I had a slight wound that they cleaned and bandaged. We became friends, and on behalf of OSS, I worked with them for the duration of the war."

Joe asked, "What exactly happened at that camp? We've found evidence of several versions, and we've deduced others, but you're the only one who knows the whole story."

"That's one of the reasons I wanted to come today. It's time to clarify things.

"Our pre-mission intelligence had been good, and we found the camp's location without difficulty. Our assumption had been that it was being run by the Wehrmacht regular army forces and that when we showed up as SS troops with prisoners, they would yield to our authority. We soon discovered that the camp also had a contingent of ten SS officers and troops. This eliminated our ability to throw our weight around to achieve our goals."

"How did you deal with the SS?"

"Wilhelm Schnacht, who later assumed my name, was second in command of the resident SS group. I sensed right away that he was different from his superior, Kurt Schmidt, who was a true believer in Hitler as the German messiah. Every time this man spoke he spouted propaganda declarations. I noticed that Schnacht and several of the others cringed a bit at his statements. We played along by being flatterers and yes-men for a while, until I could sound out Schnacht on his outlook. When I did, he surprised me by indicating his unhappiness with the regime along with his belief that we newcomers were impostors. I protested and showed our credentials, but he stated that he knew that we were on a mission and that he and some of his friends would assist us if we took them along with us later."

Joe said, "So he initiated the scheme. How did you know he wouldn't betray you?"

"I didn't, but I reasoned that there was no need for him to betray us later when he could have done so right away. We did have some doubts, but few options other than to play along with him. He ended up convincing me to trust him by his actions."

"What do you mean?"

"The day after Schnacht approached me, he told his superior, Schmidt, that we had informed him of allied paratroopers in the area. Schmidt wanted to show the new arrivals that his SS people were efficient and ready for anything, so he led them out to do battle with the paratroopers. Three hours later they returned with casualties. The report was that Schmidt and three of his men had been killed in a battle with the allies. I did observe blood spatter on Schnacht's uniform, so he must have been very close to someone who died. We never discussed what happened, but that action left Schnacht in charge of the remaining SS troops who now consisted of him and his five friends who wanted to come with us."

"What happened to the people you lost?"

"Enough time had passed for our prisoner interview misinformation about the invasion coming on the south coast of France to reach the German High Command. We radioed for air support to make our getaway. What ensued was a case of a complete misunderstanding of his orders by the responding pilot. Instead of firing his machine guns at the guard towers and in the general area to cause chaos to mask our escape, he decided his mission was to destroy the whole camp. Chaos was achieved. Everyone panicked in their rush to find cover. By the time the plane finally left, the attack had killed most of our men along with most of the real prisoners and the German regular army staff. Schnacht and his people had been waiting for us outside the camp and weren't hurt. We had remained inside because some of our people were posing as prisoners.

"The plan was for us to take Schnacht and his people out with us, but when we got hit, they headed for the coast and the rendezvous point on their own. They took our identification tags and papers so that they could pretend to be us. They chanced the masquerade because they all spoke fluent English. They also reasoned that

200

soldiers on special assignment with OSS would not have many associates who knew them well.

I was unconscious for a couple of hours, and when I woke up the camp was empty except for the wounded and the corpses. Max Griggins had survived despite serious wounds. I took him with me, but he died during our trek to the coast. I buried him in a grave overlooking the Channel."

Joe said, "After you got back to England why didn't you have the impostor Germans picked up and dealt with?"

"My first problem when I arrived in England was to reestablish my own identity without having any documents. Fortunately, our lead trainer and I had built up a relationship. He vouched for me and believed my story. It's strange how naked you feel without any identification. At least I had been smart enough to exchange my SS uniform for an American Army version before I left the camp.

"When I finally got back to London and talked with the OSS leaders, we decided to let our German converts continue their charade while we watched them closely. They never knew that I had survived or that the authorities were aware of their identities. I remained hidden from them. We had the feeling that they would be valuable intelligence assets if they turned out to be truly loyal to us instead of to the Nazis. I'll say this for them: they had many chances to drop their new personas and disappear, but they played it straight for the rest of their lives."

"What happened to that pilot, Albert?"

"That's another sad story, Joe. When he realized how badly he had screwed up and how many allies and innocent prisoners he had killed, the pilot developed what we now call PTSD, post traumatic stress disorder. He never flew again, and he spent the remainder of the war in

201

a mental hospital. I don't know what happened to him after that."

Penny joined in, "At the end was it the CIA that had the six Germans killed?"

"No, Penny, we don't work that way. They gave us many good years as agents, first in connection with the UFO business and later as one of our windows on East Germany. They deserved to live out their retirements until they reached their natural endpoints. Someone else decided to terminate their lives, and we'll help you find them."

Joe felt a bit uncomfortable as he listened. He edged into the conversation. "I hear what you're saying, and it sounds as though you really took the long term approach to monitoring these people, but how could you not want to get back with your family? You also failed to notify the families of your dead friends."

"You're forgetting something, Joe. The OSS selected us for this mission both because we spoke German and because we had no living family members. We all knew it could turn out to be a suicide mission, and they didn't want to have to tell family members what had happened to us. We knew the danger, but we also knew that we would save thousands of lives if our mission convinced the German High Command to expect the invasion in the wrong place. We went into this mission with our eyes open to its long odds, and we succeeded in planting misinformation that helped win the war."

"But how could you hope to keep close tabs on these men after they were living in the U.S. and taking your places? They could have been causing all sorts of undercover trouble."

Albert looked at Mary Byrne. An unspoken question passed between them. She nodded.

"Joe, we considered such problems at the very beginning. We knew that my namesake was the leader of

202

the group, so we assigned someone to him for long term surveillance. That is Top Secret information that has never been revealed over all the years that these men worked for us."

Penny said, "I wondered how Mandy could appear so dependent and so capable at the same time."

The others all looked at her with various degrees of astonishment on their faces. Albert's expression changed to a smile. "You are good at deduction. Where did she slip up?"

"After the other Albert's death, she seemed to be trying too hard to make us think well of him and to dispel our suspicions about his background. I guess she felt it was her duty to put a positive spin on our memories of him."

Joe said, "So Mandy was the one who tricked young Albert into noticing her instead of the other way around."

Mary said, "Don't be so surprised. More often than not, it's the woman who selects her mate and arranges for the man to think he's won her affections after a difficult pursuit, right Penny?"

"I wouldn't respond to that if my life depended on it. Of course I succumbed to Joe's well-planned campaign for my affections."

Joe put his arm around Penny. "Regardless of who was the strategist, we've worked out well together."

Albert said, "That's how my namesake must have felt, too. Mandy is a remarkable woman. In case you're wondering, she never knew about me. It would have been too much to ask of her to be his loyal wife while hiding her knowledge of my survival. She had to live as though she believed every story he told her."

Joe looked around the parking lot. Two workers were going through the motions of repairing the pavement while a third instructed monument visitors to park in the lot down the road. "Why do we have all of this extra security today?"

Albert smiled. "I'm afraid that's my fault. You see, I stopped existing during World War II, and my value to the Company would decrease if people knew about me. There are very few people who would suspect an old man with no visible background of being a spy. They can turn me into anyone they need. That being said, it's time for me to disappear again. As far as your associates are concerned, this meeting never happened." He beckoned to the driver who had been watching from beneath a tree across the parking lot. Then he shook hands once more with Joe and Penny and turned his motorized chair towards the van.

Mary also shook hands and promised to keep coordinating aspects of the case between their agencies. Then she also headed for the van as the paving repair team appeared to be finishing up its work. By the time Joe started their car's engine, theirs was the only vehicle in an empty parking lot.

The ride home was quiet and pensive. After a long while Penny said, "I feel as though I've stepped out of a dream."

"This whole case has been a cross between a dream and a nightmare. I've cycled my evaluation of those six men between negative and positive so many times that I'm completely confused. What happened to the simple western movie where you could tell the good guys from the bad guys by the color of their hats?"

CHAPTER 54 - TRACKING

When Joe and Penny returned to their agency, they found Steve DuBois waiting for them in the lobby. He appeared to be in a good mood as he sat on the waiting room couch with a cup of coffee and a box of doughnuts on the table in front of the couch. A bulging file folder on the couch beside him bore a large red asterisk, advertising its importance. Steve jumped up to greet them.

"Welcome back, you two. While you were out enjoying your lengthy lunch and afternoon break I received a whole lot of information from Interpol about our visitors to the nursing homes."

Joe interrupted Steve, partially to slow him down but also as an expression of irritation at Steve's not realizing the value of their afternoon meeting.

"Technically, we can only prove those guys were at the Evansville home. The Lexington nursing home didn't have cameras."

"I'll go along with that, but we're all pretty sure they wouldn't have had different killers visiting the Lexington home and using the same assassination technique as in Evansville.

"Anyway, if you'll let me continue, the two men in the photographs we captured from the video recordings turned out to be well known to Interpol. They call themselves Diego Garcia and Juan Terron. Interpol indicates that these are assumed names because both men have known backgrounds in Eastern Europe, and because Diego Garcia is an atoll and U.S military base in the Indian Ocean. They also have known Mafia connections and have been seen in the vicinity of several notorious killings but have never been connected to them. They frequently travel with one additional man whose name is not known and a woman who calls herself Marta."

"You mentioned Mafia connections. Were they international or American associations?"

"They were definitely European, Penny. These people normally avoid traveling to the United States. This was their first known sighting over here. That interested Interpol right away. They figured this crew had been sent in to do a touchy job and then disappear. Interpol is putting a high priority on tracking them since they now know where they were in August. By their standards, this is a hot trail."

Joe said, "We should pass this information to CIA. Let's get another organization on the trail of these killers."

"Does this case have a CIA connection?"

"We'll fill you in on that part later, Steve. Sometimes food is only the first part of a long lunch break. In the meantime, does Interpol have these guys pegged strictly as hit men, or do they cause other kinds of trouble too?"

"They've been known to lean on drug traffickers who kept more than their fair share of the profits. Garcia and Terron enforce discipline in the drug trade, but they've never handled drugs themselves."

Penny had listened to the latest exchanges between Steve and Joe, but her thoughts had been directed toward another question. "Why did these two come here? Interpol says they avoid coming to the United States. Maybe they have some old outstanding warrants over here. Somebody with some clout had to get them to take this job. That probably says that either these assassinations were ordered by some international powerhouse, possibly even a government, or someone very powerful inside the U.S. had enough influence to get them to come here, do the job, and then disappear. What do you think, Joe?"

"I'll first question that thought. How do we know they disappeared? They could still be in this country."

"I agree that they could be here, but that would only make sense if they had another job to do. Why bring in hit men from outside the country unless they were supposed to go back where they came from afterward and disappear? There are plenty of domestic bad guys to use, but they would be more likely to be detected. I think this was what the military calls a series of surgical strikes that were supposed to look like accidents and leave no evidence or killers behind."

Steve said, "In the two nursing home cases, they were literally surgical strikes."

That got them laughing. Joe took a bite from one of Steve's doughnuts. "OK, I'll concede that they probably left the country. We'll need the motive before we can decide whether the masterminds behind this were international or domestic. What was the motive, Penny?"

"We're one step closer to getting that. Without going into details, we've determined that all six of the assassinated veterans had been German soldiers and probably Nazis. The motive probably had something to do with that fact. I think it was either to get rid of them because they were once Nazis or to get rid of them because they turned their backs on the Nazi cause."

"Or because of things they did while being soldiers for Nazi Germany."

"Yes, Joe, there are variations within my motive framework."

"Anyway, we can conclude that someone higher up got these enforcers to eliminate the six old veterans. The hit men were just following orders."

Steve almost choked on his last gulp of coffee. "I think I've heard that *just following orders* line in connection with Nazis before."

CHAPTER 55 - MINDER

Arthur sat at his office desk with his best friend, his mug full of hot black coffee, musing over recent events. He had yet to tell anyone about his proposal to Irma. It felt good to have that quantum leap behind him. He guessed that comfortable feeling was the sign that he had made a good decision. What wasn't comfortable was the feeling that the case they had been investigating had moved on without them. He had thought that Irma's setting up the ABC Consultants group would have kept them in lock-step with Joe and Penny's agency, but lately everything seemed to be happening in Washington and not here in Parkville. On top of that, Arthur had been noticing that he was having trouble coming up with top grade sermons lately. The recent ones had lacked the inspiration that had been his typical strong point. Was there some truth to Irma's suspicion that he had lost his spiritual drive in favor of investigative work?

He had to learn how to better cope with slow times and dullness. He realized he couldn't share these thoughts with Irma. Somehow women didn't like to hear *slow times* and *proposal* in the same conversation.

Arthur turned on his radio and set it down on his desk so that its speaker faced upward. Then he placed his coffee mug on top of the speaker. He found it soothing at times like this to watch the patterns the sound vibrations made on the surface of the coffee. While he was meditating on his boredom and his coffee surface patterns, he heard a knock on the half-open door.

"Come on in; the Pastor's office is open for business."

Bobby Andrews' massive frame came through the doorway. "You may be open for business, but it doesn't look as though you have very much of it. I like to look at vibrating coffee patterns too. If yours is fresh, I'll join you."

"Come on in, Bobby. The coffee's fresh, and I need company. Do you have anything exciting to add flavor to my drink and my day?

"I do have something for you. I came over to share the fact that Renee and I are going to have a baby. She filled me in on it last night. Momma realized it earlier, but husbands are the last to know these things."

Arthur stood up and extended his hand toward Bobby. Congratulations, Future Daddy, you two will make great parents. You haven't done any of that gender testing yet, have you?"

"No, and if I have my way, we won't. The surprise factor is one of the highlights of a new birth. I'll love either gender of baby just as well."

"I'm sure you will. Nothing's quite as cute as a big guy cradling a tiny baby. How far along is she?"

"We still have about six months to go. I'm glad Momma's back operation is scheduled soon. I wouldn't want Renee to be in her final stages of pregnancy while she was going through the extra exertions of shepherding Momma through her back surgery process."

"Women are durable creatures, Bobby. I'm sure Renee will be fine and won't have to slow down her activities for a long time. I'm sure Momma will do well too."

Bobby drained his coffee cup and stood up. "I have a few more people I want to visit with the good news, but I wanted you to be among the first to know."

"I appreciate that. I'll come over and take you to a celebration lunch later in the week."

Bobby left, and Arthur sat and considered how his day had become a little less boring. The telephone jangled him out of his thoughts.

"Hello, Pastor Blake speaking..."

Irma's voice responded. "Hi, Arthur, clear your conference table; I'm bringing over some tourists. We'll be there in ten minutes." She disconnected before he could ask any questions, and he decided that Irma's personality had added buoyancy since he had proposed to her. This was going to be an interesting day after all.

Nine minutes later Shirley Hadley walked in and placed a tray of pastry and small sandwiches on his table. She waved but returned to the church office without saying a word. Shortly after she left Irma arrived with Penny and Joe close behind her. They all exchanged greetings and chose seats at the table. Shirley returned with a pitcher of pink lemonade and some paper cups and plates. "You'll have to do without the fine china today. That requires advance reservations."

Irma flashed a *thumbs-up* gesture at Shirley. "Your hospitality is perfect - no need for anything fancy." Shirley left, and they all took pastry and relaxed.

"Penny, Joe, what's the purpose of this surprise visit? You usually give us advance notice. Is there a breakthrough in the case of the old veterans?"

Joe nodded to Penny, and she responded. "We have made progress on the case, and some of it involves sensitive information that requires careful face-to-face discussions. However, when we stopped in on Irma, we discovered that a celebration is in order, so we thought we'd make a combination visit to you."

Arthur stared at Irma. "How much did you tell them? I thought we said my folks would be the first to know."

"These guys are such close friends and such a perfect working couple that I had to tell them. I couldn't hold it in any longer. Are you upset?"

"We may have to discuss what rules and agreements mean to us. I'm bothered because Bobby was in here, and

210

I didn't say anything about our engagement because of our agreement."

Joe turned to Penny. "It looks as though we're in the midst of their first argument. I'm glad they're not as perfect as we are."

"Watch it, Joe, or we'll have two animated discussions going on here. Anyway, congratulations to both of you; we expected the process to take longer, but we felt it was inevitable."

Irma turned to Arthur with a pouting expression. "I'm sorry if my excitement got the better of me. I'll come to confession and do penance."

"You're forgiven, but to show that I'm still a bit bothered about it, I'll drink lemonade during this session instead of coffee. Now, fill us in on what's happening with the case."

Joe got up and shut the door so that no one would overhear them. "We'll give you a status report, but we'll have to omit certain details that are classified information. I don't think you'll want to take ABC Consultants to the point of needing a secure facility in order to justify security clearances. Most of our cases won't require them anyway.

"Without indicating where we got the information, we have confirmation that our six veterans were, indeed, German soldiers and probably Nazis. The twist is that they apparently requested the Americans on the OSS team to take them along to surrender and work for the Allies. A mistaken interpretation of orders during an air raid on the camp caused the Americans to be hit, and the Germans made their escape to the Allied side by using the OSS team's dog tags and other ID's. That's as much information as I can give you, so don't ask any questions about my summary of what happened."

Arthur said, "That's fine, Joe. We know a lot more about the raid and the German impostors than we did before. I assume that somebody on our side knew about them before they came over here as discharged American soldiers."

"That's reasonable for you to assume, but I can't comment on whether it's true."

Irma said, "OK, we have a vague idea of what happened during the OSS raid, and we know that these men came to America and assumed the identities of soldiers who were on the undercover mission. From our own investigations, we have a pretty good idea that they ended up working for the CIA, eventually spying on the East Germans for them, and that they retired some time after Germany was reunified. Is there any other new information?"

"There is a rather astounding new piece of information, but I'm not sure what to do with it. What do you think, Penny?"

"I'm in the same boat, Joe. Let's put it this way, Arthur, if you had somebody start coming to your church, and you heard rumors from people of questionable reliability that he was a child molester, what would you do about it?"

"If I had little faith in the source of the information, I'd probably ask a trusted member to keep an eye on the new person. I certainly wouldn't report him to the police without more dependable information. After all, this is a church, and the Christian way would be to give him the benefit of the doubt unless he did something that required me to take action against him."

"That's exactly what happened in the case of our veterans. Albert was the leader of the group, and as the old song goes, they gave him someone to watch over him."

Irma said, "You've got to be kidding, Penny."

"No, but I have to be impressed by the dedication. I certainly wouldn't do that."

Joe laughed. "I thought you already had done it. Weren't you assigned to me?"

During the last few exchanges Arthur had sat with a bewildered look on his face. "I definitely missed something. Penny, you were saying that my hypothetical church visitor evaluation was like the veterans establishing themselves as Americans? How is that?"

"You said that you would have a trusted person keep an eye on the suspect newcomer."

"Right."

"That's exactly what the government did."

"Irma, help me on this one. Who is she talking about?"

"Arthur, you and many men have a problem with always accepting women at face value. We're talking about Mandy. They assigned her to get Albert to fall in love with her and marry her. She has been his minder since he arrived here after World War II."

"Was she paid by the government to marry him?"

Joe answered. "The government has done sillier things with our tax dollars, but in this case, we don't know the answer to your question. I would guess that this was a patriotic volunteer step on her part. If she saw something negative, she would have blown the whistle on Albert and his friends right away. When they continued to look as though they were genuinely converted to our side, she stayed and actually fell in love with him. Albert may never have discovered the trickery of their initial romance."

"I know about the difference between true conversions and cosmetic ones, so this was an intriguing, pardon the expression, undercover operation."

Arthur's statement received a chorus of groans from his tablemates. Irma gave him a brief hug. "That's my guy. One minute he doesn't follow what we're saying, and the next he's taken over the discourse. Seriously, though, I'm amazed that Mandy kept up her part over all these years. I'm not even sure we should discuss it with her now. In dramatic terms, she'd have to step out of character to answer us. She has been Albert's wife for so long that she may have obliterated her original assignment from her memory."

"Does Albert's death change anything, Joe?"

"Not really, Arthur; Mandy is Albert's widow in every sense of the word. I think her being his minder might explain why she set up that information on the group's talents for your father to find. She wanted him to see them as industrial espionage consultants rather than old men with Nazi backgrounds and the baggage of terrible acts during the war. It shows her love for Albert."

"That being the case, I suggest that we don't say anything to Mandy yet. We can always do so later. I'd like to see whether she continues to live as Albert's widow or leaves and becomes the person she once was. We also have to consider our search for the killers. We have no reason to eliminate Mandy as a suspect. After all, she knew more about the group than anyone else."

It was obvious from the way everyone stared at Arthur that none of them had thought to suspect Mandy.

CHAPTER 56 - THEORY

"Arthur, were you planning to give me an engagement ring sometime?"

"I didn't think you were a materialistic woman."

"I'd consider it a medal for a campaign well planned and executed."

"I don't think I like your selection of that last word."

They were sitting on a couch in the parsonage, or at least Arthur was sitting, while Irma was lying down with her legs across his lap. She reached for a pillow and propped herself up with it.

"When are we going to tell your parents?"

"We could call them, or we could drive over there. I'm sure Mother would want you within hugging range when she heard the news."

"Why do you use the more formal *Mother* but the less formal *Dad* when you talk to your parents? I'm still working on what I'll call them after we're married."

"You'd better work quickly. They'll expect you to use their long term designations as soon as we announce our intent. As to my usage, it's natural for a child to feel less formal with the parent of the same gender."

"Do you really think young children think like that?"

"No, but grown-ups who are asked questions about things they have always done subconsciously think like that. It's as good a reason as any. Try out a few names for them in your head, and see what sounds best to you. You could always call them Janice and Peter as you did when we visited them last time."

"That would work for your father, but I think Janice expects more than that. Since my father is no longer living, I don't think he'd mind me calling them Mom and

Dad. I'll try that and see how we all feel about it. Don't think I'm going to forget about the matter of a ring."

"In that case, you might check out the lump under the couch cushion. I think you flunk fairy tales. Didn't you ever read *The Princess and the Pea*?"

Irma jumped off the couch and lifted the cushion to find a small maroon box with a fuzzy surface. She opened the hinged top to reveal a solitaire diamond in a white gold setting. She slid it onto her left ring finger and threw her arms around Arthur. "It's beautiful - exactly what I wanted."

"My spiritual nature wouldn't let me go any larger on the stone."

"You don't have to be defensive. It's lovely. Every girl dreams of this." Several kisses later, they returned to the couch. This time Irma's sprawled with her head on his lap.

"Arthur, what did you think about that business with Mandy? What if I were a spy who was romancing you to keep track of your activities?"

"I'd say you were the nicest spy I had ever known."

"What person or group do you think was behind the murders of Albert and his friends?"

"It could be anyone that didn't want to let former Nazis die a natural death or it could be some group from Germany that they rubbed the wrong way when they were spying for the CIA."

"I have another theory."

"Fresh opinions are always welcome."

"At your office you said something about Mandy having been in the best position to get at everyone."

"I did."

"Take that thinking a stage further, and family members in all six families might want to kill the patriarchs."

"Why?"

"If I ran across papers that said my grandfather was a Nazi, I might want to wipe that blot out of my genealogy for the sake of my children's future."

"Why not destroy the records so that no one would ever know? It's a lot easier than killing the people. Beside, even if you killed the patriarchs, papers might come to light in the future that said they had been Nazis."

"That's conceivable, but the truth of such papers would be questioned in the absence of living witnesses."

"Who among the relatives would be in a position to secure the services of Mafia-connected killers?"

"Arthur, I was a little fuzzy in thinking through my theory that family members might be involved, but I think you just asked the key question. Is there a relative with Mafia connections?"

CHAPTER 57 - CONNECTIONS

It had been a good golf outing so far. They had all played well. Going into the seventeenth hole, Frank led by two strokes, but Nate, Shorty, and George had been improving as the game went on. With a par four on the last hole, only George was too far back to have a reasonable chance of winning. They had each kicked in two thousand dollars, two grand, for this winner-take-all match. Frank was already thinking about how he would use the money. He hit his tee shot one hundred yards short of the point where the fairway doglegged right at about a twenty degree angle. It wasn't a great shot, but it wasn't a disaster either.

As Nate approached the tee, he turned to Frank and asked, "Is everything complete and cleared?"

"Sure Nate, I got word from my brother John that they got out through Cuba by way of Key West, and they've passed through two other countries on their way back to their homes. They've all split up, so anybody looking for a group of three guys will get nowhere."

"I thought we had four guys on this job."

"We did, but one had a bad accident."

"What kind?

"He'd taken out his assigned victim without problems, but the cops recognized his car as stolen and chased him. He skidded trying to take a high speed corner, and his car rolled a bunch of times and burned. There wasn't much left to identify. The charred remains of him and the car ended up in the middle of a section of highway that had never been completed."

"That's too bad. Are you sure there was nothing left to trace?"

"Absolutely; enough talk - are you ready to tee off?"

"OK, Frank, but you ain't won this pot yet." Nate emphasized his point with a screaming drive that landed at the dogleg corner, giving him a direct line of sight to the pin for his second shot.

Shorty approached the tee carrying a driver that had been custom made to match his oversized frame. He knew that the club's extra length would let him really blast the ball if he hit it dead center. His oversized hands gripped it firmly, but with controlled pressure. He followed through on his strong but smooth stroke and smiled as the ball sailed toward the right completing its turn around the dogleg corner. "Three good shots out there, George; see if you can beat them."

"No way, Shorty, you guys are too good for me. I'll play my normal game and take my loss like a man." He stepped forward, took a few practice swings, and then connected to drive his ball straight down the fairway, but well short of the others. Then he turned to Nate. "There's nothing to worry about. I checked the police report. They had it down as a drunk driver who stole a car for a joyride and died after he lost control and rolled it. There was no indication they needed any further investigation. We're clean."

"That's good. This project is too important to allow an accident to screw it up. I'll tell you what. Just to show you how pleased I am with your work, we'll double the stake for everybody who's still in this contest. George, you're off the hook, but Frank and Shorty, the three of us are now in for four thousand bucks each. Don't let that get you nervous on the rest of this match."

Frank and Shorty groaned as they headed for their golf carts.

CHAPTER 58 - RICHMOND

Without any advance notice, Arthur and Irma drove to Richmond, arriving in the late afternoon. Arthur knew that his father closed Blake Antiques earlier during the fall months than during the tourist-rich summer. They rounded the corner, pulled into the driveway unobserved, and headed for the kitchen door. After ringing the doorbell they stood there looking at each other with big smiles on their faces and listening to the sound of Peter's engineer boots coming down the stairs and into the kitchen. The door opened.

"Arthur, Irma, we weren't expecting you. Did you call ahead? I wouldn't really know because I just got back from work. Come on in. I'll get Janice.

"Janice, we have visitors. Arthur and Irma are here."

Janice came running into the kitchen, wiping her hands on her apron as she did so. "I was watering the plants. Hello, you two. Welcome back. I hope this visit doesn't mean that something's wrong. Why didn't you let us know you were coming?"

Irma remembered Arthur's caution when she had first met Janice that she tended to let her comments and questions gush out in a torrent.

"Hi, Janice; don't worry there's nothing wrong. We decided that it was time for us to be in the neighborhood and drop in. We like to keep things casual."

Arthur said, "I hope we timed this visit so that you haven't prepared dinner yet. We'd like to take you two out for dinner."

Peter draped his arm around his son's shoulder. "A father always likes to hear that his son is treating for dinner. That's a rite of passage from all the times Dad picked up the tab."

"Don't make it sound as though this is the first time I've offered to treat."

"No. it isn't, but maybe I'll pull your old trick and order the fanciest thing on the menu."

"You're welcome to do so, Dad. I'm feeling generous."

"The preaching business must pay a lot more than it did in the past. I remember when Pastor Seymour at Richmond Village Church had to work a second job in the hardware store in order to get along."

Janice squeezed Peter's arm. "Stop teasing Arthur. He and Irma have had a long drive. Let's all go into the family room. You go ahead. I'll get the pitcher of lemonade and some glasses."

Irma said, "I'll help, Janice. Carrying both the pitcher and the glasses at the same time is awkward." They started toward the kitchen.

Suddenly, Janice hesitated in the doorway. "Peter!"

"What's wrong, Janice?"

"She's wearing a ring!"

"So?"

"You are an antique. It's an engagement ring!"

Peter hurried over by Janice to see Irma's ring. As he looked down at it, Janice leaned over and gave him a kiss on the cheek. He looked at her with a surprised expression. "That came out of nowhere. I always enjoy your kisses, but why now?"

With a gleam in her eye Janice said, "That was a congratulations kiss. We're going to have the daughter we always wanted."

Arthur walked over to join the huddle. "Does that mean you would have preferred for me to have been a girl? Where did this daughter business come from, Mother?"

"Arthur, it only means that we had hoped to have both a boy and a girl. After you were born I found out that I wouldn't be able to have any more children, so we had to put aside that part of our dream. Now that Irma is going to become part of our family, the dream is real.

"Welcome, Irma; you and Arthur make the perfect couple. Now I won't have to feel so guilty about my rushing you toward this day. Arthur was pretty unhappy that my anticipation was getting ahead of your reality."

"I was only hoping that Irma and I could make our own decisions at our own pace."

"You mean at your pace; I'm sure Irma would have been happy if this day had come earlier."

"Perhaps, Janice, but I had some reservations that I needed to work out. I'd say that the timing to reach this point has been perfect."

Peter said, "Irma, you are a diplomat. Anyway, we're all happy now. You can buy the dinner tonight, Arthur, but I'm springing for the champagne. Then we'll come back and have a long chat session so that I can learn more about my future daughter-in-law and she can find out about all of our family skeletons."

"Dad, don't put extra pressure on Irma. We'll have plenty of time for family gatherings and gabfests."

"That's fine, Arthur. You don't have to protect me from the family. If I'm going to be the daughter they wanted, we'll all have many years of story exchanges to catch up with each other."

Peter cleared his throat. "Excuse me, but while I'm not supposed to put extra pressure on Irma, I do have the right to add a little pressure to my own son. What's the schedule for the wedding, Arthur?"

"That's a valid question, Dad, but we need to enjoy being engaged before we throw ourselves into planning the ceremony and reception. Give us a little time to think about ourselves and our future."

"Fair enough Arthur; I'm not rushing you, only taking a few jabs at my favorite son."

Much later, when they were getting ready for bed, Irma told him, "I'm feeling more convinced that my theory might be right about those killings. Your dad joked about exposing the family skeletons to me. That's exactly what the Nazi patriarchs would be to their descendants."

"I can see how one family might take drastic action against its black sheep founder, but why would they want to wipe out the others? There has to be more to it than that."

CHAPTER 59 - WHO AND WHY

Penny looked across the breakfast table at Joe. "We've been looking at six deaths as though they were independent events. Actually, the murders were parts of a single effort by some individual or group to wipe six people off the face of the earth. These guys tried to be invisible as they arrived in the U.S. following World War II. They lived here for decades pretending to be conventional family men while they were doing covert work for the CIA. Then they were relegated to the accident statistics files during August. Americans like to think they're open to everyone around them and that they have nothing to hide, but not these guys."

"To the contrary, Penny, they always seemed to have nothing to hide. They wanted to be Americans, and they acted like everyone else; but the emphasis should be on the word *acted*."

"Changing the subject a bit, these Spanish omelets you made are great, Joe, not too spicy, but a little tang to them. If you want to keep up this Saturday morning cooking routine, it's fine with me."

"I promise I won't push my heritage and give the breakfast a Spanish accent every week."

"Either way is fine with me...Anyway, getting back to our victims, we've spent a lot of time working on who they were, but I think that we need to concentrate on why they were killed. Finding the motive will be the trick to solving the case."

"I agree up to a point, Penny, but I doubt that we'll find the motive without understanding the people, including their wives and descendants. Irma is working on a theory that they were wiped out by members of their own families who found out about their Nazi background and wanted to erase all aspects of it."

"With complete respect for Irma's thinking, I find that hard to believe."

"Don't forget that a significant percentage of murders in this country are committed by family members."

"I'll concede that, Joe, but most family murders are committed due to anger and passion without advance planning. These murders were professional hits."

"True, but family members could have hired the pros."

"I still say we need a stronger motive than pruning your family tree."

"I'll go along with your quest for a motive, but take it to the next level. You say that cleaning up your family's background isn't a strong motive. What if you needed a clean background to get a security clearance or get a high-paying job? There could be a second-stage benefit beyond the genealogy thing."

That argument made Penny think for a while. As she did so, she made what she called an Irish burrito, a tortilla rolled up with thick layers of cream cheese and strawberry preserves inside. "These are good; you should try one. I'll go along with a family culprit if there was a big reward resulting from it, but why would any family member hire hit men to kill the heads of the other five families? It makes no sense."

"Let's get really outrageous and try something a little bit different. What if the family member wasn't the originator of the murder plot? What if the Mafia people found out about the Nazi group and took action on their own to take them out so they wouldn't ruin a project they were already developing."

"That's intriguing, but you make the Mafia sound like a business cartel."

"Don't look now, but that's what they've become, a business cartel with a lot of money plus muscle when they need it."

"Why would they go after this group of old guys? They were too senior to cause them any significant trouble."

"Mobsters might have gone after them because of their Nazi background, or they might have known about their CIA ties. If you were working on a big project for the Mafia, would you want the CIA looking over your shoulder?"

"Now that starts to sound like a motive. If it were true, we'd need to identify a project big enough to justify all of those killings. Let's think about that one over the rest of the weekend. That's the kind of thinking I do best in an unconventional setting. Let's go to the zoo this afternoon."

CHAPTER 60 - VISITOR

Precisely at nine o'clock the telephone rang. Janice jumped up from the breakfast table to grab it before it rang a second time. She had heard Arthur and Irma stirring, but Peter had been sleeping when she left the room to come downstairs. "Hello?"

"Good morning, Janice. It's Mandy. I was in your neighborhood last night, and I saw Arthur's car in your driveway. I'd like to come over to see him before he leaves. Will he be there for a while?"

"Hi, Mandy, he's here with Irma. They're engaged now, isn't it wonderful? They haven't come downstairs yet, but I think they're on the way. My guess is that they'll be leaving by noon, so why don't you come over in an hour or so. I have lots of fruit and pastry for a bite of brunch."

"That is exciting, Janice. I'll aim for an hour from now. I've known you folks for a long time now, so don't worry if Peter's still in his ratty old bathrobe. Actually, I think we gave that robe to him a long time ago. I'll see you soon."

As she placed the handset back on the wall hook, Janice turned to see Irma, Arthur, and Peter parade into the kitchen. "Hello, you three. Take some pastry and fruit from the table; would anyone like some eggs or cereal?"

Irma and Peter sat down and started to help themselves. Arthur remained standing and queried his mother, "Coffee?"

"Of course there's fresh coffee in the pot for you. I even took out your oversized mug so that you can drown any problems in caffeinated muddy water. I don't know where you got your black coffee habit. It wasn't around here."

"It all started when I worked at the car races, Mother. I've told you before. Anyway, you're looking well and perky

227

this morning. It has always been fun hearing you puttering around in the kitchen before I came down."

"Thanks - Irma, what else can I get for you?"

"All of this is fine. If you point me at some bread, I can make a slice of toast myself. I always like plain toast with my coffee in the morning."

"I'll make a mental note of that. There are loaves of white and whole wheat on the counter, and there are English muffins in the refrigerator...Peter, your oatmeal is in the pot on the stove."

"Thanks, Janice; did I hear the telephone ring?"

"Oh, I almost forgot. Mandy called. She'll be over around ten o'clock to see you folks before you leave."

Irma removed her English muffin from the toaster. "Thanks for the advance notice. If you don't mind, I'll have my muffin and coffee upstairs while I freshen up."

Arthur continued to enjoy his coffee. "You look fine to me, but go ahead. I'll enjoy time with the folks down here."

As soon as Irma left, Janice gave Arthur a big hug. "Irma is so perfect for you - so perfect for all of us."

Peter stood up, and wiped his mouth. "I've always wanted to say this to a pastor. Son, you have our blessing." He made the sign of the cross over Arthur's head.

"That was very nice, Peter. Now you go up and put on some clean clothes for Mandy's visit. I don't want her to think we're sloppy over here."

Peter saluted Janice and left.

"Mother, is everything still normal between you and Mandy?"

"Sure, why shouldn't it be? I'm not one to let the gossip about Albert's background get in the way. They've both always been good friends to us, and even without Albert, I'll do my best to keep it that way. Mandy needs someone she can rely on now that she's alone."

"That's great Mother; we all need loyal friends."

Irma returned wearing a beige sweater and jeans. Arthur got up and kissed her; then he pulled out a chair for her to sit on.

"Well, thank you on both counts. Your mother obviously trained you well."

"I'm working on remembering that we're a twosome now, and you deserve my attention and deference."

"Oh, I think I'm going to enjoy this relationship. Keep going for those brownie points, Arthur; I love to be flattered."

The kitchen doorbell rang, and Janice went to the door to greet Mandy. They exchanged greetings and then Mandy walked over to Irma and Arthur who had stood up upon hearing the doorbell. She gave each of them a hug. Then she took a small box out of her purse and gave it to Irma. "I want you to have this, dear. It's a piece that Albert brought back from Europe for me. Think of both of us when you wear it."

Irma removed the paper and saw a black jewel box with a fleur-de-lis on the cover. She opened it to reveal a beautiful silver bracelet with circular daisy-like segments fitted with crowns on each end and chained together with silver links connecting the crowns, top and bottom. "It's beautiful, Mandy. I'll wear it all the time. I don't know how you sensed my taste, but it's exactly the sort of thing I would buy."

"It's supposed to be a French Etruscan antique. I have no idea how old it is, but it gives me the feeling of being ancient and modern at the same time. That's how I feel sometimes. May you two have a long and loving life together; enjoy everything you encounter."

"Thank you so much, Mandy. Both the bracelet and the sentiment that goes with it are perfect." Irma put on the bracelet and held it out for all to admire. After a series of appreciative comments, they all sat down around the kitchen table."

Peter said, "This is true country living. We gather around the kitchen table with good friends and family. It's time to exchange stories and comments and to nibble on goodies while we do. Arthur, you've been quiet while Irma held center stage; what do you have to say for yourself?"

"Well, Dad and all, I feel more than blessed as I look forward to a life with Irma. Thank you all for your good wishes. We both wanted you to know how important this family is to us. We're starting off with a great deal of support, and we appreciate it."

Irma gestured to the group. "You have been treated to his shortest sermon ever. I'll do my best to keep him succinct in the future.

"Mandy, what are your plans? Will you stay at your longtime home, or are you going to look for a smaller place?"

"I've been hesitating about breaking the news to you, but I plan to put our old house up for sale. It's time for me to move on. I'll probably take the conventional path of getting a smaller place somewhere in a warm climate. I haven't selected a spot yet, but I'd like to have some warm winters before my end comes."

Janice patted her friend on her left shoulder. "I can't say that your words come as a complete surprise to us. When a long marriage comes to an end, a new outlook on life is required, and that sometimes includes a new physical location as well."

Arthur asked, "Do you have a schedule for these changes? It might take quite a while to sell your house."

"Albert left me in pretty good financial shape, so I would be able to purchase a new place and leave the selling of the old house to the realtors afterward. Right now, I'm starting to study properties and maps with the goal of being in a new place in December. It will be my Christmas present to myself."

Janice and Peter expressed surprise at her plans for an early move. Irma and Arthur exchanged glances that indicated how Mandy's plans increased pressure for an early solution to this case.

CHAPTER 61 - SNARES

Diego Garcia rounded the protective point on the island's northern coast and slowed his boat as he entered the no-wake zone near the harbor's entrance. He saw that there were several boats ahead of him, so he coasted to a crawl while he waited. Tourist season always diminished the boating freedom of the residents, but at least it brought lots of money to the local economy. He saw that there were already more boats lining up behind him. He removed a beer from his cooler and uncapped it as he waited for the traffic to clear. The slight roll of the boat gave him a peaceful feeling.

As he tilted his head back to drain the last of the beer from the bottle, he felt the boat shudder as boats on both sides bumped into it. Someone had jumped into his boat behind him. He turned and reached for his gun at the same time, but he couldn't extend his arms. One man was holding his arms against his body while another wrapped some kind of restraint band around him. He knew there was no point in struggling, so he relaxed. He was a professional, and he recognized these people as having carefully honed skills. He would wait to see what fate had in store for him.

One man guided him into the boat on the port side of his own vessel while a second took Diego's controls. Slowly, four boats eased out of the waiting line and veered away from the coast toward a large yacht that was about a mile from the island's shore. As they approached the yacht someone lowered a cloth bag over his head and secured it. The world went dark, but at least they were being gentle with him. He smiled as he realized that he was more valuable to them alive then dead. This would not be the last day of his life after all.

They guided him onto the yacht, and he heard the engines start. Their smooth resounding bass tone and minimal vibration declared that the yacht was seaworthy and capable of deceptive speed. The cost of such a vessel told him that his captors represented a major organization. He was sure that they would treat him fairly. Cooperation might even lead to something better. It wouldn't be the first time he had changed sides.

CHAPTER 62 - MARY BYRNE

Joe answered his telephone without really paying attention. He hadn't been able to organize his thoughts well this morning, probably because Penny had again been talking about moving out of town and buying a house. Why didn't women leave well enough alone? "Joe Gonzalez speaking; may I help you?"

"Mary Byrne calling, Joe. I'd like to come over and share a progress report. We've turned one of the assassins to our side, so I'd better bring you up to date."

"That's great, Mary; how about one o'clock?"

"That's perfect. I'll see you then."

Joe walked down the hall to Penny's office and waited while she finished sending an email. "Sometimes I have trouble coping with the mindset at CIA. They always believe that the end justifies the means. Mary Byrne is coming over at one o'clock to give us a status report and to look for new input from us. They made agents out of those former German soldiers, and now she says that they've turned one of the assassins of those same soldiers to our side, and they'll probably have him spying on the Mafia."

"The spy game is definitely a world of its own, Joe. Nobody in any government wants to acknowledge how they get their intelligence information, so long as it's prompt and true. Information is more important than wealth. If you know what's going to happen before it comes to pass, you can head off the bad news and cash in on the good news."

"What do we have that's new to share with her?"

"Arthur and Irma learned that Mandy is planning to move away before Christmas. We know that she worked for CIA as a minder for our six Germans, including her husband. My guess is that once she moves, she'll disappear and become someone else. With Albert dead, she has no reason to keep up her long term charade. She has the skills to become someone else and retire."

"That should be a harmless change. She's finished up one of the longest assignments in history. What else is happening?"

"Steve has been checking out some of the grandchildren of the six veterans. He found that Warren Handley's grandson, Henry Wilson, is suspected of computer fraud. He apparently learned computer skills from his grandfather and has been using them to hack into the trading accounts of brokerage firms. They don't have as tight an oversight as banks, and he has been managing to insert a few extra transactions here and there, buying and selling shares that never existed for his own unlisted account. He inserts his transactions after moves in the market have already happened and predates them, so he almost always arranges to make money. That's why regulators got suspicious. His investments were too successful. This could be what the Mafia was after in removing the patriarchs. If Henry worked with the organization, they would have a scheme for removing money from the financial system without the risk of robbing banks."

"That's worth considering. Only the independent little guys rob banks any more. It's too easy for the outfit to pursue white collar crime, and it doesn't have the same risk. Many times the accounting systems are too slow and crude to catch up with them. Anyway, Henry Wilson's scheme is one good candidate for what they were protecting with these murders."

Promptly at one o'clock Mary arrived. She, Joe, and Penny gathered in the secure conference room.

"I came over in order to keep this face-to-face. Neither email nor the phones are as secure as we would like to think they are. My basic report is that we got lucky. We went after the hit man who calls himself Diego Garcia, and he turned out to be a soft target. Instead of refusing to talk under all forms of coercion, he volunteered to give us what he knew in exchange for our letting him work with us instead of his former employer. I guess he figured he would have less risk playing the turncoat card. Based on his information, we've picked up the other killer in the photographs, Juan Terron, plus a third man who hadn't appeared in any picture. He told us that there had been a fourth man in their crew, but that he had died in a car crash while trying to elude police after making his hit on Albert Dandrich."

Joe had been making notes and looked up from his pad. "Did the fourth man die right after killing Albert or some time later?"

"He crashed while trying to get away in his stolen car. According to the police report they identified the car as stolen and chased it before they knew about Albert's so-called accident."

Penny asked, "What else did you learn from Diego Garcia?"

"As expected, he didn't know what the outfit was up to. He agreed that it must be a big project to justify bringing them in from outside the country to do the killings. There are plenty of domestic killers available, so they went out of their way to keep their hands clean on this one. They always try to look like businessmen instead of gangsters, but they spent a lot of extra money to avoid suspicion this time. The people who ordered these hits have to be after something that is very important to them."

Penny said, "We have one possibility concerning Henry Wilson, the grandson of Warren Handley. He's suspected of creating a scheme to steal lots of cash from brokerage firms through dummy stock and bond transactions. It's all done with computer hacking, but I don't think it would justify all of these killings. It's also a crime that works well as long as the perpetrator limits its scope, but it would be easy to detect if they increased its size much. The trick is to hit brokers at random and only occasionally. Then the losses can be chalked up to poor accounting techniques. What do you think, Mary?"

"I agree that it's too small a deal for them to give it such a high priority. This would have to be something very big and something that would fall apart if its existence became known."

Joe paused from his note-taking. "I follow your thinking, Mary. That's why all of the deaths had to look like separate and unrelated accidents."

Penny said, "Don't forget that the characters behind this used international operatives because they want to look completely innocent. Maybe this has something to do with cleaning up their reputations. What do you think, Mary?"

"With all the dirt on mob figures in all the databases of police, justice, and intelligence agencies around the world, it would be very difficult for mob figures to sanitize their pasts. There's something big going on, but we'll have to do some more snooping before we find what it is. Don't worry though; we will find what's going on before it's too late."

CHAPTER 63 - OLD MOVIES

Renee sat in the waiting room at the University of Chicago Medical Center, waiting while Momma underwent her back operation. Renee wasn't worried. The staff and facilities had a great reputation, and the surgeon had assured her that this would be routine. While she sat among the others on the well-worn chairs, she watched the usual daytime television that such places offer. She stood up and paid special attention when a special news bulletin interrupted the game show. Then she hurried downstairs to go outside and place some cell phone calls. She never had understood why hospitals tell you not to use your cell phone inside the buildings.

"Hello, Irma, turn on your television news right away. Call Arthur, and tell him to watch it at church. I'll call Penny and Joe. Our case is becoming clearer."

After calling Arthur, Irma sat down to watch. If a news bulletin is considered important enough, they interrupt most of the channels, so it wasn't hard for her to find a channel that had the story. The crux of the bulletin was that little-known Congressman Paul Griggins from Florida had announced that he would seek the Republican nomination for President of the United States in the next election. He had announced plans to undertake a nationwide speaking tour to introduce himself to people outside of his home area. He had also announced that he anticipated endorsement by a large number of major organizations, although he would give no names until those recommendations had actually been issued. When asked about his financial capability to conduct a national campaign, Congressman Griggins had indicated that he already had a substantial campaign war chest and that he was sure he would receive both small and large contributions once the people got to know him. He had made his announcement surrounded by his parents, John and Lucy Griggins, his sister, Dr. Mary Waters of the National Institutes of Health, and several other friends and relatives. Congressman Griggins had announced that his campaign slogan would be: *Accentuate the Positive - Eliminate the Negative.*

Irma's telephone rang. Arthur asked her to hang on while he completed the conference connection with Joe and Penny. A moment later he asked, "Is everyone on board?" This was followed by three "I'm here" declarations.

Arthur opened the discussion. "I think Renee was correct. Congressman Paul Griggins' announcement that he wants to be President constitutes a big enough project to be the reason for organized crime to want to eliminate the patriarchs and use an international hit squad in order to keep their own hands clean. What do you pros think?"

Joe said, "I think we'd better do a very thorough investigation looking for contacts between the Congressman and his family with any aspect of organized crime."

Penny said, "Now that this is out in the open, we'll have to keep our inquiries very discrete. We don't want politicians saying that the current administration is out to smear the new candidate. What are you thinking, Irma?"

"In the context of his having possible behind-the-scenes backing by organized crime, I'm worried about what he might mean by *eliminate the negative.*"

"We could assume the potential for actual violence against opponents, but my guess is that it's a signal to his Mafia friends to remember that the President of the United States has the power to pardon anyone for any crime. That may be why the bad guys are doing their best to look like good citizens. They certainly have plenty of money to donate, and they can arrange for it to arrive as small

239

contributions from a large number of people and organizations."

Arthur said, "That's a pretty good analysis, Penny. What do we do now? Our friends at CIA have to be very careful since their portfolio is nominally international intelligence. Do you want to add any suggestions, Irma?"

"We could leak the truth about his grandfather having been a Nazi, but that could be viewed as a political dirty trick. It could also backfire if someone could document that in later years his grandfather served as a loyal agent for the CIA."

Joe said, "We'd better discuss this with Mary. CIA holds the trump card of having picked up all of the assassins. Whether their victims are viewed as Nazis or patriotic CIA agents, they were six old men who were deliberately murdered. That wouldn't go over well with the voters."

Irma responded, "We also have the small point of a presidential candidate who may have been involved in planning the murder of his own grandfather. If true, that would go beyond being disgusting to making him a felon."

Arthur said, "Trying to be charitable, I could suggest that Paul Griggins might be the innocent dupe of his relatives and organized crime. However, that argument suggests that if he were elected President, they would have no hold over him, and his value would be lost." Arthur heard Joe laugh over the phone line. "Is something funny, Joe?"

"Did any of you see the movie, *The Manchurian Candidate*? These circumstances remind me of it. I wonder if they've somehow managed to brainwash Congressman Paul Griggins into thinking he owed it to his country to eliminate his Nazi grandfather and pardon the patriotic criminals. This thing is a real mess."

CHAPTER 64 - NEXT STEPS

Mary Byrne and Penny Gonzalez strolled together around the circle of flags at the base of the Washington Monument. They took occasional pictures along with the other tourists. At one point Penny even agreed to take a group photograph of a mother and her three children using that tourist's camera. People paid less attention to individuals who talked while they walked than they did to people sitting on a bench in serious conversation. Somehow a moving conversation appears to be less intense and more spontaneous.

Penny said, "I'm not very experienced at the public relations end of things, but it seems to me that we'll have to entice the media to write their stories from our point of view if we want to bring this Congressman's campaign to a halt with minimal public scandal."

"Don't worry about working with the media. We have experts at planting both information and disinformation, as required. Whether we use the press as a weapon or not, I think we'll have to convince Paul Griggins that dropping out of the race would be his best option. First, of course, we'll have to determine how he fits into this scheme. Does he know what's been happening, or was he flattered into announcing his run for the White House?"

"I see what you mean. Politicians tend to have big egos, and they'll believe they're great if people keep telling them they are."

"If your group works on finding mob contacts within the family, we'll do our best to find who inside the outfit is behind this project and what he or she expects to get out of it."

"That's right; I forget that the push for more leadership by women applies in organized crime as well as conventional fields. I like your suggestion of dividing the labor. We'll each be playing to our strengths."

"Penny, don't forget how dangerous these people in the background are. Who knows how they'll react when they realize that someone understands their plot?"

"We'll have to get involved in a way they don't expect."

CHAPTER 65 - TACTICS

"Penny, I don't like this approach at all. Our charter doesn't say that we're allowed to put innocent civilians in danger. For all we know, the Griggins family could be part of the outfit, or they could have mobsters watching their every move."

"Joe, these civilians aren't innocent amateurs. Second, if the mob is watching, they won't consider these folks as much of a problem as law enforcement people."

"Do you think they'll even agree?"

"There's only one way to find out. Let me plant the seed of suggestion, and we'll see what happens. Are you willing to go that far?"

"I guess that's a fair approach, but if it happens, we'll need to have our professionals nearby for backup."

Penny nodded and picked up her telephone. She selected a familiar number from her memory list. "Hello, Shirley, this is Penny Gonzalez calling. Is Arthur available? Fine, I'll hold while you get him.

"He's on his way back from the Veterans Group Residence next door. I'm on hold while Shirley flags him down and hurries him up...

"Hello, Arthur, I wanted to bounce some ideas off of you regarding the best way to handle an investigation of the candidate and his family. We want to be subtle about this."

"Hi, Penny; I agree that it's tricky, especially with all the media surrounding him. What are you thinking?"

"My idea is to offer you and Irma a government-paid trip to Florida to meet the Griggins family. If you think that it would be reasonable to involve Mandy, now that we know about the candidate, I have an approach that might yield useful information."

Penny gave Arthur a summary of her plan and asked for his reaction to it.

"It sounds feasible, but a lot depends on Mandy's willingness to get involved. Of course we'll learn more about her outlook no matter what she says. We'll start the preliminaries tomorrow. If we see problems, we'll contact you before proceeding."

"Thanks, Arthur; I'll start making the travel arrangements."

CHAPTER 66 - MANDY

They had called to say they were coming, but neither Arthur nor Irma knew quite what to expect from their hostess. Up to this point everyone had taken Mandy at face value as the grieving widow and long-time friend. Now they would have to be more open and direct in their conversations with her. Arthur shrugged his shoulders at Irma as he rang the bell.

Mandy opened the door with her usual welcoming expression and invited them into the living room.

"I went ahead and made coffee for you, Arthur. You sounded as though you had something significant to discuss, and I know you like to have coffee when you're being serious."

Irma laughed. "I guess you do know him pretty well. He may need fuel for thinking, but nothing for me, thanks. I've had enough to drink already. Arthur, go get your own coffee while I relax with Mandy."

He left, and Irma sat with Mandy on opposite ends of the couch. Irma decided to head directly toward establishing a new rapport based on what they'd learned about Mandy.

"This has been a long and unusual relationship for you. You've had to be two different people at the same time over a long period."

"Oh, so we've come to that arrangement, have we? Oddly enough, it didn't take long before it all became natural. Albert always was a charmer. I blended my efforts into the fabric of our marriage so that it didn't feel all that unusual. Most housewives keep track of what their husband and his friends are doing. I was charged with doing a more thorough job of it; that's all."

245

"At the beginning, did you see him as putting on an act for you, or did you accept him at face value?"

"I think that my biggest initial difficulty was trying to avoid seeing Albert the way my instructors had described him. Once I overcame that barrier of artificiality, I was able to be natural and enjoy his many fine traits. Labels get in the way of relationships; don't you agree, dear?"

"I think you're absolutely right, Mandy. Arthur had to stop seeing me as the Medical Examiner, and I had to get by his Pastor label before we could build our relationship. Did Albert see your second self?"

"We never discussed it, and I honestly don't know. He may have suspected I had a secret life, but then he had one too, and he may have not wanted to rock the boat by talking about it."

Arthur returned from the kitchen with Albert's favorite mug full of coffee and a plate of cookies for the ladies.

"Mandy, I hope you don't mind my raiding the cookies and bringing some out, but I feel uncomfortable being the only one having refreshments."

"That's fine, Arthur, you know I've always thought of you as part of our extended family. While we're on the subject of feeling comfortable with each other, I'll let you know that Irma and I have removed our masks while you were gone. She made it obvious that she knew about my initial minding role, and I'm quite aware that she joins you in your investigations. Now please tell me why you wanted to meet with me."

"I'm more than impressed at how easily you two communicated around that potential barrier. Here's the problem. Max Griggins' congressman grandson has announced that he is seeking the Republican nomination for President. We and our associates think that the people who killed Albert and Max and their other friends are somehow connected to this candidacy. We need your help to find out exactly what is going on."

"So you found out about the other murders. You are good investigators. I thought I was the only one who could connect the dots to see what was happening. What can I do to help avenge their deaths?"

"We're assuming that you've had some contact with Max Griggins' family. Is that correct?"

"We did meet his children and wife about ten or fifteen years ago after everyone retired. Before that, they all lived completely independent lives so that no one would see any connections among them. I vaguely recall some later phone calls with them also. Albert didn't even mention the others to me before they retired, but I had known about them from the beginning. The Company originally selected me to watch Albert because they had identified him as the leader of the group. They figured that watching the leader would eliminate the need to monitor all six of them. For the most part, it worked, but I had to go beyond talking with Albert to keep up with the activities of the others. I won't go into details on that effort."

"We would like you to contact the Griggins children, or at least John, to give us an introduction. You can use your story of my being your pseudo son, the way you and Albert always used to describe me. Irma and I will be vacationing in Florida where I'll be sharing my NASA background with her. If we can become friends with the family, Irma will have a lot in common with John's daughter, Dr. Mary Waters, and I'll be able to invite the family to visit NASA's facilities at the Cape. With a little luck, we'll even get Congressman Paul Griggins involved. Our goal is to discover how the family interfaces with the bad guys who killed Albert and Max and the others. We don't know if they were part of the plot in some way, or if Paul realizes that his candidacy is being used by others for criminal purposes."

"Are you going to be mingling with the killers?"

"Hopefully, this will only be a nice vacation for us where we meet some interesting people. We're not planning to do anything dangerous, only keep our eyes and ears open."

Irma said, "You're not allowed to do anything dangerous until after the wedding."

CHAPTER 67 - VACATION

They arrived in West Palm Beach in the late afternoon due to their having had to fly from Chicago to New York and change planes for the final leg of the flight. The last time Arthur had gone to West Palm Beach he had flown to Miami and then driven to the smaller city. After arriving, they picked up a rental car and headed to their hotel. On the way, Irma reminisced about the time she had spent in West Palm during spring break along with college kids from all over the country. She had been significantly older than most of them, but had blended into the crowd without any problems. She recalled the near riot that had ensued when a tavern had offered all-you-can-drink beer for a fixed price, and then ran out of beer. It had taken extra police in riot gear to keep the students from tearing the tavern apart.

After a smooth flight followed by a back-jarring ride in a taxi with defective shock absorbers, they arrived at their hotel feeling worn out. Arthur threw his bag on the bed and placed a call to John Griggins.

"Hello, John, this is Arthur Blake calling. I believe that Mandy Dandrich called to let you know that I would be visiting West Palm Beach along with my fiancée, Irma Custis. We've just arrived, and I wondered whether it would be convenient for you and your wife to be our guests for dinner."

"Hello, Arthur; yes Mandy called and gave you a great endorsement. She referred to you as the son she always wished she had. If you don't mind, we'll take a pass on the dinner. We've had people in and out all day, and we're not on a normal eating schedule. How about coming over around seven, and we'll get to know each other around the pool. Did Mandy give you directions to get here?

"That will be fine, John. Yes, we have the directions. We'll be there at seven."

Arthur returned his cell phone to his pocket and collapsed onto the bed, testing its softness approvingly as he did so. "We're all set, but we'd better grab a quick bite before we go. It will simply be drinks and snacks by their pool."

"I assume we won't be swimming. I'll save my new bathing suit for you at the hotel pool tomorrow."

"I'll look forward to it."

"Did he sound perturbed to have Mandy, whom he doesn't know that well, throw new people at him?"

"No, I got the impression that he preferred visitors with some indirect friendship connection to all the strangers from politics and the media. We didn't talk about his son's political career, but he mentioned people having been in and out of the house all day."

"Aren't we more of the same?"

"If we play our cards right, we become friends. If we're deemed to be more of the same bunch of strangers, we're not going to learn very much."

They had no trouble following Mandy's directions, and arrived with five minutes to spare. The house was a single story ranch with a circular driveway in front of it. They walked up to the front door where they found an envelope with Arthur's name on it taped to the front door. He opened the unsealed flap and found instructions to take the path at the left side of the house back to the swimming pool.

Arthur put the envelope and note into his pocket. "I feel as though I'm on a treasure hunt. Maybe we'll find another clue when we get to the swimming pool."

"There's a bit of philosophy in that: Life is a treasure hunt. Anyway, let's follow the yellow brick road and meet our new friends."

At the end of the path alongside the garage and a jalousie windowed Florida room, they unlatched the privacy gate and passed through it to a paving stone path that led to a concrete deck and pool area. They turned the corner at the back end of the house to find the host couple waiting for them in lounge chairs by the pool. John and Lucy got up and came to meet them as Arthur and Irma waved. After exchanging introductions they moved four lounge chairs within reach of a drink table with labeled pitchers and a tub full of ice that contained beer bottles and soft drink cans. John played the genial host.

"Arthur, Irma, help yourselves to drinks. The pitchers have two flavors of Margaritas plus lemonade and water. The tub is full of bottled and canned stuff. We don't have the fanciest house in town, but if you sit out by the pool with cool drinks on a pleasant day, you feel like you're at a mansion."

Irma said, "You folks have a delightful place here. From the background splashes, I assume your neighbors have pools too."

Lucy responded, "Irma, if you were looking down from above, you'd see a cluster of four pools arranged like the letter H. Ours is the left-hand one on the bottom of the letter. At one time we wanted to remove the fences in order to have neighborhood parties using all of the pools, but the zoning people wouldn't let us. They said that each pool needed its own fence for safety. We do have hidden connecting gates. We only open them for the big parties; it's a compromise solution. Lately, we've all kept the gates locked so that the media people and photographers don't sneak in here without permission."

"We understand. We saw the television news about your son's decision to run for the presidency. This step must be changing your lives along with his."

"It certainly has made a difference. We have to be ready to be interviewed on short notice. We also try to keep this place neat all the time because we never know what important people might drop in to express their good wishes for Paul's success. We're even starting to be recognized in public because of television coverage. That's why we opted for peace and quiet by the pool."

Arthur said, "We wish Paul success too, but we're here for social rather than political purposes. If you're tired after dealing with all of the unexpected activities, we can make this a short visit and plan something else for tomorrow."

John got up to get a fresh glass of lemonade. "We're doing fine, Arthur. You're almost empty. Grab yourself a fresh beer, and let's share some background stories. I'll start to get the ball rolling...I'm a retired librarian. I used to specialize in works on American History, both fiction and nonfiction. My favorite historical fiction author is Kenneth Roberts with his novels about conflicts during the early days of our country and Canada. He was one of those authors who wrote fiction based on verifiable history. He entertained and educated you at the same time. More recently, I've started a business manufacturing Florida souvenirs. I'll show you some later."

Arthur said, "My parents are from New England, and those books were on our shelves and frequently discussed at our house. My father's an antiques dealer, and we frequently had pieces from early colonial times. I grew up with a hearty respect for history, so I'd enjoy discussing your interests some time. I started my career as an engineer, working for NASA, and shifted to the ministry after that. If your schedule permits it, I'd like to invite you to join us for a trip to Cape Canaveral later this week. I'm going to start making arrangements with some of my old colleagues and friends tomorrow. I want Irma to meet them so that she'll be able to better relate to the people I talk about from that stage of my career. My ministry outlook and experiences require much more time than an introductory gathering, so I'll save them for another time. Irma, would you like to share your background?"

"I see this is going to be a fast-paced series of vignettes, so I'll contribute that I went to medical school and concentrated on pathology. I served as a Medical Examiner in three different locations, and I met Arthur when I came to examine a body he found in the church attic. Our two professions both deal with the transition between life and death, so we grew closer discussing matters relating to people's bodies and souls. How about you, Lucy? How did you and John meet?"

"Well, I didn't have a professional background; I worked in retail sales, sometimes in clothing stores and sometimes in stores catering to tourists. I was the inspiration for John's entry into the souvenir manufacturing business. We met when I visited his library looking for genealogy resources for my family's history. He was quite attentive to my needs."

John winked at his wife. "You looked completely lost and very attractive, so I said a little prayer of thanks and did what came naturally."

"May I take it from that comment that religion plays an important part in your lives?"

"Absolutely, Arthur; I've lost count of the number of times we've been in serious trouble with regard to health, our financial status, relationships, and other matters, and every time our outlook improved when we turned to God in prayer. We try to be diligent in our prayers of thanksgiving, and not only pray when we want something. We're Methodists too, so that shared background made us even more interested in meeting you."

Irma said, "I see some long philosophical discussions coming. Before we get into them, let me ask about your interest in genealogy, Lucy. Was yours a complex family for tracing ancestry? I'm interested in that myself, but before anyone else brings it up, I'm not a descendant of Martha Washington."

John laughed. "You must get a lot of inquiries about the Custis name. I'm glad you spoke up before I followed that line of thinking. Go ahead, Lucy, tell them how successful you've been at tracing people."

"Compared to people who have a real flare for genealogy, I haven't done much, but I do have an interesting family background as does John. Both of our families came to Florida during the Great Depression of the 1930's. The great-grandparents on both sides were out of work and barely getting by, but they figured they might as well face their difficulties in a warm and beautiful place. My grandfather was mayor of Stuart, north northwest of here. He's probably the inspiration for Paul's political career. My father and mother got divorced a few years after I was born, and Mother remarried but got divorced a second time just before John and I met. That gave me multiple branches of the family tree to trace. John's mother was quite a bit younger than his father, who died a few months ago in a car accident."

Arthur said, "That would be Max Griggins. He and Albert Dandrich, Mandy's husband, were friends from Army days and died at about the same time. Albert died in a car accident too."

Arthur and Irma both studied the facial expressions and body language of their hosts to see if there would be a significant reaction to this statement, but the only response was John's brief comment about the dangers of older people continuing to drive after their health starts to deteriorate. Lucy continued her comments.

"My father is interested in genealogy too. About six months ago, I stayed with John's father, Max, when he was sick, and I found some of his old World War II papers. My father researches that period, so I loaned them to him for about a week. When he returned them I told Max about finding them, and I put them back in the same place so that he'd be able to locate them easily. Older people have trouble keeping track of things if you move their storage location."

Irma asked, "Did Max say anything about your finding the papers and loaning them out?"

"Not exactly, but he did appear surprised. I think he had forgotten about those papers and didn't think anyone would want to see them so long after the war. Anyway, I've enjoyed picking up facts about the people on both sides of the family. I'll keep doing it as a hobby. It's similar to your family's interest in antiques, Arthur."

"It is indeed. Lucy, you were saying that your mother was divorced twice. What were her different last names, and what name did you use as your maiden name when you were married?"

"My father's last name is Rothstein, he's Jewish; my mother's second husband's name is Sinclair; and my mother's maiden name was Scott. I used Scott as my maiden name for the wedding paperwork to show that I favored my mother and didn't want any competition between her two husbands. Actually, she'll be married for the third time next month. I rarely see my father any more, although he has helped Paul with some political matters. We do have interesting families. What's your family like, Irma?"

"My family's not nearly as interesting as yours. My parents are both dead; my older brother died in the war in Viet Nam; and I'm on my own. Marrying Arthur will give me a chance to be part of a family again."

John stood up and put his glass down on the drink table. "Well folks, this has been a great introductory session, but it has been a long day, and we need some rest. Let's meet here at noon tomorrow, and I'll try to get Paul and Jill to join us for lunch. As a candidate, he has a terrible schedule, but if I ask, he'll play hooky from it for a while. Irma, I'd like you to meet our daughter Mary, who's a doctor at the National Institutes of Health, but she's out of town. We'll have to make that contact on another occasion."

"I'd very much enjoy meeting her. Lots of good research work comes out of NIH. Thanks for being so cordial to a couple of strangers dropping in on short notice. We'll be back at noon."

As they walked back to their rented car, Arthur said, "We'll have to contact Penny and Joe to check on Lucy's father. He's Jewish, and if he found out about Max's Nazi background from those papers, he might have had something to do with the murders."

"That doesn't necessarily follow, but I agree that he deserves some checking."

CHAPTER 68 - PAUL AND JILL

At noon the next day, Arthur and Irma drove to the Griggins house bearing a fruit basket that Irma insisted they pick up for their hosts. She had told Arthur that it was his first lesson in acquiring some social graces. When they arrived, they parked on the street because the circular driveway was full of cars, including a lengthy black limousine. Several people stood next to the cars talking to each other in businesslike tones. The Congressman had arrived, and this was his entourage standing by for the journey to his more official next stop.

They headed for the house, Irma leading the way, with Arthur following with the large fruit basket. This time they walked directly to the pool area without debating about using the front door.

John saw them coming through the propped-open gate and came out to greet them. "Welcome back. A day does make a difference. I feel as though we've known each other for years. Hey everyone, here's Irma Custis followed by a fruit basket on legs."

Arthur stuck his head around the side of his burden. "I am back here somewhere; Arthur Blake, porter extraordinaire, at your service." He set the basket down onto a table by the fence and stepped forward to greet the others.

"Hello again; your hospitality is so generous, it's practically biblical. You must be Paul; I'll shake your hand if you're not worried about separation of church and state." Arthur reached out to shake Paul's hand while Irma groaned.

"I'm not so sure I can go through with this marriage. You all see how hard it is to cope with his humor."

Paul shook Irma's hand after leaving Arthur. "I enjoy it, Irma. Compared to the gloom and doom of Congress, it's refreshing. I want you both to meet my wife Jill. She inspires my energy and keeps me from thinking too highly of myself."

"Isn't that the job of every wife? I'll correct myself by adding that it's her job in addition to all of her household and professional duties. When I'm not being the candidate's most avid supporter, I work in the import-export business, processing voluminous shipment paperwork. Thank heaven for computers. A few years ago we had to do most of it by hand with multi-part forms marked *sign with black ballpoint pen and press hard for seven copies.*"

Arthur said, "It's a pleasure to meet you, Paul. I've never had the opportunity to exchange views with a presidential candidate before."

"Arthur, I've never had conversations with someone in both space technology and theology before. As a good politician, I'll keep you talking. What are your views on the relationship between religion and science?"

Irma said, "Watch what you ask for. He has several long sermons on that topic."

"Don't worry, folks, I can sum it up pretty briefly. It's the job of science to learn more and more about God's creation. If every human being who ever lived on this earth had been a scientist, we still wouldn't understand everything about this world and the life upon it. Science takes us only so far, and then we have to rely on faith to make our brief lives meaningful.

"What are your views on the space program, Congressman? I'm organizing a trip to Cape Canaveral to visit some of my former associates at the Kennedy Space Center, and I'd welcome your joining us if your schedule permits."

258

"Let's say that I sometimes worry about our fiscal capability to support all the science we'd like to do, but I am a Congressman from Florida, and I know that our state benefits from much more than the scientific achievements. Summing it up, I am a strong NASA supporter."

Jill said, "And if I ask him to take out the garbage, he gives me a long speech on the pros and cons of garbage disposal. That's the new language I've had to learn, politician-speak."

Irma applauded. "I can see we're kindred spirits, Jill. We both have men who like to preach in one form or another. Are you an only child?"

"No, I have a younger brother who's in the Army. He's stationed at the Pentagon, so I get to see him when I'm in Washington. I'm not sure what his duties are there. Do you remember, Paul?"

"Stan's a liaison officer. He works on the interface between intelligence and operations functions. He gets to know a lot about all aspects of the Department of Defense. If he ever joins me in politics, it will serve him well."

Arthur asked, "Does he have political ambitions?"

"He's expressed some interest, but I'm not sure if he's ready for the rigors of this career."

John struck an old-fashioned hanging steel triangle to announce that lunch was ready, and motioned everyone to visit the long table with its array of deli meats, cheeses, and other sandwich fixings.

"Dad, I'm going to have to run to my next appointment. I'll take a doggy bag of this stuff with me. If I stay any longer my staff out front will be after me. Arthur, Irma, great to have met you. I hope we'll have some more time together in the future. Jill, I'll see you at home later." Paul scooped up some meat and cheese slices, hugged his mother and father, kissed Jill, and disappeared around the corner of the house."

259

Jill said, "Now you see him; now you don't. This candidacy thing is a whirlwind experience. At least I don't have to trail along everywhere. I will join you for the NASA outing, Arthur, if the invitation is still open."

"That's great news, Jill. You're more than welcome. I'll keep you all posted on the arrangements. For right now, that food looks delicious."

As they lined up at the food table, Arthur made a mental note to ask Penny and Joe to check for more details on Jill's brother Stan.

CHAPTER 69 - LOOSE ENDS

Joe sat in Penny's guest chair alongside her desk while she used her computer to search several databases doing relationship and criminal background checks. He drummed his fingers on the edge of her desk.

"Joe, stop the rat-a-tat-tat. It makes me nervous and breaks my concentration."

"I'm only doing it because I'm a bit nervous about what we might find. It's pretty touchy stuff to come out with something negative about a presidential candidate unless you are absolutely sure of your information."

"First of all, we haven't found anything negative yet, and we won't share any such information we do discover unless it's corroborated by multiple sources. What else is bothering you?"

"I'm not happy about having Irma and Arthur doing undercover work. They're out making friends with people who may be ruined by what they uncover. It won't be good for their reputations if the two of them are exposed as phonies."

"You're being a worry-wart, Joe. Irma and Arthur have all the proper credentials for what they're doing. If things go sour, they'll be able to handle it.

"I've checked Lucy's mother. Her first name is Dorothy, but she goes by Dolly on everything except legal documents. Looking at Dolly or Dorothy Scott, her maiden name, I've found no signs of any legal problems or criminal records. Under the second husband's surname, I've checked Dolly and Dorothy Sinclair and found nothing except a preliminary foreclosure notice from a bank. That was issued while they were in the process of getting divorced, and I see nothing dated more recently. She's also clean under Dolly or Dorothy Rothstein, her first married name."

"Did you find Lucy's father's first name?"

"That's coming up right now in the marriage license files. Here it is. His name is Nathan. Now I'll check Nathan Rothstein for criminal background...We have something. I show no indictments or convictions, but there's a notation to check the organized crime database."

"Now that sounds interesting."

"Here we are: Nathan Rothstein, known associate of Pablo Miguel Manteres and Willie Gaberti; no known indictments or convictions; suspect in several cases of money laundering and bribery. Subject has taken frequent international trips to Germany, Turkey, and Israel; has dual American and Israeli citizenship."

"Well, the last item may or may not be important. Israel has a law conveying automatic citizenship to Jews who move there. On the other hand, he could have passed information on the Nazi background of his daughter's father-in-law to Mossad, Israel's intelligence and special operations agency."

"That's possible, but we already know that Diego Garcia was one of the hit men and that he was working for the Mafia, not for any government's agency. Also, Mossad tries to expose Nazis and bring them to trial to remind the world of their terrible deeds. They don't usually kill them."

"I'll grant you that, but there are always exceptions. Anyway, Nathan Rothstein has associations with known organized crime bosses who might owe him a favor."

"That's what the file says, Joe, but the fact that he's never been convicted of anything doesn't mean that he's not a crime boss himself. We'd better take a closer look at him."

"Arthur suggested that we look at Jill's brother Stan. He's in a sensitive position in the Pentagon. I'm not exactly sure what we should look for, but I've learned to trust Arthur's hunches."

"For starters, let's look at how he got into that sensitive position. Does he have the qualifications for it? My guess is that Arthur saw Paul running for President and Stan in a key post in the Pentagon and told himself that there's the potential for too much power to be concentrated in a single family."

"There have been families with more power than that, but they didn't tend to have Nazis and Mafia in their backgrounds."

"Some people might dispute that statement, Joe, but let's get on with the checks on Stan...I'm searching for Paul Griggins' wife. Jill comes up with a maiden name of Hupther. That means that Stan's last name would be the same unless Jill had a previous marriage we don't have listed."

"I may be getting hyper about this Nazi connection, but Hupther sounds as though it might have a German origin."

"You are off base, Joe. Paul didn't even know about that background. Why would he have chosen a wife to match with it?"

"There's always Hitler's old concept of Aryan racial purity."

"Enough speculation from you; I'm taking a break while you get back to your logical investigation mode of thinking. You're thinking like a politician or a gossip columnist." Penny pushed her chair back and walked out.

Joe shrugged his shoulders and headed for the coffee pot. There was something in Penny's comments. He wasn't his normal self today, and he couldn't quite put his finger on what was bothering him. Maybe he was jealous of Arthur checking out people in person while he was stuck with computer searches. Still, research was a basic part of his job, and it hadn't bothered him before. He might have to listen to Penny's continuing comments about buying a house somewhere else. The Washington scene was turning him into a paper shuffler and meeting denizen.

Penny came back into the office. "Have you cleared your head of meandering thoughts? I'd like to make some progress before we run out of daylight."

"I took my dose of caffeine, and I'm ready to concentrate on foreground thinking. The background thoughts are the ones that mess up my mind. Let's get back to it."

Penny sat down and brought her search screen back to the point at which they took a break. "I'm looking at military records: Stanley Hupther, Lt. Colonel U.S. Army, is assigned to liaison with intelligence operations. He interfaces with GS-12 level Intelligence Research Specialists and Intelligence Operations Specialists. Those people are high enough in the chain of command to be considered experts and to author significant reports that trigger important decisions. Looking at his rank history, I see something interesting. Stanley has had three substantial promotions within the last two years. I'd consider that unusually fast advancement. There's no cause-and-effect evidence in these things, but the Army may have wanted to stay on good terms with Stan's brother-in-law, Paul, who is second in seniority on the House Armed Services Committee. Arthur said something about a discussion of Stan's eventually getting into politics. His position at the Pentagon may mask an effort to enhance his resume for a political campaign. There's nothing illegal there, but it is a sign of power politics at work."

"It does say that Paul plays the game of doing favors for relatives, and probably friends too. If he were elected President, he might be willing to listen to requests from his grandfather, Nathan Rothstein. If Nathan is part of the white collar section of organized crime, he would rank as a VIP in those circles."

"Yes, but it doesn't say anything about why Max Griggins and the others were killed."

"I can think of two motives. Lucy said that she showed Nathan some of Max's old papers from World War II. Nathan could have pinned the Nazi label on Max and his five buddies and decided they were a threat to Paul's election. Nobody would vote for a candidate whose grandfather was a Nazi."

"Don't forget that his other grandfather is in organized crime."

"That's suspected, but not yet proven in court. The other prospect is that Nathan had some relatives who were killed in the German death camps and that the assassinations were his personal vengeance for that."

"Following that line of thought, Nathan could have wanted personal revenge, but he might have convinced the mob to do it for him. He would have argued that the six former Nazis were a potential threat to Paul's success in the presidential election. Nathan would have needed to keep his hands clean so that he would be in a position to influence Paul later on."

"Now I think we're seeing the pattern in the tapestry. I think it's time for us to discuss our findings with Mary Byrne. We need a plan to capture the bad guys and prove their guilt."

CHAPTER 70 - SETTING THE BAIT

Following a meeting with Joe and Penny Gonzalez, Mary Byrne initiated their agreed plan by contacting Diego Garcia. She knew that her newly converted hit man couldn't name the mastermind behind his recent assignment, but he could work through his contact to assist them in tracing the network of people who had been involved. He had agreed to implement the plan, but she had people watching him and monitoring his cell and land line phone conversations to be sure his new allegiance to the CIA held true. Mary listened in on his conversation with John Twinings.

"John, it's Diego calling. I need you to take care of something for me. There could be a problem if the police find the truck we used to dump the shop equipment for that crash in Dallas. I did some checking on the supplier of that special triggering mechanism, and it turns out that they keep records by serial number of their devices matched to credit cards used and photographs of people calling for the merchandise. When Juan bought and picked up that unit he didn't have enough cash, so he had to charge it on your card."

Mary could hear the other end of the conversation. "What a stupid thing to do. He could have come back for more cash."

"Don't sweat it, John. We can still make this right. I parked that truck in Smitty's brickyard with an old tarp covering it. All you have to do is get someone down there to dismantle the dumping mechanism and destroy the triggering unit. It'll take two people, but the place is abandoned, so they can take their time and do the job right."

"You said it, Diego. It had better be done right. I'll get down there with my brother so that we don't have any more screw-ups. Juan must have been high on something when he did that."

"Juan's a good man. He never gets high, especially when he's on a job. He cut a corner when he ran out of time. That's all. Make the device disappear, and there's no problem. I've got to get back to being a witless playboy. Let me know when the job's done."

"OK, Diego, we'll take care of it. You sure gave yourself a cushy life with that witless playboy cover. I give you a lot of credit for thinking that one up. I'll be in touch."

Mary smiled to herself at the way the playboy had pulled it off. Maybe he would be a useful operative for them, especially when they needed a hit man who would be linked to a totally different organization.

CHAPTER 71 - BRICKYARD

John and Frank Twinings slipped through the gap in the brickyard fence after carefully removing and stashing the loose board. Their dark clothing blended into the early evening shadows. The tools they carried were in a soft-sided case with each item separately wrapped in a towel to minimize the noise of tools bumping against each other. They expected the brickyard to be deserted, but they had encountered stranger things than winos and nosey neighbors before. Once, Smitty had discovered a family of homeless people living between two piles of concrete blocks underneath a precariously balanced sheet of corrugated steel. After that, he had installed a nighttime sound system that played random samples of junkyard dogs growling and barking.

Frank motioned John toward a remote corner of the brickyard where something lurked in the shadows draped with an old military-issue canvas tarp. He picked up a corner and nodded affirmation to his brother. Having identified the left front fender, he moved to his right until he reached the rear of the vehicle. Together, Frank and John rolled up enough of the canvas to reveal most of the cargo space on the flatbed truck. John hoisted the tool bag onto the truck and climbed aboard.

"Come on up, Frank. Here's the dumper drive. We'll have to unbolt it to get to the trigger mechanism underneath it. Oh, there goes that junkyard dog recording. Smitty said it would be realistic."

As John picked the proper socket from his set and started to turn the first bolt, floodlights went on, bathing them in blinding light.

"Hold it right there you two. Put down the tools, and don't reach for any weapons. You're surrounded."

As John and Frank's eyes adapted to the lights, they saw at least twenty people in black clothing and protective vests. Two were handlers for large dogs straining at their leashes.

John said, "I guess that wasn't a recording of dogs growling."

One of the handlers responded. "The first time it was a recording, but it startled my dog who answered it, and we had to move in."

Frank noticed that one of the people surrounding the truck had turned away, revealing his vest's imprint of Homeland Security on the back. "Hey, why are you guys from Homeland Security? We aren't terrorists. We're loyal Americans."

Joe Gonzalez stepped forward but didn't identify himself. "You're both involved in an international plot that assassinated retired government agents. You're going to be up for treason charges."

Frank and John looked at each other and shook their heads. John said, "Look, we're loyal native born American citizens. The only time I was out of the country was when I was in the Army. I'll admit that I'm no angel, but don't say I committed treason, and my brother didn't either."

"Thanks, John; you always did try to take care of your little brother."

Joe said, "This is all very touching family relations, but unless you give us the full story on those six murders and convince us that they were motivated by something else, you're going up for treason, and your families will forever be ashamed of you. We already have you on board the truck that was used as one of the murder weapons."

John said, "We'll cooperate, but only if we get a written guarantee that our names won't be linked to treason charges. All we did was arrange for some old guys to have accidents. They were so old that they would have died soon anyway. That's what I never understood about this whole thing. Anyway, that's all I'll say without that written guarantee and without a lawyer."

Joe motioned for the armed men to move in. They handcuffed John and Frank and led them to a van. Before he allowed himself to be guided into the back seat, John called out, "Honest, we're loyal Americans."

CHAPTER 72 - SPILLED BEANS

Mary Byrne sat with Penny and Joe in her conference room. She laughed as she described the interrogation of John and Frank.

"Sometimes you get lucky. It doesn't happen often, but when it does, it's something special. Those two were raised with patriotism as an absolute requirement in their lives. It was pure luck that they reacted the way they did to that Homeland Security vest label. That was a big break. Even bigger was Joe's genius in having them brought to CIA for questioning. As soon as they saw the building and logo, they waived their rights to attorneys and spilled everything. We hit their weak spot. They didn't mind being called criminals or killers, but they'd do absolutely anything to avoid the traitor label. It's good to know that our traditions about American values mean so much to some people."

Penny said, "I'm afraid we don't have as many patriotic people as we once did, but who knows? Maybe the pendulum will swing back the other way. Anyway, what did they reveal about the plot?"

"They didn't know anything about why they had to assassinate their six victims. As John indicated earlier, he thought it was a waste to put all that effort into killing old men.

Penny said, "Mary, are you saying that John and Frank couldn't reveal who ordered the murders?"

"I'm not saying that at all. Frank said that they were ordered by Nate Rothstein and that while Frank was playing golf with him and two other friends, Nate asked him whether the project had been completed without leaving any evidence behind."

Joe said, "That's why they rushed into the trap in Dallas. They had assured Nate that there was nothing left around as evidence, and Diego Garcia said there was some in that truck."

Penny said, "OK, folks, we have our connection to Nate Rothstein, not just as an associate, but as the person who ordered these hits. What are we going to do about it? We have to be subtle and careful, because he's the grandfather of a presidential candidate. We don't want this to look like a political hatchet job."

Joe responded, "You're right about having to be cautious, but as far as relationships go, don't forget that this grandfather of the candidate had the other grandfather of that same candidate killed. Mary, CIA is used to working behind the scenes on sensitive matters; what course of action do you suggest?"

"I've given it a bit of thought, and I see only one approach that would minimize harm to a lot of people. We can gather corroborating statements from John, Frank, Diego Garcia, Juan Terron, and their other associate. This will give us a large amount of evidence against Nathan for the assassinations. We'll also use CIA resources to get evidence against him on the money laundering and other white collar crimes he has so far evaded."

Joe said, "Are you sure you can find the evidence for that?"

"I'm sure. Some of it is already in our files, and Mossad and other agencies will give us more. The only reason he wasn't charged and convicted earlier was that such a conviction was lower priority than other things we were doing. It now has increased importance. Anyway, my advice is that we privately present the assassination evidence to Congressman Griggins and suggest that if he withdraws his presidential candidacy Nathan will be prosecuted for the money laundering and related charges rather than for the murders. His political career might withstand that approach. If he chooses to continue his candidacy we would have to prosecute for the assassinations. If we took that course, I'm sure that the electorate would turn their backs on him."

"That prosecution would also publically reveal the black sheep in five other families."

"Yes, Penny, but we're hoping that Paul chooses the other path. CIA doesn't like to say too much about retired agents who served us well."

Joe said, "It's all up to Paul. We'll soon find out how good a politician he is."

CHAPTER 73 - PAUL

Congressman Paul Griggins had just returned home from a campaign stop at a nursing home. He felt relaxed for the first time in several days because he had nothing more on his schedule for the day, and he had the house to himself. Jill and her parents had joined Arthur and Irma for a private tour of Cape Canaveral. He wondered if he would ever have an afternoon of solitude like this if he were elected President. Paul had sat down to enjoy a cold bottle of beer when the doorbell rang. He headed for the door, a bit irritated that his pause for relaxation had been taken away from him. He opened the door to find two women and a man standing there.

"I'm sorry, I need my privacy. I'm not giving any interviews today."

The taller woman said, "We're sorry to intrude, Congressman, but something has come up that requires your immediate attention. My name is Mary Byrne, and I'm with the CIA. My companions are Penny and Joe Gonzalez from a different domestic intelligence agency." All three showed Paul their credentials.

The man spoke. "We need to have a confidential conversation with you. We have information about pending legal matters that will affect you, and we would like to give you the opportunity to learn about them before anything appears in the media."

Mary said, "We can discuss these matters here, or if you prefer we can do it at a government office where we would have complete security and privacy."

Paul thought for a moment. "No one else is at home, so please come in, and we'll talk right here. My neighbors are quite used to my having political people visiting, so they won't think this is anything unusual. I have an office at the end of the hall. Make yourselves comfortable there, and I'll join you with some drinks."

Paul left them, and they headed for the office. It had a large mahogany desk, a couch with a sturdy coffee table in front of it, and a wingback provincial chair. Paul returned with a tray full of assorted bottles: soda, beer, and green tea. He put the tray on the coffee table and spread out some coasters and napkins.

"Please sit down. I hope you don't mind drinking from a bottle. My wife would insist on glasses, but I'd like to get right to our conversation." He sat at the desk and turned off the telephone ringer. Joe took the provincial chair, and the two women sat on the couch. Each took a drink bottle.

Penny spoke first. "Congressman, we know that your candidacy for high office puts you in the spotlight for potential criticism. That's why we wanted to give you every courtesy in informing you of new developments. They affect both public matters and your family."

Paul sat forward on high alert. "My family is on a visit to the Kennedy Space Center at Cape Canaveral. Nothing has happened to them, has it?"

Penny continued in a calm subdued voice. "No, this has nothing to do with their visit. Your Grandfather, Max Griggins, died a while ago in an apparent automobile accident. We have evidence that it was a case of murder. Five of his longtime friends were also murdered within the same month in apparent accidents."

"That's shocking! Who would want to murder a man of his age, and five others also? What tied these deaths together?"

Mary took up the story. "These six men were World War II veterans, but they were originally members of the German Army. During the course of a special operation by OSS, they tried to change sides and accompany American soldiers back to England. Unfortunately, their American companions were killed in combat. The German soldiers assumed their identities and went to England pretending to be their American counterparts."

"Do you mean that Max Griggins was once a German soldier?"

"Yes, all six of these men were."

"Were they Nazis?"

"We know that some of them were, and they all had to swear allegiance to the National Socialist cause, because they were Waffen SS troops."

"Good God! Have you only just discovered their identities this long after the war?"

"No, we found out about them shortly after they switched sides and identities. We found that they were truly committed to their new roles as American soldiers. They fought well against the Germans for the duration of the war. Then they continued their impersonations through the discharge process and came to live in America. We approached them during the early days of the CIA and turned them into a Cold War team of agents working in East Germany. All of this is, of course, classified information. They served the CIA well and retired after Germany was reunified."

"So, they lived out their lives as Americans. Were they naturalized citizens?"

"No, they couldn't be, because they continued to impersonate native born Americans. The real Max Griggins died in France before D-Day."

"In other words, my father is the son of an illegal immigrant."

"Yes, if you want to look at it that way; that is a correct statement."

"So, you're telling me this because you think it might affect my candidacy and my political credentials?"

Joe finished his soda and returned the bottle to the table. He said, "I'm afraid our subject matter goes beyond that. The murders of these six men were ordered by someone with connections to organized crime, your other grandfather, Nathan Rothstein."

Paul twisted uncomfortably in his desk chair and pounded the desk with his right fist. This was not going to be a good day for him. "That's a very serious accusation to make. Do you have proof that will stand up in court?"

"We have all of the actual assassins and their mob contacts in custody, two in the United States and three in other countries. They have all confessed, naming Nathan as the mastermind behind the plot. We also have a specially-modified truck that was used as the murder weapon in one of the killings."

Paul stood up and paced back and forth as he spoke. The others sat quietly, sensing his frustration. "So you're saying that my paternal grandfather was a Nazi, and he was killed by my maternal grandfather who is a mobster. Now that is a proud pedigree for a politician! When is all of this information going to be released to the public?"

Mary stood up and faced Paul. She wanted to monitor his eye movements and expression changes as she continued. "What becomes public and when it happens depend partly on your actions. You have a political career to protect, and the CIA wants to protect the anonymity and reputations of its agents. If we can reach an agreement that protects the best interests of our country, it may not be necessary for everything to become public."

"What are you proposing?"

"I have been authorized to suggest that if you withdraw your candidacy for President and serve out your term as Congressman, Nathan Rothstein will be tried for money laundering and other white collar crimes instead of for six murders. Further, his case will not come to trial for another year to separate his court appearance from your withdrawal."

"Who authorized this approach?"

"I'm not at liberty to say, but it comes from someone with sufficient authority to make these procedures happen."

"And if I choose to continue my candidacy despite the information you have given me?"

"Then legal measures will begin immediately, and Nathan will be charged with six murders."

Paul blinked several times and sat down. His voice quavered slightly. "Why are you making this offer?"

Mary's words confirmed her assessment of Paul's body language. "We don't think that you took part in these crimes, and we want to give you the opportunity to complete your service to our country."

"Even if I do what you say, I doubt that I could be reelected with Nathan facing even the lesser charges during the period of the campaign."

"That is a likely outcome, but your family and the families of the other five veterans would be spared the trauma of sensationalized media coverage."

Paul stood up again, regaining his composure. "I would like a little time before I give you my decision. It's not easy to give up one's lifetime career, and I would like to discuss these circumstances with Nathan."

Mary said, "You may do that, but be assured that his every move is being watched, and if your discussion triggers his attempt to flee the country, the possibility of lesser charges will be cancelled, and he might even be shot during his escape attempt. The full facts would be given to the media."

Paul sat once more, fully subdued. "I understand."

"You have one week to make your decision. We'll show ourselves out."

CHAPTER 74 - NATHAN

Nathan sat in his car in the parking lot of Grassy Waters Nature Preserve. It was the first time he had visited this place, and so far he didn't like it. He felt itchy, thinking about the huge number of mosquitoes that had to populate the winding trails through this wetlands preserve. Nathan had arrived a few minutes early for the meeting requested by his grandson, and he had used his extra time to assure himself that there were very few other visitors in the area. Paul was a presidential candidate, and he didn't want their meeting to be documented by the press. Paul had selected this place in the hope that it would be isolated enough for frank conversation, and the low attendance today confirmed the wisdom of his choice.

Nathan felt himself getting a little bit tense. Paul had a reputation for being absolutely punctual. For the first time in memory, he was significantly late, and Nathan had to wonder whether there was a message in his grandson's tardiness. He got out of his car and walked toward the buildings and the water behind them. Sounds of wildlife surrounded him, but he wasn't expert enough to know what he was hearing. He reversed his steps when he heard a car entering the almost-deserted parking lot. Paul had arrived, and he deliberately parked far away from Nathan's familiar bronze Cadillac. Nathan sat down on a bench in anticipation of his grandson's approach.

"Have you been waiting long?"

"Not too long; I've been here only long enough to get a feel for the place. It's definitely different from most parks I visit."

Nathan stood up and shook hands with Paul. He noted that the short crisp handshake was a distant imitation of Paul's normal enthusiastic politician's grip.

"Is everything OK, Paul? You sounded a bit strained on the phone."

"I'd have to say that everything is definitely not OK, Nathan. In case you didn't notice, I was doing pretty well in the early stages of running for the presidency, and you had to do your best to knock my ship of state clean out of the water."

"What do you mean? I've been staying in the background, and I haven't had anything to do with your campaign."

"Let's walk down one of these trails as we talk. I don't see anyone nearby, but you never know. We'll keep moving.

"Nathan, I've always wondered about the crowd you hang out with, but I've tried to look the other way and give you some slack in our relationship. Apparently you couldn't stay away from ruining my life and goals; you're more evil than I could have ever imagined."

"Don't get self-righteous on me. There's not a politician alive who should use that word evil. You guys all manipulate everybody for your own benefit. As to my friends, there's nothing wrong with my knowing some powerful people too."

They took turns ducking beneath a branch overhanging the trail.

"I'll grant you that politicians don't always have the best interests of the public as priority number one, but at least we don't give orders for six old men to be killed."

"So that's what this is about. I didn't think anyone had seen any connections among those accidents. Even so, those weren't normal old men. They were Nazi soldiers who probably killed their American counterparts and assumed their identities. I saw Max's old wartime papers.

280

Lucy found them when she was taking care of him, and she showed them to me. Do you think you could be elected President with a Nazi grandfather and his SS buddies standing behind you? We made sure that everything looked accidental so that your campaign wouldn't be affected."

"Careerwise, it would be bad enough for me to have had a grandfather who was once a German soldier, but it's much worse to have another grandfather who's a serial killer."

"I never killed any of those guys; some other people did."

"You ordered their deaths which is the same thing. And for your information, I know that those guys did not kill their American counterparts during the war. I've been briefed on everything about them. They even worked for our government later on."

"That means nothing, Paul. They were the evil ones. The Nazis rounded up and killed almost all my relatives. They took them away to the death camps and systematically wiped out my mother, my father, my two older sisters, and my favorite aunt and uncle. They were six people who meant everything to me when I was a little kid, and when I had the chance to get six of theirs in return, I took it. It felt good, and I'd do it again. They were old, but they didn't have the right to die peacefully; they got what they deserved. You can whine about your political career suffering a setback, but it's nothing compared to what the Nazis did to so many people. You never would have been elected in the first place if Max's Nazi roots had been discovered earlier. People have long memories when it comes to Hitler and his crew. You had a chance to run for President, and I'm glad that you had that opportunity. I had a bigger opportunity. I served God as the angel of death, and I'm proud of it."

"You said that I was being self-righteous. You took revenge for things that happened more than sixty-five years ago on people who were so ashamed of their government's actions that they found a way to switch sides in the war. They ended up fighting against their own countrymen for the last year of the war. Don't look now, but two of our country's strongest current allies are Germany and Japan. Times change, and people have to learn to forgive each other, or we get eaten up by hatred."

"You speak like the politician you are. If you ever get to heaven, try that political speech on my mother, father, and sisters. See if they'll agree with you."

"They probably would, or they wouldn't be in heaven."

"Don't give me any of that crap, Paul. I'm sorry if I hurt your career; but I did what I had to do. I knew about these Nazis, and I was in a position to take care of them, so I did. I had them make each case look like an accident so that nothing would hit the press. I did it for your career too. I didn't want Max's past treachery to hurt your campaign. It still hasn't come out. People can speculate all they want, but there's no evidence connecting me to anything."

"I'll give you the politician's favorite, 'No comment!' on that one. Stay out of my life and Mother's from now on. I'll tell the family you told me you were going overseas for a while."

"That might be a good idea. I could get away from the hypocrisy of election year politics. Good luck with straightening out your career, Paul. I was looking forward to having the President for a grandson."

They took the trail branch that led back to the parking lot. As they approach Nathan's car Paul said, "Remember, I don't ever want to see you again."

"You remember your flowery speech, Paul. Someday you may want to take back those words and forgive me.

Don't be surprised if my friends cancel their commitments to donate to you and support a different candidate."

CHAPTER 75 - DECISIONS

The flight back from Florida had been delayed by bad weather in the Midwest. Rather than waiting it out at the airport, Arthur and Irma rescheduled their flight for a day later and telephoned their hotel to ask for one more night. Their undercover work had been a success, and that they had even enjoyed mingling with the Griggins family. Arthur was surprised when the hotel reservations person said that they could have their same room for the extra night.

He ended his phone conversation and turned to Irma. "We have the same room. Either they're very slow in cleaning up after departing guests, or they're not very busy. Anyway, it will be like going back to our vacation cottage."

They caught the hotel shuttle bus and an hour later found themselves continuing the same conversation in their old hotel room..

"Your cottage comment was a good idea, Arthur. When we get back to Parkville, let's talk about getting a vacation cottage in Wisconsin or Iowa."

"That's a possibility. It also brings up one of the million or so relationship topics we've never discussed. Do you like to vacation in the same place every time, or do you like to travel all over the place?"

"Either one is fine, but I like the idea of a familiar vacation spot within hours of home."

"You do realize that as a United Methodist pastor, I'll be getting moved to a different church in a different community every few years?"

"That's another reason for a vacation cottage that's all ours. It would be our home away from wherever they assign you. Parsonages are fine, but they're not homes."

Arthur looked at Irma for about ten seconds before he spoke. "You know, there's still a lot we have to learn about each other. Everything has been so casual up to now that we haven't got into much of the deeper stuff."

"Deeper stuff such as whether we should buy a vacation cottage?"

"Such as whether we do a lot of long term planning or take each day as it comes."

"Nobody is so casual as to not plan ahead at all."

"I plan ahead in the sense of being sure I have the resources to handle whatever comes along. I take what God gives me rather than trying to tell Him what I want."

"He already knows what's in store for you. Maybe you should share your outlook more with family and friends, and even your fiancée. I'm ready to share my life with you. You ought to at least share your plans and dreams with me."

"I'll work on that, but I've come this far on a *taking what comes* basis, and I find it hard to formulate my wishes for the future and to force them on other people."

"You have a problem. We have a problem. This conversation is going to have to get a lot more attention before we'll be ready for marriage."

Arthur got up and went to the door. He'd had this conversation once before when he had been married to Cindy. Fortunately, she had walked out on him before they'd had to discuss it further. He opened the door and picked up the newspaper that lay outside. He always enjoyed a hotel that gave him this extra hospitality touch.

As he walked back toward Irma, he unfolded the paper and read the headline and lead article.

"Let's table that discussion for today. Big things are happening."

"What things?"

"The headline reads *CONGRESSMAN QUITS PRESIDENTIAL RACE.* The lead article continues: *Congressman Paul Griggins has announced that he is withdrawing his candidacy for President of the United States because of personal family problems that require his attention. The Palm Beach Post has learned that the Congressman's maternal grandfather, Nathan Rothstein, has died in a fishing accident. At approximately seven o'clock this morning, his boat was rammed by a freighter approximately two miles east of Boynton Beach, southeast of the Palm Beach area. Congressman Griggins indicated that this accident followed by only a few months the death of his paternal grandfather, Max Griggins, in an Everglades automobile accident. The Griggins family has requested that the public respect their privacy during the funeral preparations. Congressman Griggins' public relations assistant has indicated that in deference to the tragic circumstances, his office will not comment on any political matters for one month. The Post has learned that the Congressman's wife, Jill, had been close to both of her husband's grandfathers, and that she has been particularly shaken by these events.*"

"Well, Arthur, there's an argument for your practice of taking things as they come. With Nathan dead, he won't be prosecuted for either the assassinations of the six veterans or his money laundering activities. Paul Griggins will be able to stay in politics as long as he doesn't seek higher office, and the six families won't have to face reporters sensationalizing the backgrounds of the six former German soldiers. Everything is now very neat."

"Everything is too neat. I'll bet that Nathan wasn't even an ardent fisherman. Someone arranged that accident."

"Who do you think would have done that?"

"There are motives all over the place. It might have been done by Nathan's organized crime associates to avoid a potential mess during his trial. Political operatives may have wanted to save Paul's career. Our government may not have liked the idea of courtroom attention for our six veterans regarding how they switched sides and then worked for the CIA during the Cold War."

"My guess is that everything will simply quiet down with time."

"You're absolutely right on that one, Irma. No one gains by publicizing this any further."

"What about John and Frank Twinings over here and the three hit men overseas? Do they walk away from this unscathed?"

"I suspect that Diego Garcia will be in good shape because the CIA will want to use him in the future. The others are already in custody, and their cases will be handled very quietly, assuming they make it to court."

"You really don't know which of the three factions eliminated Nathan Rothstein?"

"No, and I don't want to know. May God have mercy on Nathan's soul."

CHAPTER 76 - FAREWELL

The flight back to O'Hare Field in Chicago and the drive back to Parkville were uneventful except for the fact that both Irma and Arthur devoted most of their thoughts to the question of whether they had opened up an incompatibility issue during their hotel room discussion. They both hoped that it would go away with time. After all, what couple's outlooks were perfectly matched?

As they drove past the *Welcome to Parkville* sign, Arthur grasped Irma's hand. "Do you want me to drop you at your apartment, or do you want to head for the parsonage with me?"

"I don't want you to drop me anywhere. You're pretty much stuck with me, especially after this trip. That was the longest period we've spent on our own, and we did everything as a couple."

"I hope we didn't contribute to long-term rifts in the Griggins family. They were so accepting of us, and we did our best to tear their relationships apart."

"No, Preacher, we weren't the implements of God's vengeance. Nathan brought it all on himself and his family. I remember your sermon after your dad reacted so traumatically to Albert's Nazi photograph. You talked about forgiving others so that others would forgive us too. If Nathan had been able to forgive Max, they'd both be alive, and he'd be facing nothing more than a money laundering charge with a low priority for prosecution."

"*If* is a powerful little word."

"And *if* you hadn't found a body in your church attic, I might never have met you."

"That seems like a very long time ago. Anyway, here's the parsonage. This is the end of the line; time for everyone to get out.

They each took some luggage and headed for the front door. Arthur heard the telephone ringing. He dropped his suitcases, unlocked the door, and ran for the telephone.

"Hello, this is Pastor Blake speaking; may I help you?"

His mother's familiar voice responded. "Hello, Arthur, I've been trying to reach you for a couple of days. Have you been away? I haven't been able to reach Irma either."

"That would probably be due to the fact that we were in Florida together, and before you ask, it was a vacation."

"Good for you. I know you both deserved a getaway. Have you just now arrived home?"

"Yes, I dropped the luggage on the doorstep when I heard the phone ringing. Why?"

Irma brought the luggage inside, and stood listening to Arthur's side of the conversation, trying to deduce its other side.

Janice continued, "I hate to ask this of you so soon after arriving home, but would you be willing to visit us? We've learned that Mandy succeeded in selling her house, and she's planning to leave for a vacation and house-hunting trip to Arizona. She sold all her furniture with the house and put her other belongings in storage. If she finds a house on this trip, she may not come back."

"When is she leaving? Can you give us a day or two to transition between trips?"

"She delayed her trip for three days to handle all of her goodbyes, but I wasn't able to reach you for the first two of those days."

"In other words, Mother, you're telling me that we have to get there today?"

"I'm afraid so, Arthur."

"That's fine. We'll be there. I'll have to check that there aren't any church emergencies. I'm going to give the phone to Irma so that she can get the schedule squared with you while I run over to the church." He cupped his hand over the mouthpiece.

"Irma, I don't know if you got all that, but Mandy sold her house and is leaving town tomorrow. If we want to see her and say goodbye, we have to go to Richmond today. Talk with Mother while I check for any church problems." Arthur handed her the phone and semi-slammed the door on his way out."

"Hi, Mom, we had so much leisure on our trip that we forgot that things can get hectic here. Please tell me when we should be there."

"I heard that door slam. I hope I didn't upset Arthur."

"No problem; the wind blew it shut."

"Nice attempt to cover for Arthur; you'll be a great wife. I remember that the door opens inward, so it would be pretty hard for the wind to slam it."

"Anyway, do you have a particular plan and schedule for today?"

"We'll play things loosely. Try to be here before suppertime. We thought we'd all go over to Mandy's house with some pizzas. We'll get some half-and-half pizzas with assorted toppings so that we don't have to take orders in advance. We'll also bring beer and soda pop."

"That sounds fine, Janice. We'll be there in three to four hours, depending on whether Arthur gets involved in things at the church. He'll get free as soon as he can; you raised him to be responsible, and he took your teachings seriously."

"Thanks, Irma. I'd better get going now. Peter needs my help minding the shop while he makes a delivery."

Ten minutes later, Arthur returned from the church with a smile on his face. "I've been informed that I'm not necessary to the operation of the church. Shirley has all the office matters under control; Wally Sanborn has written a layman's sermon for Sunday; and Donna Frieden has been calling on sick and shut-in members of the congregation, sometimes with Bill Martin in tow. They are a well-matched couple."

"As are we, Mr. Casual; your mother and I have a definite schedule for this trip, so if you'll do a quick clean-up and change your clothes, we'll be on our way."

Fortunately, the parsonage had two bathrooms, so they each managed to be ready for departure within a half hour. The trip to Richmond went smoothly, punctuated only occasionally by chatter because of their fatigue from all of their traveling. They pulled into the Blake driveway right behind Peter as he returned from work. They climbed out of their cars and exchanged hugs and handshakes.

"This will be another major change in your relationships, Dad. You've had Mandy as a friend for a long time."

"It's been a very long time, but we'll still stay long-distance friends. Maybe we'll even visit her in Arizona when winter gets terrible here. There aren't many winter customers at Blake's Antiques, so I can shut it down for a vacation now and then."

They headed inside through the kitchen door and found Janice on the telephone ordering the pizzas. When she finished, she called Mandy and said that they would arrive in about forty-five minutes. Then she greeted everyone with hugs and kisses.

"I ordered the pizzas as soon as I saw you in the driveway. You made good time. Arthur, I'm sorry you didn't get time to rest, but I'm sure you'll appreciate seeing Mandy before she leaves."

"That's fine, Mother. I will enjoy having the chance to say goodbye."

"Peter, you're supposed to pick up the pizza in twenty-five minutes. One advantage of living in a small town is that everything's pretty close together, so driving time is low."

Irma told Janice and Peter about their trip and the visit to the Kennedy Space Center while they waited for the pizza pick-up time. Then Arthur joined his Dad to pick up the food while the women drove directly to Mandy's. They timed it so that they would all arrive at about the same time. During the pizza jaunt, Arthur brought Peter up-to-date on the case.

"So it's pretty much solved now? Albert and his friends were killed by mob associates of Nate Rothstein."

"That's it, Dad. Rothstein and Max Griggins had been friends as well as relatives by marriage, but when Nate saw the old papers indicating Max's roots as a German soldier, he snapped. Nate had lost most of his family in the death camps, and he saw his chance to strike back at someone. I think he had a case of survivor guilt. He lived because he had been sent to the U.S. to live with relatives, and he felt guilty because his parents and other relatives stayed behind and died."

"That's not that much different from the way I felt when I saw that picture of Albert in a Nazi SS uniform. I didn't have relatives in Europe during the war, but I'd seen pictures of the piles of dead bodies and the emaciated camp survivors. I wanted nothing to do with anyone who had participated in that."

"We still don't know what Albert did in the German Army, but we do know these six men risked their lives to switch sides."

"What's going to happen to the Congressman who wanted to be President?"

"The only thing he'll have to give up is his ambition. Paul Griggins will be free to run for reelection, and my guess is that he'll probably win. He does know that there are people behind the scenes with information that would kill his political career if he becomes ambitious again. He gets to continue being in Congress and all six families, including his own, avoid nasty publicity."

"Enough talk about that for now; I'll be right back with the pizza." Peter climbed out of Arthur's car and hurried inside the restaurant.

While he waited, Arthur reflected on the relatively short period of time that had passed since his father had come to church with his surprising information about Albert. Now they were on their way to bid Albert's widow safe passage to her new home. So many things had happened and he had learned so much about the differences in people's attitudes. He had the luxury of giving glib sermons that preached positive messages, but life wasn't as simple as his sermons. There were good aspects of bad people and bad aspects of good people. Arthur mentally filed his thoughts and popped open the back hatch as his father returned with the pizzas. A man followed him carrying a carton filled with assorted drinks. They both loaded their burdens into the back of the car, and the second man returned to the restaurant.

Peter climbed back in on the passenger side looking pleased. "I told Tom this stuff was for a farewell gathering for Mandy, and he gave me the drinks for nothing. He said she and Albert had been regular customers for years, so he wanted to help with the party. He's a good soul."

They arrived at Mandy's house just as Janice and Irma were climbing out of Peter's van. Then they headed for the front door single file. Janice led the way followed by Irma; then Peter took his place carrying the pizzas, and Arthur trailed the group carrying the drinks. Janice pushed the bell button four times, once for each of them.

Mandy opened the door just as Janice was finishing her fourth ring. "What are you trying to do, Janice, wake me up? Everybody come on in. Thank you for this big sendoff. Perch anywhere you can. A lot of my stuff is already in storage, so the place looks bigger than usual. The real estate person said that the house would be easier to sell if it didn't have so much stuff in it, and she must have been right because we found a buyer in only two weeks.

Irma said, "That is a short time for selling a house nowadays. Either you were lucky, or your price was right."

"I didn't ask for as much as I might have a while ago. It's time for me to move on, and at my age, what am I going to do with tons of money anyway?"

They gathered around the kitchen table, paused for Arthur to say grace, and spread out the food. Very quickly the sound level rose as several people began to talk at the same time. After a few minutes, Mandy tapped a glass with a fork to get everyone's attention.

"Thank you all for coming and for being such good friends, now and in the past. I want to give special thanks to Arthur and Irma, both for their willingness to come out here for my party and for their tireless work with various agencies to track down those serial killers. They have all been caught, haven't they?"

Arthur said, "Don't worry Mandy, the mastermind died, ironically in an accident which may have been arranged by parties unknown, and the actual killers are all in custody, facing unpublicized prosecution. You and the family members of Albert's friends who were killed have nothing more to fear; and your lives won't be marred by hostile publicity either."

"It is true that I'm moving to Arizona because I want to start over, even at my old age, without any more talk about things that happened in the distant past. I had thought that my fresh start might require that I change my name, but thanks to the success of your investigations I'll be comfortable with remaining Mandy Dandrich. As you discovered during your search for the murderers, I have some background with the CIA that will be useful when I restart my life in a new place. I also have to announce that I won't be living alone. I will have a companion."

Mandy's words took everyone by surprise. They stopped eating and drinking. The door to the basement opened, and Albert walked into the kitchen.

Everyone started to talk at the same time. Then Albert motioned for them to quiet down and listen to him.

"Thank you all so very much. You have remained our friends during some very trying events. I know you're surprised to see me, but I assure you that I am not a ghost. I avoided the assassins by being prepared for them. They made a big mistake because they didn't come after all six of us at the same time. I had been in pretty constant touch with the others, so I saw the pattern of what was happening before they could get to me. Max had told me earlier that some of his old papers had been seen by others, but that he didn't know whether we would suffer any consequences because of it. I warned Peter Rodwin and Sam Spincus, but they thought they would be safe within their assisted living facilities. Unfortunately, they misjudged their degree of safety. May they all rest in peace."

Arthur and the others murmured, "Amen."

"As you no doubt discovered along the way, I was active in the American Legion veterans' group. Two of my best friends there are members of the Wisconsin State Patrol. When I saw the pattern of assassinations, I confided in them, and they helped me set up a trap. I spent several days performing errands frequently driving between Richmond and Lake Geneva, Wisconsin on a short multilane stretch of U.S Route 12. It was short enough for me to summon assistance when on one of my round trips I detected a maroon car following me in the southbound lanes. My State Patrol friends responded to my cell phone call in time to keep me from getting killed, even though my pursuer managed to sideswipe my car before they arrived on the scene. Before my assailant could get out of his car to finish the job, they chased him, and he died in a fiery crash off the end of the unfinished road."

Irma asked, "Did you stage the shot through the driver's window and the apparent bullet hole in front of your left ear?"

"Yes, and we must have done a pretty good job on those photographs if they fooled you. We also tampered with evidence a bit, and took some of the assassin's cremated remains as my own. Fortunately, you didn't ask to examine them, or you would have seen that the quantity of ashes was too small."

Janice asked, "Why did you pretend to be dead?"

"The murderers were still out there. I was the only one they failed to kill. As long as they thought they had killed me, I was safe. I hoped to wait until they were caught before I returned from the dead. I didn't even reveal myself to Mandy for quite a while so that she would remain a believable grieving widow. Peter, you passed by my hiding spot in the basement when you came to look at my papers. Your visit coincided with my covert return to look for my pistol. I thought I might need it if they tried again to kill me.

"I waited another week before revealing myself to Mandy. If you hadn't tracked down the killers by the time we had completed the real estate arrangements, Mandy and I would have simply moved and lived under new names."

Peter mumbled, "You've done that before."

"Yes, my friends and I did live under assumed identities, but it wasn't supposed to have happened that way. We thought we were simply going to go to England along with your OSS raiders. We had enlisted in the SS because it was the only way we could avoid being deemed traitors by the German government. We had to be very careful because there were Nazi zealots all around us. We took a big chance in setting up our desertion with your people. Everything would have been different if the support plane had hit the right targets. Once we saw how badly the attack had gone, we took our only way out by switching identities with the OSS team."

Arthur said, "I believe that you and your five friends proved your loyalty to our country during your many years working for the CIA. I'd like to know how you and Mandy fell in love when you were trying to hide your background, and her job for the CIA was to determine your true loyalty. How long did it take you to learn about Mandy's CIA connection?"

"You just informed me about it...Seriously, I suspected before too long that she had another layer to her identity, but that just made her more attractive to me. I was living a multi-faceted life, and she was too. We were obviously meant for each other. And what man hasn't had second thoughts about whether he or his spouse had been the pursuer during their courtship?"

Peter looked at Janice. Arthur looked at Irma. Everyone started to laugh. While they were still laughing, the telephone rang, and Mandy went into a quieter room to answer it. She returned a few minutes later smiling.

"There's been a slight change to our plans. That was Mary Byrne from CIA on the phone. I don't know how she knew about Albert having survived the attempt on his life, but she said she wants us to travel to Phoenix by way of Washington, DC, so that Albert might be reunited with an old friend."

Irma looked at Arthur. "Did you arrange that?"

"All I did was text Penny that Albert was alive and well. She must have passed the word to Mary. I don't officially know about anything, but I hope you'll make that extra stop on your trip. I suspect your friend requested this meeting."

Albert said, "We'll go. I had heard a rumor once during the period when we worked for CIA. I hope this trip confirms it."

As the party ended, Peter approached Albert, shook his hand, and hugged him. During their embrace, Albert whispered something to Peter that nobody else heard.

Irma nudged Arthur and also whispered something. "They're still being devious. Supposedly, Mandy didn't know Albert had cheated death until much later, but she would have had to identify the body and arrange for the cremation if events had occurred as originally related."

Arthur whispered back, "They certainly are well suited for each other."

CHAPTER 77 - PENNY

Penny looked up from her magazine as Joe entered the kitchen carrying a large box tied with a red ribbon. He set it down on the table in front of her.

"What's in the box, a puppy?"

"It doesn't have air holes. Don't guess; open it up."

"It's not my birthday or anything special that I can remember."

"Open it up."

Penny slid the ribbon off the end of the box. Then she removed the shallow cover. The four sides of the box all fell outward to lie flat on the table. She stared at the world globe that was revealed inside. It was a painted metal design, and Joe or someone else had added a red outline around the continental United States.

"It's very nice, Joe, but what do I do with it?"

Joe reached into his pocket and withdrew a small square jewelry box. A string tag dangled from it as he handed it to her.

"Ooh, this is getting more exciting. The tag says 'With all my love...' Thank you, Joe, whatever it is." She gave him the kind of kiss that said she really meant it. Then she hinged open the box very carefully. "What is this? It looks like a little green house from a Monopoly game."

"It's a very special Monopoly house. It has a magnet on its bottom. I told you that after we finished the case of the World War II German soldiers, I would take you looking for houses. We said that we can live anywhere in the country because of all the traveling we do, so all you have to do is put the magnetic house on the globe where you would like to live. I'll let you choose for us."

Penny gave him another long kiss for that one. Then she started to study the globe with the magnetic house in her hand. "This might not be as easy as I thought. Do I have to make the choice by myself?"

"That's the idea. I'm granting you your wish, but you have to decide what you want."

"You're mean. This may take me a while."

"That's fine. We'll live here until you make your final decision."

"Are you thinking that you can finesse the prospect of buying a house because I'll never be able to make up my mind?

"You said that; I didn't."

Penny plunked the magnetic house onto the globe. "Decision made, and it's final."

Joe looked down at the globe and smiled. "At least we'll know some people in the neighborhood."

The house was attached to the globe at the approximate location of Parkville, Illinois.

CHAPTER 78 - WHISPERS

"Dad, why did you ask us to come down into the workshop with you? We have to start back to Parkville soon." Arthur knew he would be driving late at night already, and they were still worn out from their previous trip. He had to keep reminding himself that they had started this day in Florida.

Irma said, "Don't worry, Arthur, I'll split the driving with you."

Peter said nothing until he had once more set the smoking table out on the workbench. "I asked you to come down here because Albert whispered to me that there's another secret compartment in one of the table legs. That guy is full of surprises. This is either significant, or he's having fun at my expense."

Irma said, "How do you feel about Albert now, Peter? In a sense you were right when you were so upset before. He was a German soldier, but now we know about a lot of circumstances beyond that fact. Have you forgiven him?"

"After all this adventure and excitement, how could I not forgive him? I do have to admit though, that if I had no further information beyond what I first found, I might still be stewing. Don't forget that even the second set of papers we found in this table were lies, somewhat resembling what happened but twisted to make him look innocent and to manipulate our feelings."

While he talked, Peter examined each smoking table leg, tapping and twisting in a precise pattern of moves. In the middle of his examination procedure for the third leg, his expression changed, and he raised his head.

"Here it is. This leg was made by turning a single length of wood on a lathe, but then the craftsman cut it in the bottom of a groove and reassembled the leg with a dowel on its centerline. He worked the two pieces apart, gradually revealing the hardwood dowel. The dowel came free with the lower section of the leg, and he felt something moving within the top portion when he shook it. Peter removed a long thin pick with a slight hook on its end from his toolbox. Then he probed the leg cavity to retrieve its contents. After about four minutes he had enough sticking out to use a pair of tweezers on it. He pulled out a thin object about three inches long that had been wrapped in an old sheet of paper.

Before anyone could reach for it Irma said, "Don't touch it."

She reached into her purse and removed a laboratory test tube with a rubber cork in its end. She also took from her purse a sealed plastic bag containing sterile surgical tweezers and a second bag with sterile gloves. As the others stood back, Irma cleaned her hands with hand sanitizer, put on the gloves, and carefully removed the object from its wrapper with the sterile tweezers. Then she opened the test tube and placed the object within it, replacing the rubber stopper afterward. Finally, she used the tweezers to unroll the paper that had wrapped the long thin object. The paper imprint read *Ohio State University Department of Physics and Astronomy.*

Arthur said, "What do you think that is?"

Irma replied, "In an investigative sense, it's a smoking gun. In terms of pathology, it's a bone unlike any I've ever seen or studied on Earth. That's why I had to keep human beings from touching it with their hands."

"And it was wrapped in paper from the department charged with questioning the existence of UFO's." Arthur looked very amused.

Peter said, "What's so funny?"

"When I left NASA, my colleagues said I'd be sorry for not being there when they brought back artifacts from space that might reveal the existence of life on other worlds."

- END -

ABOUT THE AUTHOR

Richard Davidson is the author of the self-help guidebook: *DECISION TIME! Better Decisions for a Better Life*. He has written the five-novel Lord's Prayer Mystery Series: *Lead Us Not into Temptation, Give Us this Day our Daily Bread, Forgive Us Our Trespasses, Thy Will Be Done*, and *Deliver Us from Evil*. He has edited an anthology, *Overcoming: An Anthology by the Writers of* OCWW. His latest three novels, *Implications, Impulses*, and *Impostor*, from his new series, the Imp Mysteries, continue to chronicle the exploits of Arthur Blake and the investigative associates who aided him in the earlier mystery series, taking their interests in new directions. Mr. Davidson is Past President of Off-Campus Writers' Workshop, the oldest ongoing group of its kind in the U.S. and is the founder of the ReadWorthy Books Book Review Blog. He is the founder of the Independent Mystery Publishing Society (IMPS). Mr. Davidson is a Certified Lay Servant Speaker and a former Lay Leader in the United Methodist Church. He is also an aeronautical & astronautical engineer and a businessman.

Richard Davidson

WORKS BY THIS AUTHOR
NONFICTION:

DECISION TIME! Better Decisions for a Better Life,
VBW Publishing, Inc.
ISBN 978-1-60264-063-4 (paperback)
ISBN 978-1-60264-064-1 (hard cover)
RADMAR Publishing
ISBN 978-0-9829160-7-0 (2nd edition paperback)
ISBN 978-1-4581-8395-8 (Smashwords eBook)
ASIN B0052GOZEO (Kindle Edition eBook)

Where you are in life today is the result of all of the past decisions you have made or which have been made for you in response to the various situations and events that have impacted your life. The decisions that you will make from this point forward will determine the degree to which your future will be positive or negative. *DECISION TIME!* gives you insight into the subjective decision-making process as applied to both small and large choices you will face. It includes dynamic aspects, cultural effects, and morality as applied to decision-making for individuals, teams, corporations, and societies. *DECISION TIME!* prepares you to face the continuous impacts of decision situations confidently and without hesitation.

FICTION:

Lead Us Not into Temptation (The Lord's Prayer Mystery Series, Volume I),
VBW Publishing, Inc.
ISBN 978-1-60264-407-6 (paperback)
RADMAR Publishing
ISBN 978-0-9976381-0-3 (2nd edition paperback)
ISBN 978-1-4581-7381-2 (Smashwords eBook)
ASIN B0052MGI6Q (Kindle Edition eBook)

Arthur Blake, former NASA engineer turned minister, receives an emergency appointment to be pastor of the United Methodist Church in Parkville, a distant suburb of Chicago, following the bizarre sudden death of the church's unusual former pastor. Pastor Blake's attempts to unravel the mystery that shrouds his predecessor become involved with tracking the child of a possibly bigamous soldier in World War II England, art and jewelry treasures plundered by the Nazis and their sympathizers, and the eventual results of childhood sibling conflicts in combined families. Arthur's allies in his investigation include Parkville Police Chief Bobby Andrews, County Medical Examiner Irma Custis, and the married team of Penny and Joe Gonzalez who work for a clandestine government agency. During the course of *Lead Us Not into Temptation,* the reader discovers how seemingly minor historical events lead to major present-day dislocations in church, village, and family relationships.

Richard Davidson

Give Us this Day Our Daily Bread (The Lord's Prayer Mystery Series, Volume II)
RADMAR Publishing
ISBN 978-0-9829160-0-1 (paperback)
ISBN 978-0-9829160-5-6 (2nd edition paperback)
ISBN 978-1-4580-6717-3 (Smashwords eBook)
ASIN B0052MQI66 (Kindle Edition eBook)

Arthur Blake, Pastor of Parkville United Methodist Church, has to deal with the aftereffects of a traumatic communion incident. He works to assist the authorities in investigating the cause while doing his best to convince members of his congregation that it is safe to return to church. Working with the police and federal agencies, he discovers that the terror of the initial event is minor compared with the potential chaotic impact of future disasters being planned by the perpetrator. The investigation is interwoven with several relationship situations that affect the final outcome.

Forgive Us Our Trespasses (The Lord's Prayer Mystery Series, Volume III)
RADMAR Publishing
ISBN 978-0-9829160-1-8 (paperback)
ISBN 978-1-4657-3739-7 (Smashwords eBook)
ASIN B005SULQ6Y (Kindle Edition eBook)

Arthur Blake, Pastor of Parkville United Methodist Church, tries to assist his father to resolve his trauma after learning that his best friend, recently killed in a car accident, may have been an imposter with a heinous background. The investigation reveals that the presumed accident was but one link in a chain of murders. Blake works to determine the true identity of his father's friend, while also discovering the man's past activities and affiliations. Arthur works to solve the murders in conjunction with his colleagues at ABC Consultants. He also draws on assistance from associates at a covert government agency with which he has worked before. The coordinated effort to solve the puzzle examines incidents that span the period between World War II and the present in order to defuse the personal, national, and international dangers resulting from them.

Richard Davidson

Thy Will Be Done (The Lord's Prayer Mystery Series, Volume IV)
RADMAR Publishing
ISBN 978-0-9829160-2-5 (paperback)
ISBN 978-1-3013-4293-8 (Smashwords eBook)
ASIN B009JU6EZM (Kindle Edition eBook)

The sudden death of a young woman attending Parkville United Methodist Church infuriates her brother and leads to congregational outrage over his outburst and subsequent murder. The investigation of that slaying by Pastor Arthur Blake and his associates leads to revelations of a previously undetected criminal organization operating in the area. Unraveling the mystery and scope of this group entangles Arthur and his associated investigators in a web of conspiracies extending from Illinois to both U.S. coasts and through Mexico to Guatemala.

Deliver Us from Evil (The Lord's Prayer Mystery Series, Volume V)
RADMAR Publishing
ISBN 978-0-9829160-3-2 (paperback)
ASIN B00EBDUXFY (Kindle Edition eBook)

Arthur and Irma's wedding day has finally arrived, but an unexpected interruption leads to their need to investigate a possible murder committed by someone close to them. With the aid of friends and federal agents Penny and Joe Gonzalez, they follow a series of clues, crisscrossing the United States to learn more about the murder, related subsequent events, and the significance of a rare object brought home by a veteran of the Iraq War. A second murder close to Pastor Arthur Blake's church involves them in a new investigation, assisting Parkville Police Chief Bobby Andrews. Are these murders and the tracking of that strange object connected? Will marriage deteriorate or improve the relationship between Arthur and Irma? Character flaws in many relationships color the outcome.

Richard Davidson

Overcoming: An Anthology by the Writers of OCWW
Edited and with an Introduction by Richard Davidson
RADMAR Publishing
ISBN 978-9829160-4-9 (paperback)
ASIN B00E80NN4I (Kindle Edition eBook)

This anthology covers many aspects of overcoming life's problems, obstacles, and challenging developments. The contributing writers have used fiction, non-fiction, memoir, poetry, historical chronicle, and drama to highlight our continuing need to overcome our problems, rather than dwell on them. The reader will learn from many talented writers the skills needed to respond constructively, energetically, and sometimes humorously to whatever obstacle bars one's path. Apply their lessons to your own needs and to those of others you cherish.

Implications: An Arthur Blake Mystery Novel (Imp Mysteries, Volume 1)
RADMAR Publishing
ISBN 978-0-9829160-6-3 (paperback)
ASIN B00LY9IBWK (Kindle Edition eBook)

Bishop Howard Chandler has assigned Pastor Arthur Blake to investigate the burning of a church in the small city of Amboy, Illinois. He learns from that church's pastor that she had to overcome past improprieties by former members. During the investigation of the fire's cause, Arthur and the other state fire investigators uncover disturbing aspects of the ninety-year-old church's design and history. Arthur calls on his federal associates for assistance, as the investigation of a local church fire expands to seeking solutions to related crimes occurring from the present to recent years and back to the Prohibition Era. Progress in the investigation intertwines with new developments in Arthur's family life.

Impulses: An Arthur Blake Mystery Novel (Imp Mysteries, Volume 2)
RADMAR Publishing
ISBN 978-0-9829160-8-7 (paperback)
ASIN B012LFQXYI (Kindle Edition eBook)

Several disturbing dreams cause Arthur Blake to wonder whether he is trying to do too much for the many people who seek his services. These qualms are complicated by Bishop Howard Chandler's suggestion that Arthur temporarily set aside his official duties and take an extended sabbatical leave. His resulting internal debates about career moves are set aside when the pastor who replaced him at the Parkville church dies in an apparent suicide possibly linked to several deaths at the Parkville Rehabilitation Home. The bishop assigns Arthur to determine the circumstances behind the new pastor's death, while Arthur and Irma, his wife and constant investigative partner, also study a mysterious shipment at his father's antiques shop. The sudden disappearance of a young associate provides another mystery and leads to questions of life after death and reincarnation. Events that initially appear simple become increasingly complex as the true natures of many people come into question.

Impostor: A Genealogical Mystery (Imp Mysteries, Volume 3)
RADMAR Publishing
ISBN 978-0-9829160-9-4

When Debbie Danforth discovers a flaw in the genealogy of her live-in boyfriend, Jeremy Hadley, he and his family try to discredit her findings, but eventually admit they must be true. Jeremy and Debbie run a private detective business, the Sandley Agency and commit their skills and resources to learning about the impostor Debbie has discovered in the Hadley ancestry. They are assisted in this effort by Penny and Joe Gonzalez, principals in a covert federal agency, with whom Jeremy has previously worked as a consultant. Their joint investigation uncovers both unique details concerning the mysterious Hadley impostor and little-known facts about events leading up to World War II in both Britain and the United States. Was the person who masqueraded as a Hadley a villain or a hero? Did other Hadleys know he was a fraudulent member of their family? Did his actions assist or impede the British and the Americans as they faced the growing menace in prewar Europe?

Learn more about the writings, humor, and random thoughts of Richard Davidson at: radmarinc.com davidsonbookshelf.com betterlifedecisions.blogspot.com and at the Independent Mystery Publishing Society (IMPS) https://www.mysteryimps.com
Richard Davidson's author page on Amazon is located at https://www.amazon.com/author/richarddavidson
Follow and *Like* Richard Davidson, Author on Facebook at https://www.facebook.com/richarddavidsonauthor?ref=hl
Follow him on Twitter @mysteryimp